A Column of Smoke

A Novel

Rebecca Nesbit

Brambleby Books

ISBN 978-1-908241-313
eISBN 978-1-908241-412

First published in 2014 by BRAMBLEBY BOOKS
www.bramblebybooks.co.uk

Cover design by Tanya Warren – Creatix
Cover image from istock

Printed on FSC paper and bound by
GraphyCems, Spain

To my family

About the Author

Rebecca Nesbit grew up in Tewkesbury, Gloucestershire. In 2005, she graduated from the University of Durham with an excellent honours degree in biology. Her PhD was based at Rothamsted Research, Herts., where she studied butterfly migration. Her interest in the environment began as a young child, but during her time at Rothamsted she became interested in sustainable agriculture, particularly the complex social and environmental issues surrounding genetically modified crops. She now works in science communication in London. This is her first book.

Go to www.rebeccanesbit.com to contact the author directly.

Acknowledgements

Writing this would not have been possible without the encouragement and advice of fellow authors at Cambridge Writers. Too many people have provided valuable feedback on drafts for me to name them all, but my mother deserves a special mention.

I first decided to become an author when I was still at junior school, and I have Mrs Wilson to thank for this. For their support in my scientific career, I would like to thank my colleagues at Rothamsted.

Finally, I am grateful to my husband Phil for his support for my science and my writing.

Chapter 1

A policewoman came forward to make the first arrest, and a ripple of booing spread through the crowd. Impervious to the shouts, the policewoman snapped a pair of handcuffs onto a protestor's wrists. Immediately he began to chant: "Put a stop to GM crops."

His bare chest was painted with 'ban GM' and the skin on his back glistened with sweat. The policewoman began to lead him away; he didn't struggle but his chanting grew more elaborate. "No GM, protect our wildlife, No GM, save our farmers, No GM…"

Around 20 protesters joined his cries, pushing forward towards the police cordon. Two police horses tossed their heads as banners surrounded them, their faces shielded by plastic riot guards.

"No GM, stop the pollution, No GM…" More of them were swarming in, and another pair of handcuffs was brandished.

Just a few metres away Sally stood transfixed. She knew to move backwards if trouble started, to be away from the field long before the first stone was thrown or pepper spray was first threaten. Let the police protect the crop. But she had forgotten what this kind of excitement could feel like. Her whole body seemed to have woken up from months of interminable writing, proof reading and daytime TV. She glanced at the group of fellow on-lookers, all showing silent support for the modified crop faced with 'decontamination', all convinced that genetic modification could be used for good.

"No GM, no power to business, No GM, no lies from science…"

Suddenly the man next to her stepped forwards. He was young, attractive and seemingly gripped with rage. '*He's going to shout,*' she thought, '*and they're going to turn on us.*' She froze, waiting for the inevitable, for 300 protestors to notice the awkward cluster of scientists, farmers and hangers-on, and realise they had the perfect target. But no shout came, and Sally stepped forward to touch his arm.

"It's not worth it," she said. "The trial's protected, we'll only make things worse."

The man looked at her, and for a moment she was the focus of his anger. But then he relaxed and stepped back into the group. He ran a hand through his thick brown hair. "Sorry, I just can't deal with them turning scientists into the bad guys." They were silent for a moment and then he shrugged and reached out to shake her hand. "I'm Darren by the way."

"Sally."

As the chanting became louder, a young policeman politely told the group of onlookers to move away, smiling as if the whole event amused him. Reluctantly, they dispersed and regrouped on a grassy bank.

If Sally was honest with herself, her main motivation for coming wasn't to support the scientists who risked losing their work but to meet people, to break the tedium of living with her parents. Spurred on by this, she made sure she stayed close to

Darren in the crowd and sat down next to him. She picked at the daisies and found the courage to speak.

"Are you a scientist?" she asked.

"Yes, a researcher at Cambridge University. You?"

"I'm a geneticist." It was true; that's who she was, though as the weeks of unemployment wore on it felt increasingly like a lie.

"Where do you work?"

Already she'd been found out. Her daisy picking became more frantic. "Actually, I've just finished my PhD and I'm writing papers while I apply for jobs."

He smiled. "We've all been there. What's your area?"

"Plant genetics, but I'm not limiting myself, anything that's interesting and I'm qualified for." She sounded desperate.

"Are you in to all this stuff?" He gestured vaguely towards the field trial. "Because we've got a grant proposal which looks like it might be funded, so we're on the lookout for a post-doc."

At the thought of a job the excitement of the arrests paled into insignificance. She replied as calmly as she could manage. "Yes, definitely, when will it be advertised?"

"As soon as the funding's confirmed. Here, take my email address." He scribbled it on the corner of the GM information booklet they'd been handed and tore it off to give to Sally.

"Thank you."

They sat in a moment's awkward silence until the organiser of their 'counter-protest' walked past, tactfully telling everyone it was time to go; they'd made their point and didn't need to antagonise the situation. As the group started to break up, Sally scanned around her for Paul. She knew it was fruitless, that he was living in America with his wife, and who knows, maybe even kids. But it was a habit she had developed whenever she was in a group consisting largely of scientists. Anyway, situations change; he must spend some time in England at least. She wasn't willing to relinquish the hope this gave her. With a last look at the chanting protesters, Sally and Darren got up to leave.

Sally smoothed the creases out of her skirt and glanced up to see if Darren was looking at her. She had dressed carefully; blending in as an environmentalist was the only way she could think of to show that scientists weren't all in the pockets of corporations, they were just environmentalists in different ways to the protestors. Despite understanding that cotton was horrendously bad for the environment and probably GM anyway, she had worn a floral cotton dress. They walked together to the train station.

"It's not fair how we're judged by different standards," Darren said. "They can shout dodgy slogans and send death threats to scientists. We say one thing that isn't PC and we're intellectual elites with hidden agendas."

Sally had read the briefing emails, explaining the importance of staying polite, open to discussion, but she knew better than to repeat this to him. "I guess we just have to go along with it. That's kind of what all of this is about, not wacky ideals but working with the situation we've been landed in, even if our situation includes some nutcases."

Darren was right; none of this was fair: that a few extremists could hold back valuable research, or that big businesses could have such power over farmers. But ultimately it wasn't fair that some people chucked out excess food while others starved. Science was the only way she could think of to make any difference at all.

Chapter 2

Six weeks later Darren directed Sally to the interview room and left her at the door. As she entered, the information she had absorbed through days of cramming and fretting seemed to evaporate. Along with the overwhelming panic which replaced it, there was also mild disappointment. Despite the name, Professor Vangelis Papadakis's middle-class accent instantly revealed him to be English. Not only that, but his deep frown lines and the grey streaks decorating his hair confirmed he was a good 10 years older than the university website would have you believe.

The room was clearly his office, and it seemed he felt no need to keep up appearances. He hadn't tidied for the interview; instead stained coffee cups collected in the corner of his desk, and piles of papers were stacked alongside his computer. The shelves were crammed with textbooks and PhD theses, the names of each of his students embossed in gold along the spines.

He gestured for her to sit down on a tired office chair and, with the briefest of introductions, began the interview.

"What can you tell me about our lab's research?" Vangelis asked.

She had spent three solid days preparing for this one. "You are genetically modifying wheat so that it's resistant to insect pests, particularly aphids, beetles, and moth caterpillars."

Vangelis didn't smile. "So you've memorised our website, very good, but you're forgetting one vital piece of information – why?"

Sally opened her mouth to give the answer, but Vangelis didn't leave time for her to speak.

"This is what I mean about seeing the bigger picture, not getting so absorbed in your lab work that you forget your ambitions for it, where it fits in. This isn't about adding genes, it's about reducing the need for pesticides at the same time as reducing pest numbers." He tapped his pen impatiently on the table. "And do you know what genes are involved?"

Sally fought to dredge up the information from the back of her brain; somewhere she knew the exact names. "A regulatory gene which switches on…"

"That will be a no then." Vangelis scribbled on a piece of paper in front of him.

Sally tried to conjure the feeling she'd experienced when she'd passed her PhD: the feeling of knowing everything she needed to, of believing she'd earned the right to call herself a scientist. But instead she felt the pinch of her skirt, bought by her mother when she was about to have her first interviews as an undergraduate. Beyond that, all she felt was humiliation.

"Tell me about your research – very briefly," Vangelis said.

This was where Sally could speak with total confidence, and she recovered slightly. But he quickly completed his dissection of how she'd spent the four and a half years since her graduation, 200 pages of PhD thesis brushed over in less than five minutes.

"Presentations?" he asked.

Perhaps he hadn't read her CV.

"Last year's biotechnology conference in Florida."

"My son had bronchitis and my wife forbade me from going. Very disappointing."

Sally had invested in a haircut for the interview, a rare treat now her savings were dwindling, but the hairdresser had cut it too short. She kept pushing strands of blonde hair behind her ears, only to have them fall back again and obscure her view. She focussed on the time when she would be the professor and vowed to make interview candidates feel inspired not crushed.

The discussion became a monologue, and Sally willed herself to concentrate. Interviews always meant hearing about somewhere you may well never work, and this left her wondering what it would be like to get the job rather than paying attention to what was being said. She pictured herself sitting in this office, making intelligent comments in a meeting and not sitting there as she was now – nervously picking her nails under the desk. It was a hard jump for the imagination.

"A position in my lab would be tougher than you're used to: I expect a lot from my post docs, and GM crops come with their own problems. And journalists love the controversies, most of all if they can get a crazed scientist to give a statement on giant carrots that taste like fish and talk like monkeys. I had a grad-student who spoke like that, back in the '90s, before GM safety had been proven."

Sally imagined Vangelis being able to sabotage the reputation of GM food with arrogance far more than a student could with careless stories.

"Tell me," he said. "Are you happy to take on research which will make you unpopular?"

"Yes," Sally said honestly. "If I'm confident what I'm doing is right, then I won't be scared off by sensationalism."

For the first time Vangelis looked almost impressed.

By the time the interview was over Sally's hope had dwindled. She still believed she had the dedication and ambition to deal with life in Vangelis's lab, even if he hadn't let her show it. Annoyingly, she also still saw a brilliant professor who would support her ambitions; she hadn't prepared for disappointment by reassessing the situation as an arrogant man who would happily squash his employees' egos. With a firm handshake he showed her into the corridor and made an absent-minded promise to be in touch.

Outside Vangelis's door Darren was waiting for her.

"Did Vangelis give you a grilling?" he said with an engaging smile.

"You could say."

"That's promising. He doesn't go gently in interviews, or in reality for that matter."

He led her along the corridor, past labs and equipment rooms.

"This is our lab." Darren paused and Sally looked enviously at the busy laboratory. There was a wide glass window onto the corridor, and conical flasks of clear liquids were lined up along it, each with magnetic beads inside to act as stirrers. She could see the back of someone working at the far bench, reaching for solutions with an efficiency that only existed in her life at the moment when she was folding her mother's washing.

"Have you been here for long?" Sally asked.

"Four years of a five-year contract."

"What's it like?"

"Best place I ever worked: labs to die for and the most knowledgeable, supportive boss you could get. Hard work, but worth it."

Sally wasn't quite sure whether he was showing off about working hard or warning her. His positive words about Vangelis as a boss didn't tie in with her experience in the interview room.

When they had reached the end of the corridor Darren used his access badge to let them onto the stairway. Sally knew this was probably still part of the interview, that Darren would report back on every candidate, but she instantly trusted him and thought some honesty might establish the rapport she'd failed to create with Vangelis. "I'm not sure I'm quite what Vangelis was looking for."

"What makes you say that?"

"He seemed hard to impress."

"He's easier to impress when you're generating results for him."

"It looks really good here." Sally forced a laugh and, against her better judgement, said, "Tell him the other candidates made up all their results and published data they'd fabricated during their lunch hour."

At the bottom of the stairs Darren paused in the open doorway, a gust of cold air rushing in.

"Nice meeting you," he said.

"And you. I hope we get to meet again."

With a nod goodbye, Sally let the door close behind her. Outside, the air smelt fresh and stormy. A cold wind rushed through the naked branches of the trees. Sally pulled her coat up around her face and buried her hands deep into her pockets. Out on the street she dodged bicycles and students, all as oblivious to her presence as they were to the revving of impatient cars. The light had already faded and the streetlights flickered on. The excitement of the day was ebbing, and exhaustion flooded over her. She tried to fight it with some chocolate, but just felt sick.

The idea of returning home to her parents' house filled her with dread. As she had left that morning, her mother had straightened her jacket and said, "Now, don't be too disappointed if you don't get it, will you dear?" Sally closed her eyes and wondered how she would keep going if she was rejected. She was 26 and living with parents who loved her but had forgotten she wasn't 16. It was 9 months since she received her last pay cheque, and she was beginning to fear she'd become Dr Jones just so she could work on the supermarket checkout.

Instead of heading to the train station, she found a bench by the river and tried to let her thoughts drift away from the interview. The murmurings of a pub on the far bank reached her, muffled by the wind. Sitting there alone, it seemed impossible that five years had passed since Cambridge was her home. The events of her undergraduate life felt vivid, and she was no closer to understanding them.

Her solitude was broken when a grey-haired lady laden with carrier bags joined her on the bench. She had the distinctive musty smell of someone whose clothes get washed only in the rain, and clearly had no home to go to that night. Sally peered at her collection of bags, somewhat less subtly than she'd intended. They held a strange assortment of possessions, no doubt essential for life on the streets – a sleeping bag, a teapot, some yellowing newspapers.

The lady turned to Sally and smiled, displaying a surprisingly healthy array of teeth. "What's up, pet? You look sad."

"Just tired, thank you. I had a job interview, and I don't know it went that well."

"Is that all m'love? Yer look so pale. Tell me what's been bothering you, I won't hurt."

Sally was touched by the stranger's concern and vaguely amused at the idea of sharing confidences with a bag lady.

"Well, I'm OK really, but really need a job, and at this very moment I just wish I wasn't infatuated with a married man on another continent." Sally laughed at the absurd levels she had sunk to, the laughter diffusing the day's tension. "I've never said that out loud before!"

The lady tutted, "It'll all end in tears. A pretty young girl like you shouldn't get mixed up in that. You hear me?"

"You're right." Sally sighed and they lapsed into companionable silence, Sally wishing the lady's advice were as easy to follow as it was wise.

Paul hadn't been married when they met, and he'd lived on the other side of Cambridge, not the other side of an ocean. She didn't see that as an excuse for her obsession, but it explained a little of how it had happened.

They met as teacher and pupil, the professional divide between them making Sally nervous. He was a graduate student earning extra cash by giving tutorials. She was an undergraduate and slightly geeky. At 20 she was too old for a schoolgirl crush, but young enough to feel detached from his life. The five years between them felt as wide as the gap between reading her chemistry textbook and understanding it.

Throughout her undergraduate days, her desperation to impress left her awkward, never quite comfortable in the presence of anyone who knew more than her. But as time went on, the nervous, tongue-tied Sally began to relax, with her friends at least. Every evening when she left the bar she'd swear she would be more confident, that the ease she felt then would still surround her in the morning. Of course she just woke up with a headache. Looking back, she wished desperately that she'd had the same confidence then as she did now, confidence that came with growing up and becoming less incompetent.

In her final year she did a dissertation in the lab. Paul was there to coax the students through their first, unsuccessful attempts at lab work, and counteract any disasters. She shared her project with two other girls, more acquaintances than friends. They were the kind of people who could turn up looking immaculate, whatever the parties of the night before, and had the charisma that Sally desperately envied.

In retrospect, it was clear that Paul had aided her transformation from clumsy teenager into confident scientist. He gave the impression that he took everyone seriously and exuded a permanent sense of calm. Even when she spilt hydrochloric acid over a thousand-pound piece of lab equipment, he seemed totally unfazed. She liked the way he saw their endless failed attempts as jokes not problems, the way he teased them. She began to stay late in the lab, initially to get more work done, but it soon became about Paul as much as about the experiments. As the lights in the other labs went out one by one, Sally and Paul would remain.

When there was no more labwork to keep them, they'd walk home together. Sometimes they'd walk in silence, enjoying the sound of the river and watching the green of spring appear on the trees. But often they'd talk. His distance from her life left her free to tell him things she'd barely admitted to herself, safe in the knowledge he would never meet the people she spoke of: her mother, her brother, her long-suffering father.

Sally's brother was 10 years her senior, and she'd always been in the shadow of his achievements. This just intensified the guilt she felt at the thought of all her parents had sacrificed to afford to send her to Cambridge. Sally's passion for study and biology left her mother baffled. She never let on, but Sally knew that her mother's only consolation was that she would meet a man with 'sensible' aspirations, like her brother. Sensible of course meant a healthy pay cheque to feed the family.

But then Paul did meet her brother. In her final year, Sally's grandfather passed away, not unexpectedly but without warning. Her brother, Michael, came to Cambridge to break the news, no doubt sent by her grieving mother. He turned up unannounced and delivered the news as if it was business. They spent an awkward morning as he tried to fulfil his older brother duties. Certain nobody would be around and, uneasy about how to entertain him, Sally took him to the lab. Fortunately she had promised she'd move Petri dishes from an incubator once the bacteria colonies had grown into furry lily pads.

He found everything quaint: the white coats, latex gloves and whirring machines. He saw her life as a second-rate reproduction of a crime-scene drama, without stopping to think that it might be the other way round.

When Sally had heard enough of *Do they really still use those?* and *Don't you need a grey beard to go with that scientist look?* she tried to draw him into to talk of their grandfather.

"What did he want done with the house?"

"Don't worry, I'm sure there'll be a floral teacup left for you to inherit when he's divided his grand estate between us all." Michael had little respect for the cousins he would share his meagre inheritance with.

Irritation held back Sally's tears, and she continued with her fruitless attempt to find out whether her brother was in any way upset by their loss. "Who's going to clear out his house? You couldn't open any of the doors upstairs, everything was hoarded behind them, decades of interesting things, things we might want."

"I never went upstairs."

"What, you never went to the toilet?"

"Not that I remember."

"The flush was broken, you had to pour a bottle of water in the cistern to make it work, surely you'd remember that?"

"Look, Sally, I never went up there and I've no doubt his hoard of stuff was all junk."

Just as Sally realised that their grandfather featured no higher up his priority list than she did, Paul came in. Relieved to be freed from any pretence of having paid attention to their grandfather, Michael busied himself with his BlackBerry, then made his excuses and called a cab. Paul took Sally out for coffee and he listened to her stories instead.

The first time Paul told her he was engaged Sally had been flattered that he would confide in her. It seemed the taboo had been lifted on the final subject they were unable to speak about. But even then she felt irritated in a way she couldn't quite justify.

He had met Katie just a year before and described their meeting as no less than love at first sight. She was a scientist too and, like Paul, was coming to the end of her PhD. They had met in the lab, Katie having come to do some final experiments. When, after just a month, she had to return to her parents' house in Winchester so she could write up, they had seen each other every weekend. Their choice had been clear: they would marry as soon as he'd finished his PhD, and he'd follow her to wherever she worked.

"She took a job in America, a much better one than she'd have found over here. She was going to turn it down, but I said take it and I'd make sure I joined her."

"You're moving to America?" Sally's parents had been a little unsure about her moving to Cambridge.

"Yep, my passport's with the embassy as we speak and, come July, I'll be there." He seemed to notice the sceptical look on her face. "Some jobs are just worth moving for, even if you end up in Luton they're worth it."

"What's your job then?"

"Her job's the good one. I've got something to tide me over though."

"But what about your research?"

"There's time." Paul sounded impatient (or was it bitter?).

Sally let it drop, and Paul filled the silence with his enthusiasm. "It's beautiful in California – humming birds visit her garden... our garden."

"Sounds nice." Sally couldn't muster any more enthusiasm.

"She can take day trips to Yosemite."

"And has she?"

"Well not yet, but it'll be easier when I'm there." Sally was silent again, and Paul noticed. "Sally, have you never known someone was just right?"

"Well I guess I'd still be with them if I had."

He paused, looked at her. "When you do, you'll realise why they're worth taking risks for."

She begrudged his 'you'll understand one day' tone. Keen to get away, she picked up the tray of dirty glassware and carried it off to be sterilised.

Sometimes he would speak more openly, and she wondered if a niggle of doubt was creeping in. But then his face would freeze, and he would retreat into bland compliments of Katie. It was as if by saying them he thought could make these things important. These were the conversations Sally replayed in her head, wondering how much Paul believed his perfect world, but they were shadowed by conversations when his descriptions would be so sincere that Sally wondered if she'd invented any doubt herself.

As time went on, Sally found it increasingly difficult to endure Paul's obsession with Katie and almost impossible not to let her annoyance show. She lived in fear that he would notice and laugh because his student had fallen for him. It wasn't helped by the fact that Paul's good looks had caught the attention of her two labmates.

"Don't you think Paul's romantic, Sally?" Bored of their work, her labmates had moved on to gossip. They were sitting at the lab bench with Paul, not even pretending to work. He seemed to be enjoying the attention.

"What?" Sally sat at the fume hood and resisted the temptation to turn and face them.

"Moving to America for his girlfriend."

"Fiancée." The second labmate giggled.

"Very sweet," Sally said with thinly disguised sarcasm.

"Katie's a lucky girl, wouldn't you say?"

Sally turned up the fume hood's fan to block them out.

That evening, when the rest of the lab was deserted, Paul confronted her.

"Why do I get the impression that you disapprove?"

"Disapprove of what?" Sally focussed her attention on the solution she was making, each chemical measured to the nearest drop with slightly shaking hands.

Paul perched on a lab stool and passed her each chemical in turn. "Of me going to America."

"You can do whatever you like."

"That doesn't answer my question."

She was caught between the desire to say yes to please him and to say no to hurt him. As she searched for what to say, he took silence to be her answer.

"When you've made something work long distance like we have, and we really have – across continents – then you know that what comes next will be easy."

The day ended with awkward silences.

As her final year at Cambridge drew to a close, the university became claustrophobic, and Sally was increasingly fretful. Just as everyone she knew seemed to forget that they existed in a bubble, Sally started to feel trapped inside it, institutionalised. Knowledge was beaten into her by ageing academics, with no apparent interest in whether she would actually use it.

Spring turned to summer and, with no more labwork, Sally began to engineer chance meetings with Paul. She'd happen to walk past his office at coffee time, or buy lunch from the same sandwich shop. Her exams came and went, and she spent her last few weeks celebrating. She knew the pubs he went to in the evenings and made sure she ended up there.

At the end of every night friends would tug them both away and they'd return to their separate lives. Then, one cool summer's evening, they left the pub together. One by one their friends had drifted off, and so they had the walk home to themselves. At the end of Paul's road they paused. "My house is just down here, if you'd like a final drink?"

Sally nodded.

His house felt like a transition zone, as if the occupants were just treading water until they started new lives. Cardboard boxes lined the hall, and there was a stale smell of stirred-up dust. Paul led Sally into the kitchen, where scrubbing for the landlord's inspection hadn't masked the years of abuse it had taken.

"What do you fancy?" He gestured towards an extensive collection of bottles, most of them almost empty. "I can't take all this with me, and you'd be saving my housemates from themselves."

"Actually I'm not sure the tequila from either of the pubs on Mill Road has kicked in yet so I think I'll wait a while."

"Cup of tea?"

"Now you're talking."

While Paul put on the kettle, Sally leant on the work surface and laughed at the stories he told of his housemates. The microwave clock turned to midnight and Sally yawned. Goose pimples were starting to rise on her bare arms.

Paul came to stand in front of her. He placed a steaming mug in her hand but didn't back away. They stood, feet touching, Sally still leaning on the worktop. She couldn't meet his eye.

"When are you leaving?" he asked.

"Next Friday."

"Will I see you again before you go?"

"I don't know." Sally busied herself taking slurps of scorching-hot tea.

"Sally, look at me."

She lifted her gaze and felt the breath catch in her chest. He reached out a hand and stroked her hair. Then he withdrew it. "I'm sorry, Sally."

Sally's heart pounded. Disappointment, frustration, fear and desire all competed for her attention. She put down her tea, the mug banging on the worktop, and turned to leave. Then she saw the look of confusion on his face and regretted every time she'd been angry with him for loving someone. She touched his arm, and felt his body relax. "Don't be sorry," she said softly.

He turned to her and smiled unconvincingly. Then he embraced her. She pressed her cool hands against the heat of his back. He buried his face deep in her hair. Sally pulled away, just enough so she could look at him. The look was meant to be a question, but it turned into a kiss.

When Sally woke up, the first of the morning light revealed Paul's room in silhouette. Outside the window a robin announced the arrival of dawn with its jubilant song. Without waking Paul, she sat up. Her head felt fuzzy, her back stiff. Silently, she swung her legs down to the floor, kidding herself that she was just going to get a glass of water. But standing naked on the cold floorboards, she knew she wasn't going back to bed. Hastily, she groped for her discarded clothes. Then she sat, motionless, panic rising. She rummaged through her handbag for some paper and a pen, flinching at every rustle, all the time listening to ensure Paul's breathing remained steady. She found a scrap of notepaper and began to write. But she had got no further than 'Dear Paul' when she noticed a photograph that had been hidden by the darkness the night before. It was Paul, with his arm round a delicate brunette.

Tears flowed silently down her cheeks, though she didn't yet know what she was crying for. For herself? For Katie? For what might have been? She dropped the pen; she had nothing left to say. Without a glance back, Sally crept down the stairs and let herself out.

With only a few days until she left Cambridge, the schemes she'd devised for chance meetings meant it was easy to avoid Paul. No amount of coaxing from her friends could get her to enter into the festive spirit. She devised melodramatic speeches to explain to them what had happened, but instead shared nothing. She maintained her stony silence until everyone began to wonder what they'd done to offend her. She counted the hours until she could put this time out of her mind and begin her life.

On the day of her graduation, Sally knelt in front of the chancellor to receive her degree. First class honours from the University of Cambridge and all she could think was, 'if I don't see him today, then I never will'.

On the park bench five years later, Sally could feel the bag lady's gaze on her, and her ears were starting to ache from the cold. She gave the rest of her chocolate bar to the lady and continued back to the station, just as the first large drops of rain began to fall. Being back in Cambridge hadn't made things any clearer; it had just made her cringe even more at her idiocy.

* * * * *

When she awoke the next morning the air was still, as if the weather were embarrassed by the anger of yesterday's storms and was now hoping to go unnoticed. The winter sun gave Sally the eerie feeling that the storms, the interview and the lady on the bench hadn't actually happened, that it was the desperate fabrication of someone who had emerged from student-hood into the depression of unemployment. But she turned on her phone to find a message from Vangelis, asking her to be in reception at 9.30 for her first day on Monday.

Chapter 3

The second time Sally entered Vangelis's office she did so as a colleague. She was no less nervous – in fact more so once she had signed the contract and committed herself to 3 years under his guidance. She was surprised how her fingers shook as she held the pen.

The state of his office suggested that it had in fact been cleared for the sake of appearances during her interview. She had to push aside a pile of undergraduate essays so she could lay out the forms she'd been given. She was offered tea from the stained mugs, which she politely declined.

Vangelis spoke with the same enthusiasm he had at her interview, and slightly less of the arrogance. "It's an exciting time for us. We have some work that's all coming together. Results from trials round the world are pointing in one direction. It's going to be high-profile."

"Field trials?" Sally tried to sound confident and switched on. The interview had focussed entirely on lab work.

"Ones we've conducted locally, and ones that our collaborators in the States and India have been doing. I've arranged a lab meeting this morning to get you up to speed. Darren and Amy are both speaking at a food security conference in 2 weeks' time, and I thought you'd be interested to hear them practise their presentations."

Vangelis handed her a wad of health and safety forms – working alone, working with dangerous chemicals, handling genetically modified organisms... Dutifully Sally pretended to read them, and signed and dated them in turn. Just as she reached *what to do in a fire* Vangelis jumped up and announced they were going to be late for their meeting. She gave up her pretence of reading the forms and just added hurried signatures.

Vangelis led her to a small seminar room, where her new colleagues were already gathered. "This is Sally," he announced, "we're very pleased that she's chosen to join our group and," he turned to face her, "I'm sure I can say from us all that we're looking forward to working with you."

There were murmurs of agreement, and Sally felt colour rise in her cheeks as Vangelis introduced everyone in turn. "Darren you've met, Amy is just about to write up her PhD, Günter models the growth of our crop varieties."

Günter rose to greet her, his bald head towering above both her and Vangelis. "Keep me away from the lab always – just give me a computer, I could not even recognise the plants we are working on." His German accent was harsh, but not unattractive. "I'm very pleased you will be joining with us."

"And finally, this is Judith, the best technician in the department."

Sally tried to force her face muscles into a smile, but could feel the look would be unsuccessful. Sitting next to Gunter was the technician she'd known from her undergraduate days, her coarse hair slightly greyer but otherwise apparently unchanged.

"Hello, Sally," Judith said coldly, and Sally feared she may still be answerable for mistakes she'd made in her first fumbling attempts at lab work.

Darren moved to the front and flicked up his PowerPoint presentation, crowded with graphs and diagrams. "Can everyone see OK?" Sally nodded. "Since its introduction in the USA in 1995, Bt cotton has reduced pesticide use and increased yields. Now almost half of the area where cotton is grown is planted with Bt plants, and we've seen widespread benefits to the environment, farmers and local communities."

This was about the most famous GM crops success story, and everyone at Darren's conference would be familiar with it. But Sally found the familiar territory both reassuring and unsettling in equal measure, like when she thought about the environmental impacts even of restocking her wardrobe.

"But most varieties of Bt cotton only protect against certain caterpillars and beetles. Our aim is to expand this protection more widely into food crops, and to increase the number of pests we protect against."

He exuded not just confidence but also calm. When the red dot of his laser pointer highlighted sections of genetic code – the letters TAGC in a garbled order – it was completely still. If Sally hadn't met him before, his self-assurance might have been intimidating. He never broke eye contact with his audience, and most of it was directed at her.

He went into elaborate and slightly unnecessary detail, so took a good 20 minutes to get to the important point. "The modification we have been developing has worked in both maize and wheat. Commercial varieties with this gene therefore have the potential to prevent the use of millions of tonnes of pesticide annually, and to empower farmers around the world to deal with the devastating loss of crops to insects."

Darren nodded to show he had finished and Vangelis flicked on the lights. "Thank you Darren. Thoughts, anyone?"

Sally debated whether she would look intelligent or pushy by joining in. But her decision was made for her by the fairly tedious debate that Darren and Günter got into about something to do with modelling the rate of insect death on the crop. Vangelis had to stop the discussion to move on to Amy.

Amy didn't have the conviction that Darren had, and her presentation lacked his finesse. When she spoke her voice sounded as if it was being squeezed out of her throat, and Sally had to strain to hear her. Her science, however, was good and Sally instantly warmed to her. Her talk may not have been elegant but her manner was sincere, and it seemed a bit of modesty wouldn't go amiss in this lab. When the meeting was over, Vangelis stayed seated at the front, his head bowed in concentration as he listened to Judith talking. Judith's skin was dry, and the flesh on her cheeks seemed to sag, dragging down the corners of her mouth. Sally moved forwards to try and talk with Amy. However, Darren blocked her way, saying he had an exclusive tour of the glasshouses in store for her.

The air in heated glasshouses can be oppressive. As Sally first stepped in from the cold, the warmth was as welcome as sunshine after a cold swim. But as heat seeped through her layers of winter clothing, the temperature seemed at odds with the grey sky still visible above them. Pensioners might go cold that night, but these plants felt eternal summer.

Wheat seedlings, not more than 5cm tall, lined the room. Each shelf was labelled with its variety, although the plants themselves looked identical. On the other side of the glass walls there were more rooms full of plants, from spindly weeds to fully-grown cotton bushes. White puffs of cotton sprayed out from the end of every twig.

"Good talks," Sally said, hoping to hear Darren's take on her new colleagues.

"So what do you make of us all?" Darren's tone suggested he wanted her to give the honest answer.

"They seem like a good bunch."

"They are. Good scientists but good fun too. Judith can take a bit of getting used to. She's a reliable technician, but you have to ask her in the right way. Though I guess I'd be grumpy if my job consisted of mixing up chemicals for people half my age."

"I knew her when I was an undergraduate."

"Lucky you. At least you're used to her."

Sally wasn't sure she'd ever get used to working with anyone who was so wilfully obstructive.

Darren pulled the greenhouse door open with a creak and gestured for her to go through. A sticky yellow fly-trap dangled from a paper clip next to the exit, covered in amorphous black dots. Sally ducked to avoid it, but it stuck to the wool of her coat. Darren gently prised it off and slid the glass door shut behind them.

* * * * *

It was dark and windy when Sally began her walk home. The traffic was gridlocked and she was relieved to be able to take a path across Midsummer Common. With a gloved hand she turned on her phone and almost immediately got a call from her mother.

"How did your day go then?"

"Really well, thank you."

"Did you meet lots of nice people?"

"Yes thank you, they're very welcoming. We had a good meeting about the project – they're working on resistance to insect pests. They've got trials here, and in America…"

"Sounds fascinating dear, now how's your house?"

"Full of boxes."

"I rang you there this afternoon in case you were allowed home early, I spoke to your hippy housemate."

"Liz isn't a hippy, Mum."

"Well, why wasn't she at work?"

"She doesn't have the kind of job that you go into work for."

"What kind of job doesn't involve working?"

"She's a poet." There was a disapproving silence on the other end of the phone, and Sally searched for a way to make Liz sound vaguely impressive. "She writes, kind of modern stuff."

"Can you make a living out of *modern stuff*?"

It was a question Sally had asked Liz many times when they were undergraduates. "I guess you don't need to make much of a profit when your father pays your rent."

Her mother was silent again, and Sally hoped she was finally thinking there were worse paths her daughter could have chosen than becoming a scientist.

When Sally arrived home the house was silent. The heating hadn't quite taken the chill out of the air, and the cold of the floor tiles permeated through her socks. She stood in their smart new kitchen and ate a piece of toast, not sitting down for fear she'd be too exhausted to get back up.

Carefully gripping a cup of tea, she climbed the stairs to the bedrooms. She viewed hers with satisfaction. It was spacious, with a double bed along one wall and a full-length mirror reflecting the skeleton trees in the garden. Liz's room was opposite, and the bathroom overlooked the road. They were similar in size, the bathroom possibly slightly larger. The overwhelming impression inside Liz's room was of paper. Her tiny desk clearly didn't have enough space to work on, so open books and notepaper covered in spidery handwriting were scattered over the floor and bed.

On the top floor Mel's room stretched from the back of the house to the front and was lit by huge dormer windows. The room sizes represented their relative salaries; it was Mel's lawyer paycheque that meant they could afford a house on Carleton Road with a built-in dishwasher and heated towel-rail.

Sally had left a narrow pathway from the door to her bed, surrounded by boxes full of all her worldly goods: clothes, jewellery, CDs, too many books. She unpacked her shoes and neatly lined up barely-worn stilettos next to the ingrained grime of her walking boots. Then she filled her drawers with tops and jumpers, knowing that the careful colour scheme of each drawer wouldn't last beyond her first wash. She shivered as she hung summer dresses in her wardrobe and was relieved to finally hear the sound of the front door.

Mel had just thrown her handbag down on the kitchen table when Sally came to join her. She unwound the scarf from round her neck and opened her coat to reveal the tailored suit beneath. She greeted Sally with a broad smile. "Sally, you survived! Tell me all."

"I met lots of people, learned about how we're going to feed the world, went on a tour of the glasshouses."

"I want the lowdown on all the people, but please spare me the glasshouses." Mel rolled her eyes at the thought of 'gardening', as she liked to call Sally's dealings with the crops.

"They're all smart, all friendly, except the lab technician who I knew from before and who goes out of her way to make everyone's life difficult."

"Any eligible bachelors?" Mel didn't hold back on the question Sally knew her mother had been desperate to ask.

"Well, if I meet one I'll give him your number."

Mel laughed. "Make it my work phone, or he'll never get hold of me."

Her laughter was infectious, and for the first time that day Sally began to relax.

"What kept you so long?" Sally asked.

"Same old, same old – partner landed 30 pages on my desk at 5.30."

"That's just cruel." Despite Sally's dedication to science, she hated being told when to work.

"Don't get me started. But before I bore you with case reports do you fancy some supper?"

"You've been working all this time, I'll do it."

"Rubbish, if I couldn't do things for my friends every time I worked too hard then I wouldn't have any left. Do you eat bean sprouts? We're having a stir fry."

Sally sat down gratefully. "I'll cook next time."

Soon the smell of soy sauce filled the kitchen, and Mel placed a steaming plate in front of Sally.

Only once they had finished did a click of a key in the lock announced Liz's arrival home. By the time she'd shed her coat and boots, Mel had already brought out a third wine glass and filled it to the brim.

"Liz, you're just in time to join us for some brain-rotting TV!" Mel raised her glass. "Cheers!"

Whatever Sally's mother had said, Liz would make a hopeless hippy. Maybe she wasn't accustomed to the hard work that Mel was, but she took both the writing and the selling of her poetry seriously. For all Sally joked about modern poetry, it seemed that Liz was actually talented. However, the thick wool of the jumper that swamped her tiny frame did give her a vagrant hippy look. Her trousers had wide flares, and their legs were frayed at the heels. She was also prone to strong views she was keen to argue about but had no desire to act upon. Sally's experience was that she was great to start a debate with, until you realised she had no intention of listening to alternative points of view. GM crops was a favourite, and when they'd been undergraduates together they had indulged in hours of circular arguments, much to Mel's annoyance.

The three girls spent the rest of the evening slouched in the deep sofas, hurling the occasional insult at the television, until finally sleepiness forced them to their beds.

Chapter 4

Mornings in Sally's new household began the way they would go on. Sally stumbled into the kitchen, hair washed but not dried, and began opening cupboards. She did this without a system – by the time she'd opened each door she had forgotten what she hoped to find behind it.

Mel, in contrast, gave the air of effortless efficiency. She was pristinely dressed, yet poured out her coffee with no danger to her white shirt. She pressed cancel on the toaster to save an extra few seconds, then calmly ate the toast while Sally flapped around her. Liz watched the whole escapade in silence, both hands wrapped round a mug of hot chocolate.

Sally had barely managed to pour herself some orange juice by the time Mel was ready to leave. She turned back at the kitchen door. "Sally – I want details on every man of marrying age, single or otherwise. And Liz," Mel said in mock exasperation, "do some work."

"You'll be lucky!" Sally called after her, then saw Liz's disapproving look. "That was about the men - she'd be lucky to get me paying attention to them, not she'd be lucky to get you to work." Sally suddenly felt far too hot, but didn't know how to stop digging. "How is your work anyway?"

"OK, thank you. You can't work all the time – you've no

control over when inspiration comes. Though I guess Mel doesn't need inspiration."

"Yes, I guess it's a bit different," Sally said feebly. To her relief Liz poured away the dregs of her hot chocolate and slipped off to her room.

When Sally arrived in the lab she was amused by the similarity to life in the kitchen. Amy was gazing at her lab bench as if the assortment of chemicals and Post-It notes meant nothing to her. She picked up a pipette in one hand then tried to unscrew a bottle top with the other. Just in time she realised that it wasn't the bottle she wanted. The pipette's slender tip hovered over the bottle then she withdrew it and selected a different one.

Darren, who was preparing Petri dishes to grow bacteria in, appeared as calm and precise as Mel had been over breakfast. Next to him a Bunsen burner flickered with a yellow flame, ready to sterilise his tools. He was using a glass rod, bent into a neat triangle at the end to spread the bacteria over the dish. Having dipped the glass in alcohol, he brought it quickly to the flame to sterilise it. The excited flash as the alcohol briefly ignited seemed to bring him to his senses.

"Morning Sally, how did your unpacking go?"

"I've got lots of junk, but it's getting there. How are you?"

"Busy, but I'm about to take these to incubate in the 37° room, if you'd like me to show you where everything is?"

"Yes please."

"This is your bench for a start. The window on one side, and me on the other – prime position." He winked at her. "I've set you up ready with the most important things you'll need."

A few lab essentials were lined up on her bench – distilled water, latex gloves, various sizes of measuring cylinders. They reminded her of the welcome pack that appears on students' beds on the first day of freshers' week – with special offers on textbooks, free samples of tomato ketchup, and a pack of condoms.

Darren led Sally through a maze of corridors, too fast for her to properly get her bearings. As they walked past doors to labs and offices, he told her about the people within. His tone was conspiratorial and he was a good storyteller.

"This lab is one of the best. They're studying the genetics of the immune system – why are some people more prone to allergies than others and all that."

"If I could have two careers, then immunology is what I'd do with the other one. Did you know that people can smell each others' immune systems?"

Darren looked sceptical. "I've never exactly been able to sniff out who's likely to die if I feed them half a peanut."

"No, subconsciously, so we choose partners with different immune systems to ours. Then our children will inherit both sides. Another way our body plays about with our mind without us even knowing."

Darren's gaze rested on her, interested, intense, and she wished she hadn't said anything.

They passed an office door with the glass window blocked by a poster. "Dr Parks, now he's one of my favourites. He's as gentle as a teddy bear during the day. But he spends his weekends living as part of a religious cult."

Sally pictured bearded men, pointed hats and ritual sacrifice. "What do they believe?"

"I don't know, but, apparently, they dress all in white and eat raw meat."

"Did one of his students spread this rumour? I'm not sure I know many scientists who would swap rational thought for a religious cult on a weekly basis."

"You'd be surprised. Not everyone's as rational in real life as they are in the lab."

Darren drew back the heavy door sealing of the 37° room and placed his Petri dishes on the table. Next to them mechanical shakers were rotating so that murky-brown liquid sloshed continuously in conical flasks. Sally watched them, mesmerised by the movement, and pictured the billions of bacteria dividing in the flasks.

She stood back for Darren to close the door and they continued down the corridor, now surrounded by biohazard signs. At the end of the corridor Darren paused.

"This store cupboard has our consumables in if you need anything."

The windowless room smelt unpleasantly synthetic, the stale smell of new bin liner. The shelves were stacked to the ceiling, and the open boxes were tightly packed on the tables below. Sally shuddered at the sheer amount of plastic – tubes, pipette tips, gloves – all destined to be used only once.

They returned to the office in silence.

Sally watched the tree outside their office window as a blue tit investigated the bare branches in a determined search for insects. She didn't yet have any emails to check, but Günter had set her up with a computer and she was searching for journal articles. The more she read the more she found she didn't know, so she was relieved when Darren asked if they were ready for a lab meeting.

"Of course, but didn't we have one yesterday?" Sally asked.

"We did, but this is different. You're a chosen one – allowed into the inner circle."

Günter laughed. "You and your chosen ones! Anyone would think we were carrying the ring to Mordor."

Darren ignored him but spoke more seriously. "We have

these meetings with just the people in charge of decisions."

"Yes, Gandalf!" Günter saluted Darren, and Sally struggled to keep a straight face.

"Now we're bringing our *Nature* paper together Vangelis wants us to get on top of it all."

Sally liked the way Darren spoke of their *Nature* paper, just assuming that the world's leading journal would automatically accept it. Günter caught her gaze and rolled his eyes. Dutifully they followed Darren into Vangelis's office.

Darren and Günter had taken the wise move of bringing their own cups of tea to avoid the public health hazard of Vangelis's mugs. As Sally reluctantly accepted tea from Vangelis she wondered what bacterial ecosystem was fighting the heat.

Vangelis picked up some sheets from the printer and passed them round. "Here's a list of the experiments we need to complete before we submit the paper. I've divided it up so that we know who's responsible for what, and how we're going to get all of this cleared up as soon as possible."

Sally was a little alarmed to see how much of his list had her name next to it.

"I thought Amy was meant to be doing more sequencing," Darren said.

"She's run out of time, she needs to start writing."

"She can't leave the lab yet, she needs more results. We need more results."

"If she doesn't start to write her thesis now she will run out of time. What's the news on the field trial?"

Darren didn't look entirely happy that Amy wouldn't be helping them in the field, but he moved on to his update. "The winter wheat has been sown, 20 hectares in total, equal areas of our GM wheat and the non-GM wheat the farmer normally grows commercially."

42

"How soon can you get the results?"

"It's due to be harvested in June, weather permitting, then Sally and I can process the samples in, I guess, 2 weeks."

"Huh," Günter said. "I will believe it when I see it."

"We're going to do it. Sally will be helping."

"That's good," Vangelis said. "I want to publish as soon as possible. We now need to get the whole paper written ready to slot this data in."

Sally looked around the table; they were all reading Vangelis's sheet of duties. Her attempts to piece together exactly what was going on were failing, and she decided it was not the time to ask. "Which trial is this?"

Sally interpreted Vangelis's look as 'keep up', but he said, "Sorry, we should have explained. We've shown that our GM varieties protect against pests; if they're not treated with pesticides, the GM wheat does significantly better than the non-GM variety. What we need to do now is show that the GM variety is just as good as the conventional one when there are no pests."

Darren pushed a diagram over to Sally, showing the arrangement of GM and non-GM crops carefully designed to eliminate bias caused by conditions in the field. "This time both of the fields have been treated with pesticide, even though the GM one doesn't need it, so neither variety should suffer pest problems. We're sure our GM variety will have the same yield as the non-GM version."

They moved on to Günter's work. It was painfully mathematical, and Sally struggled to keep up, but she found his words therapeutic. As he and Vangelis discussed the inherent problems of modelling gene expression, Sally thought with satisfaction about how this would sound to an outsider. If Paul could see her now, he'd be impressed.

As her understanding of the conversation slipped further away, she realised how little there was in Vangelis's office to give away who he was. Unless of course the chaos of books and papers really said all there was to know about him. The wall behind his computer was covered not in pictures but in a diagram of a cell-signalling pathway – lots of A4 sheets fixed next to each other so they didn't quite line up. On them, an elaborate network depicted the language of cells, where every word was a protein, whispering sweet nothings to each other – 'stay here' or 'make more' – and entering into arguments that would regulate the cell's activities, and acting as passwords to open the cell's entrance and exit channels.

The only hint of a life outside science was a photograph of three children, all under the age of 10. The oldest was a girl, and it was already clear she was going to be beautiful. Her arms were draped around the shoulders of two boys, both with the same olive skin and dark eyes.

"Thank you, everyone." Vangelis stood up and added his papers to a pile on a bookshelf. They filed out, Sally was relieved that her confidence hadn't taken the same battering as it had when she was first in Vangelis's office.

Back in the lab Sally started to arrange her bench. She looked up when Judith and Amy entered the lab, deep in conversation.

"You should know this," Judith said. "If you don't put the order in by Friday lunchtime then you've missed your chance." She let the door slam closed behind them.

"I'm sorry, my experiment didn't work, and I wasn't planning on repeating it, so I didn't know I'd need more antibody."

"Planning, Amy, is a basic skill and you'll never learn if I bail you out every time you mess up."

Darren bent close to Sally's ear and whispered, "Judith wouldn't bail out her own mother unless there was something in it for her."

"I need to finish these experiments because I have to start writing my PhD. And I need them for my thesis." A hint of desperation had crept into Amy's voice.

"You'll never get your thesis written if you can't organise yourself."

"Please, it will only take 10 minutes for you to put the order in."

"The answer, Amy, is still no." Judith walked off, with a noble look as if she'd done Amy a favour by not giving in. Sally came towards her to try and salvage some of Amy's confidence, but couldn't find the words. If Paul was there, he would have known what to say, and Sally fought to remember the kind of reassurances he had given her.

To her surprise it was Darren who came to the rescue. "Here we go." He handed over a tiny vial. "This should tide you over." He smiled and gave her shoulder an affectionate squeeze.

Chapter 5

Sally was reading the paper at the kitchen table when Mel walked in. It was gone 8 pm and she'd finished her supper but not yet summoned the energy to wash up.

"Good day?" Mel asked.

"Things are taking shape. I might actually get some work done soon and not just talk about it."

"More talking, less working – sounds good to me."

Sally smiled. "You can't feed the world by talking."

"Made any enemies?"

"Only friends I'm afraid and, before you ask, none of them are tall, dark and handsome."

"You're very coy about this Sally."

"You mean I've been there a week and haven't met mister right or slept with mister wrong?"

Mel didn't laugh. "Who was that guy you were after?"

"I wasn't after anyone." The words came out more forcefully than Sally had intended.

"Don't lie."

Sally nervously shuffled around the sections of the newspaper. She knew she couldn't hide from Mel, and that knowledge made her heart thump not just with fear, but excitement. As the story shot through her mind – the fiancée, the warmth of Paul's bed, the morning walk of shame, her unreasonable obsession ever since – the idea of sharing the thoughts she'd kept trapped within her head felt liberating.

Mel looked amused. "Everybody knew you were after him, all they didn't know was what happened to him."

"They didn't know anything."

"So you have something more to tell."

Sally sighed. "He was called Paul, and he was a postgraduate in my lab…"

"And you met when you did your dissertation."

"He helped us with our practical work. And sometimes we'd see him in The White Swan."

"I know, I was there, but did anything happen, did he know how you felt?"

"I hope he never knew, but I've no idea whether he did or not."

"Sally, you're too shy, you need to say these things. Otherwise people drift out of your life because they never knew."

"He was engaged."

This stalled Mel's flow, but didn't stop it entirely. "Sometimes that's when people look for a way out."

"He was so into his fiancée, he loved to talk about how he'd known it was right and all that. I don't think he was looking for a way out."

"Sickening. Are you sure?"

Sally breathed deeply, ready to tell her how he'd cheated on his fiancée by sleeping with her. The words that would follow began to form in her head, and the details she could offer wove themselves into an engaging story; the way they'd jumped apart with the creak of the kitchen door, the lack of suspicion on the housemate's face when he entered, how Paul's hands had found her again before the door had even shut behind him. The reckless feeling of being sober enough to know what she was doing, but drunk enough not to care came back to Sally and threatened to overwhelm her once again.

But the attention-grabbing story and her melodramatic desire to tell it repulsed her. Was it any more than a wish to dispel Mel's misconception of her innocent life? In the end her desire to tell was the reason that she fell silent.

"You're not still into him?" Mel asked.

"Well, kind of. Is that ridiculous?"

"Fairly, but we'll cure you." Mel smiled, and her confidence persuaded Sally to believe her.

* * * * *

Sally and Darren were alone in the lab with only the whirr of the PCR machine as it split apart double helices of DNA and built identical copies along the remaining single strands. The morning had disappeared with work and chat, but now the conversation had died as Sally reached a crucial moment in her experiment. With gloved hands she pipetted a few microlitres of solution into tiny wells sunk into a plastic tray. Darren watched in amusement as she used her left hand to steady the right.

Just as she had filled every well and placed the plate in an incubator, Vangelis walked in. "Don't worry, I'm not checking up on you. Are you at a good place to stop for lunch? We're heading to the canteen, in honour of Sally joining us."

Sally guessed from the pleased look on Darren's face that this wasn't a usual occurrence.

The canteen was full of students copying each other's lecture notes, and it amused Sally to think of herself a few years earlier, freely handing out notes and explanations to grateful friends. She helped herself to a large plate of risotto – the kitchen had clearly gone up in the world since she was a student. They ate the first few mouthfuls in silence, a little shy of Vangelis outside the world of the lab. In the end he was the one who struck up conversation.

"I read a study about how your position amongst your siblings affects who you are. Now that's a study which makes crop research seem easy – how do you score people's personality traits, how do you control for the influence of economic status, education, genetics…"

Judith had joined them and seemed more relaxed than Sally had seen her before. As Vangelis spoke she even seemed interested.

Günter looked sceptical. "That makes their experiments easy – easy to make up whatever results they want."

"I think there's something in it." Sally replied.

"I had a girlfriend who always said…" Darren began, but Amy immediately interrupted him. "You had a girlfriend?!"

He pulled a face. "My girlfriend's brother was always difficult and she said it was because he was the middle child."

"Was he actually difficult? Never trust a sister's view."

"He was definitely difficult," Darren said. "He was grumpy most of the time and hideously uncooperative. I think he was a bit insecure, he was dismissive of everything."

"Brothers are always protective of their sisters," Vangelis said. "Maybe that's why he was being difficult with you. Firstborns and only children are meant to be the most intelligent – they had more adult influence when they were growing up."

Sally had read the same article. "And youngest siblings are more creative. Once the parents are confident the older sibling is going to do something sensible, the younger ones are allowed to be a bit more risky." She thought of her own stereotypical family. "That's how my mother views science."

* * * * *

Lunch together had left Sally with a new air of confidence, and only as she stood looking at the thick winter coat obscuring the window in Vangelis's door did she realise how tense she'd been before. She raised her hand to knock, but instantly someone grabbed her arm.

She spun round to see Darren.

"What are you doing?" He sounded alarmed.

"Asking Vangelis something."

"Good job I was walking past."

"What's wrong?"

He looked furtively along the corridor as if he was playing detective. "Let's not talk here," he said. "Come to the office."

She followed him in silence until the office door was closed behind them. "Sally's already discovered our best gossip," he said to a disinterested Amy.

"You're forgetting I still don't actually know what this gossip is."

Darren turned to her with a grin. "Our master and leader has become romantically involved with our technician."

"With Judith?" Sally heard an edge of horror creep into her voice.

"Yes, why not?" Darren seemed genuinely perplexed by her reaction.

"It seems wrong, I don't know, they work together."

"Is that a problem?"

"No, yes, I don't know, but I mean, what, how?" Sally wasn't quite sure what she meant.

"Don't ask questions if you might not like the answer."

Sally looked to Amy for more information, but she seemed to be ignoring them.

"How did you know to stop me?"

"The jacket over the door – it's the sign."

"Do people know that?"

Darren thought for a moment. "Well his students know only to turn up exactly when he's asked them to. I guess most people know that actually. We're the only ones who turn up whenever we like." Again, he seemed proud of his exclusive rights.

"Does he know everyone knows?"

"Probably."

Sally shook her head. "I don't get it."

"Come on, I'm off to get some old samples from the freezers, would you like me to show you where everything is?"

"Go on then."

Darren slipped into guided tour mode and Sally was pleased to stop talking about Judith. It had been hard enough to get along with Judith before, but now?

By the freezers Darren was chatting and joking as he sifted through the samples, but Sally couldn't match his good mood. Only as they returned to the lab did he finally manage to get her to relax.

* * * * *

Sally ate her supper with Liz but struggled to concentrate on what she was saying. Even when Liz shared confidences about her relationship with her father, Sally could barely manage more than monosyllabic answers. It was a relationship Sally had previously viewed as hero-worship, but Liz was fretting about the weight of his expectations: "I actually have no idea what he thinks of the last poem I sent him, he just said thank you. Even when he makes suggestions I don't know what they mean, does he actually like any of it anymore?" Sally tried to look sympathetic, her mind wandering to Vangelis and Judith.

When Liz returned to her poetry, Sally stayed in the kitchen and waited for Mel. Her wait was soon rewarded and Mel walked in, already grumbling about her boss and her empty stomach. The complaints stopped when she saw Sally.

"Sally you look perplexed."

"I've had an odd sort of day."

"You spend your life putting monkey genes into my breakfast and you're worried about having an odd day?"

"We don't put animal genes into crops, or into anything for that matter. And anyway it's not the science that's bothering me."

"Good, I've spent the last 12 hours on a case about the ownership of a data centre, so I want gossip not science."

"My boss, the one I told you about, who's dedicated his life to crop improvement…"

"Yes."

"He's having an affair with the technician."

"That's good."

"How can that be good?"

"It means he's up for offers." Mel's look was mischievous, but Sally got the disturbing impression that she wasn't entirely joking.

"He's married."

"That's not your problem."

"But I can't ignore it." Sally had imagined Mel would be as indignant as she was.

"You have to."

They lapsed into silence. Sally went to fetch the biscuit jar and placed it on the table with a thud and carefully dissecting a Bourbon. As she licked off the cream, her irritation at Mel's attitude receded and gave way to fascination.

"Would you ever sleep with your boss?" she asked.

"You mean to get somewhere, or just would I do it?"

"Either."

Mel reached for another biscuit. "I never have but I know people who've done it."

"Did it get them anywhere?"

"Sometimes, and I don't think any of them regretted it."

"I wish things didn't work like that."

"So do I, but if I can't change things I might as well take advantage of them."

Sally had always enjoyed feeling that she and Mel occupied different worlds. When Mel talked about her job she evoked a life that seemed at once glamorous and ridiculous – with strict hierarchies and farcical dress codes. But this evening Sally felt their worlds shift a little closer in a way she wasn't quite comfortable with. A career dedicated to something other than money didn't protect her from the fickleness of human nature.

Conversation drifted to more mundane events of the day while Mel ate her salad. But before Mel left for bed she put a hand on Sally's shoulder. "I know it's a shock when someone you admire does something you don't. But, ultimately, people always let you down."

Sally squeezed Mel's hand, too tired to find out exactly what she meant. "Good night Mel."

Chapter 6

The tinny sound of The Divine Comedy's 'Mother Dear' came from Sally's handbag and she groped for her phone. This was the ringtone she'd saved for her mother – a warning to herself only to answer when she was feeling diplomatic and had excess time on her hands.

"Sally?" Her mother's voice was high-pitched with excitement. "I had to call you - I was reading about mosquitoes and how scientists are going to stop malaria with genes."

"That sounds interesting, what did it say?"

"They put genes that stop malaria into the mosquitoes, and they're special genes that jump. So they jump to people when the mosquito bites them, and the people are immune to malaria."

"I don't think so Mum."

"I think you'll find that's what it said. Aunt Pat showed it to me."

Sally's heart sank. Aunt Pat wasn't really an aunt, but a revered family friend. Sally's mother had always considered her to be infallible, regardless of the fact her views were lifted directly from the tabloid press. As a child Sally had naturally seen her mother as the fountain of all knowledge and so, by default, assumed Pat must be too.

This meant she hadn't thought to question it when Pat told her that global warming was invented by John Major to make sure the Middle East couldn't get rich from oil. She'd spent the next 2 weeks making badges with her school friends and chanting 'Britain needs oil not lies'.

Ironically, her love of science and evidence could possibly be traced back to this event. Upon discovering that Sally was responsible for the Middle Eastern propaganda that was circulating through the more studious members of year 8, the school's head of Biology invited her into his office. He explained how the average temperature on Earth would be around -19°C if we didn't have an atmosphere. He drew diagrams on the whiteboard in pen that smelt like ethanol, and described the runaway greenhouse effect that caused Venus' oceans to boil away.

Now it was her reluctant duty to offer the same kind of education to her mother. "You're right about modifying mosquitoes so they don't transmit malaria, but genes don't jump into humans."

"No, they said that you couldn't get enough mosquitoes for it to make a difference so the genes had to jump."

"You're totally right about the jumping, Mum, but it's not into people. The genes jump between mosquitoes."

"When mosquitoes bite each other?" If Sally hadn't known better she'd have thought her mother was being perverse.

"No, when the mosquito breeds."

"I think you've missed the point about the jumping, Sally." Her voice was weary.

"No, the genes do jump but they insert themselves into different parts of the mosquito's own DNA. That way there's more chance of the genes being passed on to the next generation of mosquitoes."

"Perhaps that makes more sense. Anyway, I've got to go, but thanks for the explanation. Pat was very interested when she told me about the mosquitoes, and I said you did the same thing for food."

"You didn't tell her that I made genes jump from plants into humans did you?"

"Well I was sure that's what the article said."

"Now you know that's not exactly what it said, could you tell Aunt Pat that?"

"I'm seeing her next weekend, I'm having a little gathering. In fact, why don't you come too?"

When Sally was an undergraduate she had resigned herself to the fact that her mother would rather take second-hand *Daily Mail* views from Pat than listen to information her daughter had learnt from university professors. But, sadly, Pat's influence went beyond Sally's mother. The local WI and parish church regarded her in very high esteem, and the extensive family she'd spent her life creating seemed to be placed strategically round the country for maximum effect. So, if Sally didn't want Pat's disciples believing she put genes into crops that would jump into humans, she had some explaining to do.

"OK, I'd planned to set up an experiment on Sunday night, but I'll look at train times and see what I can do."

* * * * *

It was cold and raining as Sally got off the train and into her parents' overheated car. She turned down the blowers and leant over to kiss her mother.

"How was your journey?"

"Fine thank you, but it was a long time without food, I'm ravenous."

Her mother beamed: she loved to feed people, particularly her children. "There's a roast in the oven and crumble to follow. But I hope you're up for some baking."

"Of course." When Sally thought of baking as lab work without the latex gloves it made the idea easier, but somehow the instructions in recipe books weren't as exact as lab protocols, and you never had all the ingredients. She always managed to break egg shells into her mixing bowl and leave the kitchen coated in a fine dusting of flour.

"Good, because I need you to ice a carrot cake and we've got three batches of scones to prepare."

"How many people are coming?!"

"Enough." Her mother said smugly.

"OK, I'll do some baking on one condition. I want to practise my explanation of genetic modification on you ready to show Aunt Pat." This line was sure to be a winner – it involved impressing Pat.

"Can you do it while I chop vegetables? I need celery, carrots and cucumber for the dips."

"No problem."

Pleasantly full from lunch, Sally sat at the kitchen table with a pile of vegetables, and began her explanation.

"Have you heard of Bt cotton?"

"I'm afraid not, dear."

"It's a cotton plant which has been genetically modified to improve its defence against insects. There's a type of bacteria that is often used as a biological alternative to a pesticide. It's called *Bacillus thuringiensis* - that's where the name Bt comes from. The cotton has been modified so that it contains the natural pesticide gene from the bacteria."

"And how, exactly, did they put a bacteria gene into a plant?" Her mother had taken to wearing narrow glasses on the end of her nose, so she could look over them at Sally while she paused during the vegetable chopping. To Sally this was endearing, and it even made her look intelligent.

"That, mother, is exactly what I'm here to explain. We use a second type of bacteria to transfer genes into a plant. Have you heard of crown gall disease?"

"No."

"It's a natural disease of trees, caused by a type of bacteria which transfers some of its genes into the plant DNA. The genes from the bacteria make the trees' cells grow into the galls which you see on trees. So we use this *Agrobacterium* to transfer useful genes into crops, genes which protect against insects for example."

"I can see you're going to have to convince Pat it's safe; she knows what she's talking about you realise." Her mother tipped her chopping board full of potatoes into a waiting saucepan and reached for the broccoli.

"Of course we know it's all safe, and they've been using bacteria like this since the 70s. Once the crop has the Bt gene and is resistant to insects you can just breed the crops, no need for the bacteria anymore."

By this time Sally's father had come to join them. He normally made himself scarce during party preparations, but with Sally talking he could feel safe from demands to help.

He smiled indulgently at Sally. "I'm under strict instructions that the house must be cleaned top to bottom before our first guest arrives, but next time you come you've got to convince me of how you know that it's worked."

"Antibiotic resistance genes…"

"Save it for next time." He smiled, already trying to attach the right nozzle to the end of the vacuum cleaner.

58

The phone rang in the next room and her mother jumped up to answer it, with effusive greetings to Pat at the other end. Sally sighed.

Her father was still fighting with the vacuum cleaner as if it was beyond his technical skills. "If it's any consolation, I'm impressed. And, coming from you, it seems pretty convincing."

"Thanks Dad."

"If we survive this party then I would genuinely like you to tell me more."

Her mother returned looking flustered. "Pat can't come. She's laid up with the 'flu. I said she should go to the doctor; she's been in bed for the last three days. She'll be along to our anniversary party though, you can see her then Sally."

"Your anniversary party?"

"Yes our wedding anniversary, didn't I tell you? Nothing too fancy. It was Pat's idea in fact."

"It would be nice if you let me know when these things are."

"Oh come on, it's not until May, there's plenty of time for invitations. What could you possibly have organised already that's so important?"

"Um, experiments!"

Her mother shot her a disapproving look.

The guests, when they arrived, were an eclectic mix, mainly members of the WI or her mother's swimming class along with their long-suffering husbands. They seemed to have a common skill of asking Sally what she did but somehow be talking about their Poinsettias or their rheumatism before she'd had the chance to answer. When the last of the scones had disappeared and rumours of Trivial Pursuit began, Sally took refuge in the kitchen. Her father was already there, carefully drying teacups.

"Where does she get them from?" Sally rolled her eyes.

"Her friends? Who knows, but she recruits them well. And they adore her, especially her cooking."

"I don't know if I've spoken to a single person who's listened to what I've said."

"I know what you mean." Her father balanced the cups on their floral saucers. "But I'm afraid your duties aren't finished yet. I get to do the washing up, but you need to be shown off a bit more."

Reluctantly, Sally returned to the slightly tipsy guests. The Trivial Pursuit board was already laid out and there was a debate raging about how to split a prime number of people into reasonable teams. Although she was seldom able to banish Paul from her thoughts, it was rare that she thought about the generic advantages to having a boyfriend. But as she watched her mother's friends squabble over who would have her on their Trivial Pursuit team Sally was struck by how much easier it would be if she had someone there with her, and not just to make an even number. If Paul was here she could at least look forward to laughing about this on the journey home.

"Sally counts for two people, with her brains," said Margaret, a boisterous lady with skin that reminded Sally of a newly ploughed field.

Her mother glowed, but Sally was quick to defend herself. "Seeing as this set dates from at least a decade before I was born, I'm probably not the best team member."

She was instantly outvoted and placed in a team with Margaret and her husband Howard. Howard's hearing and memory were fading in inverse proportion with his waistline, and tact had never been his strong point.

By the time her team took its first go, Sally still hadn't heard of any of the people mentioned in an entertainment, sports or arts question. She pretended to look enthusiastic as their first question was read out.

"What was the most popular toy in 1957?"

"I know this one!" Howard stood up and gyrated his hips, his belly wobbling at Sally's eye level. He struggled for the right word while his hips moved in ever-decreasing circles.

"Hula hoop?"

"What?"

"Hula hoops," Sally shouted, and this time a grin spread across his red face.

"You're right, roll again."

As Sally reached for the dice her phone rang, and she was relieved for an excuse to escape. It was Darren.

"How are you doing?"

"I'm playing Trivial Pursuit with the WI. I can't describe how hideous it is."

Darren chuckled. "I didn't have you down as a WI girl, what do you do, win the largest vegetable competitions with GM tomatoes?"

"I can assure you I'm not there yet. It's my mother's party and it's a little more than I'd bargained for. I actually used to think I'd join the WI when I got to the right age, you know, make jam, grow vegetables and talk about interesting things. I just have to hope that the Brighton group is an anomaly, made dotty by my mother's influence."

"Your mother hasn't turned you dotty," Darren reasoned.

"Don't count on it, today could be the end of me."

"Well, I'd better get in there quick, because I need to ask you about your experiments."

Someone called her from the Trivial Pursuit game.

"Sorry, Darren, I'll just let them ask me this one thing."

"Sally, what's the nearest star to us? Is it the moon?"

"Did I just hear that correctly?" Darren asked. She could picture the look of amusement on his face, and wished he was there.

"I'm afraid so. Give me strength." She shouted through to her teammates, "No, of course it's not, it's the sun."

Darren was laughing.

"I'm sorry, I can't believe I've made you go into work to set up my experiment so I can explain the difference between the sun and the moon," she said.

"Don't worry, I was going to be in anyway. And I've got Amy with me, she's in the office writing her thesis. Actually I think she's pretty stressed. Would you mind talking to her tomorrow?"

"Sure, I'll see what I can do. What's she worried about?"

"Normal stuff, doesn't know if her thesis is good enough or whether she'll get a job, same kind of thing we all worry about."

"Well, I can reassure her that her thesis is OK, at least."

"Thank you, I think she's become immune to my attempts to sound positive. Anyway, you wanted me to culture some cells ready for tomorrow."

Sally explained which varieties of wheat she wanted cells from, the conditions they needed to be kept under and how many of each she needed. When she had explained in minute detail all of her requests she could no longer delay the moment she had to return to the party. She hung up and thought with amusement about all her mother's parties, gatherings and excursions she had endured over the years, and how planning experiments finally gave her the sanity needed to face more.

Chapter 7

Sally waited at the end of her road for her labmates. She had agreed to a Saturday night pub crawl with Günter, Amy and Darren but, predictably, they were late. She paced up and down in front of the last houses in the terrace, practising walking in Mel's shoes.

The plants in her neighbours' front gardens boldly announced the arrival of spring, with buds and leaves swelling into life. As the evening set in, however, a chilling wind had replaced the sunshine.

She picked at her fingernails; waiting was making her nervous. She began to wonder if she'd put too much make-up on, and gently dabbed at her lipstick in an attempt to make it more subtle. She was used to wearing a lab coat and she worried how people would react to her skirt and heels.

By the time they arrived, Sally's fingers were numb with cold. Amy and Günter were already laughing, teasing Darren about his sycophantic behaviour towards Vangelis. They stopped as they reached Sally.

"You look nice." Darren smiled at her and she struggled to look him in the eye.

"Thank you."

She fell in step beside him and they walked on in silence, Sally almost regretting that she'd come. But Amy and Günter were oblivious to her nerves and dragged her into their teasing. By the time they reached the pub she was laughing along with them, her fears subsided.

As soon as they all had drinks, Amy launched into a speech about the world's perception of GM. This was somehow connected to the accusation that Darren would believe it was right to genetically engineer human babies if that's what Vangelis told him.

While her friends argued and laughed, Sally surveyed the bar. It was packed and had an unpleasant smell of stale beer and too many bodies. But it was surprisingly upmarket, giving the impression it was full of lawyers and bankers who never quite made it in London.

Surrounded by sophisticated young professionals, she was glad she'd made the effort to dress up, and even Darren had exchanged his faded t-shirts for a proper shirt. But she still couldn't help feeling detached. The rest of the pub probably never gave a thought to the future of agriculture. Her work meant nothing to them. Their clear understanding of money and fashion, conversely, was lost on Sally. Her fashion credentials were made quite clear when she wore knee high socks on her first day of secondary school, and a career in academia was hardly going to lead to riches.

Her eyes drifted past smug couples, men in tailored jackets, elegant girls in formal but suggestive dresses and large groups staring intensely at a plasma screen displaying the football. Behind the bar drinks were being served by two overworked teenagers. One of them was mixing cocktails, carefully filling a row of martini glasses. But just as the bright blue drinks were handed out Sally froze.

Standing by the bar was Paul.

He was oblivious to Sally's presence, and she was torn between waving her arms and screaming to attract his attention and retreating into the shadows of the corner. She'd lived this moment in her head in endless permutations – in some she'd reacted with anger, some joy. Sometimes she had confronted him, demanded an explanation, sometimes she had declared her love. She was so engrossed with the surreal feeling of dreams becoming reality that she'd lost the thread of the conversation. Darren had noticed and was looking at her with interest.

She bought herself time with an attempt to join in the conversation on GM crops. "Nobody wants them to work, nobody wants them." Even in her head the words seemed shallow, irrelevant, completely missing the light-hearted mood of the discussion.

"Don't want what to work? Because it looks like the alcohol's working," Darren said with amusement.

Sally felt an irrational surge of anger and struggled to think of a harsh reply. But Paul was finishing his pint, and she realised if she didn't move now she would lose him.

Without a word to the others Sally began her fight towards the bar. She could feel Darren's eyes on her back, but the crowd soon engulfed her. On her way to confront Paul, her mood swung from fear to excitement. As she neared the bar her stiletto heel caught on a rough floorboard and she lurched forward. Steadying herself on the bar she received a disapproving look from a stick-thin girl with a fake tan.

Now, as she was on the other side of the crowds, everything looked different and she struggled to work out where Paul had been standing. Scanning the group of strangers he'd been with, she realised her mistake.

It wasn't him.

Cursing her idiocy she looked around, suddenly feeling exposed. Her throat tightened and she was alarmed to feel the threat of tears. Only then did she realise how firmly she'd clung to the belief that she'd see him again. Surrounded by her fellow drinkers, the idea that she loved someone she hadn't seen for five years seemed crazy, but love was what it felt like.

She hovered at the bar; there was no way she could face her labmates, yet she couldn't just leave. Then he turned. It *was* Paul. No longer trusting her judgement she stepped towards him, still with no idea what to say. It was only then that she realised Katie was probably with him. She paused, unsure if she could deal with meeting her. But then he saw her and it was too late.

"Hi." She stared at him.

"How are you?"

"OK. You?"

"Not bad."

Her eyes darted across his group of friends, searching for the petite brunette she'd seen in the photograph. To her relief it was Paul who spoke.

"Do you come here often?"

"No. My friends are over there - I just came to the bar." Five years thinking she'd do anything to see him again, and now Sally's pride wouldn't let her admit that she'd walked across the bar to speak to him.

"Do you live here?" he asked.

"I work at the university."

Paul nodded. "Who with?"

"Vangelis Papadakis." For the first time Sally saw interest flicker across his face, and she made a desperate attempt to hold his attention. "We're doing some exciting stuff – resistance genes for more insect species, crops that could be used on a large scale. It's a great lab to work in; we're just finishing the last trials to make a high-profile paper."

"That sounds good." His voice didn't reveal whether or not he was impressed.

"I got a PhD." Sally fought for lost ground.

"Well done."

The stilted conversation made her want to laugh. She had spent years imagining what they'd say to each other, saving up stories he would love to hear. Now, in real life, they were struggling to exchange pleasantries.

With the conversation dead she stared unashamedly at his friends, hoping to learn more from them than she had from talking to Paul. There was still no sign of Katie. She was relieved to feel Darren tap her on the shoulder. He was waiting with her coat; the others had already fought their way through a crowd of pink-shirted men to the door. He looked at Paul, intrigued. Sally could tell he was expecting an introduction but she wasn't going to give it. After all, she'd already decided she never wanted to see Paul again.

But she did have a shred of dignity to maintain. "Well, it was nice to bump into you," she said, for Darren's benefit not Paul's.

Without a glance back she followed Darren out of the pub.

Chapter 8

It was nearly lunchtime when Mel emerged on Sunday. Sally was still in her dressing gown, sitting with her legs tucked up on a kitchen chair, her chin resting on her knees.

"It was a good night then?"

"I've had better."

"So what were the good bits?"

Sally didn't answer. Still waiting, Mel put out two mugs and dropped a tea bag into each of them. The kettle whistled as it boiled.

"OK, scrap the good bits, out with the bad."

"I saw Paul."

"And that's bad?"

"Oh yes."

"Did you speak to him?"

Sally nodded.

"So where's he living, is he back in the UK?"

"I didn't really ask."

"You didn't ask him what he's doing?"

"We didn't exactly have much to say."

"I'd have thought 'which country do you live in?' would have been a good place to start."

"I thought he'd be there with Katie, and I really couldn't face meeting her so that kind of put me off, and neither of us had anything to say."

"So what's the problem – he's moved on and you don't even like him anymore?"

Sally managed a laugh. "When you put it like that I seem even more ridiculous than I did before!"

"We know you're ridiculous, you're obsessed by plant DNA, but that's not my point. Tell me what's wrong."

"I don't even know anymore." Sally smiled weakly; Mel's reassuring presence had snapped her out of self-pity.

Mel studied her for a moment, just long enough for her to feel uncomfortable.

"There are other men out there. Do you think it's time to let this one go?"

Sally nodded, acutely aware of the hole it would leave in her life. Not a hole left by Paul, but one left by dreaming of him.

Mel leant forward on the table, forcing Sally to look her in the eye.

"Sally, I know he was the first and he was perfect, but you're too young and too beautiful to be chasing married men."

"You're right, that I'm too young anyway."

"Come on, what do you want for breakfast? Bacon?"

"Shouldn't you be in the office?"

"It's Sunday."

"Like that normally stops you."

"Some things are more important than work." Mel gave Sally's hand a squeeze then delved into the cupboard for a frying pan.

"Thanks Mel."

Sally's phone beeped and Mel tossed it towards her. She opened the text then sighed.

"Is it him?" Mel asked.

"Nope, I'm saved that one. He doesn't have my number."

"Why the sighing then?"

"It's just someone from the lab asking if I was OK. I think they noticed something was getting to me."

"Sally, do you know what one of my colleagues would do if they'd seen me upset?"

Sally shook her head.

"Land me more work to make sure that none of my cases – that means how much they can bill my clients – are affected by my 'personal problems'…"

"You put up with so much, I don't know how you do it. I wouldn't last two minutes."

"So count yourself lucky to have colleagues who care. Beyond you, Liz and my mother I'm not entirely sure anyone would worry if I worked myself into a very early grave." She laughed, but again Sally got the impression this wasn't entirely a joke.

"I am grateful really that labmates text me; I just don't have any sensible answers for them."

"And you wouldn't tell them even if you did?"

"I guess you're right."

"Anyway, who from the lab?" Mel's question didn't sound entirely innocent.

"Darren."

"Which one's he?"

Sally was saved from Mel's interest by Liz walking in, dressed in her poetry-reading clothes which were just a bit too calculated to give a natural 'I'm an artist' look.

"Bacon?" Liz's tone was disapproving. She liked to give Sally a hard time about eating meat, pointing out that the problems Sally was trying to tackle with biotechnology could be solved far more easily if we ate the food we grow rather than feed it to animals. But she saw the look on Sally's face and sat down next to her.

Mel tipped the sizzling rashers of bacon onto three plates. "Sally, bread please."

Obligingly, Sally coated chunks of bread with a thick layer of butter – the kind of luxury that she saved for low moments. It worked, and by the time they were half way through their butties Liz was reciting her poetry and happily deflecting accusations that her words were randomly generated.

* * * * *

On Monday Sally walked to work as slowly as possible, a knot tightening in her stomach at the thought of how to brush off any probing questions. The office was silent when she arrived, so she checked her emails. Deleting the auto-alerts for journal articles she would never read didn't take too long but it fortified her to face her labmates.

Judith was in the lab emptying the glass bins, the yellow biohazard bags exuding a chemical smell which Sally found vaguely reassuring.

"Where's everyone else?" Sally asked. "We went out on Saturday night, but they can't still be in bed!"

Her joke was met with a frosty stare.

"They're in the field. The forecast was right for harvest."

"Already?"

"Yes. Already."

"Even Günter's gone to collect samples?"

"You weren't here."

"I'm sorry, I didn't know."

"I think Vangelis wants to see you."

Without a word Sally left the lab and went to knock on Vangelis's door. She had the uncomfortable feeling that she'd been sent to see the headmaster about her school report.

"Ahh, Sally, good to see you." Vangelis gestured for her to sit down. "Are you OK to hold the fort here this morning?"

"Of course, and I can do sampling whenever you need it, I'm ready to go out and help, whatever you want."

"This afternoon if that's OK. I've sent Amy out there. She doesn't have much time to spare from her thesis, but she needs her name on this paper if she wants to submit a grant proposal to stay here. That means she's got to do some work to earn it." Vangelis waved a thick wad of paper which Sally took to be the grant proposal. He wasn't going to take too kindly to a rejection. "So why don't you drive there at lunchtime, give the car to Amy and Günter, then Darren will give you a lift home when you're done. But for heaven's sake don't let Amy drive. Gaffer tape fixed her last mishap but we might not be so lucky next time…"

Sally took the car keys from him. She hated driving. She didn't own a car so the only ones she ever got to drive were the old and clunking estates the university reserved for fieldwork.

"No problem, it's a long time until it gets dark, with all of us together we can get lots collected."

Vangelis had already turned back to his computer.

* * * * *

After an unproductive morning in the lab Sally eased herself into the driving seat of the biology department's worst car, the one which had lost its left wing mirror. Sun streamed through the windscreen, highlighting the flecks of dust suspended in the air around her. She took a deep breath and gingerly negotiated her way out of the car park.

She met her third red traffic light within half a mile of the department. She relaxed into her seat a little; every delay meant longer until she had to face her colleagues.

The light turned to green and the cars ahead rushed off. In her haste to follow them she let the clutch shoot up too fast. The engine hiccoughed and died. Behind her a lady in a four by four beeped her horn. Infuriated, Sally started the car just in time for the light to turn red. For the rest of the journey she kept herself entertained with what she would like to have said to the impatient woman. She pictured herself sliding out of her car and pointing accusingly to the fuel cap of the black Land Rover while she preached about declining food production in Africa as the world slowly cooks. She chose an appropriate explanation of why she stalled: she was virtuous for not owning a car, not useless at driving. By the time the lady was allowed to proceed through the lights she would have understood the importance of the experiment Sally was about to go and harvest, and would think twice before beeping at battered old cars.

The journey gave her long enough to calm down before she reached the farm, and her silent rant provided the inspiration she needed to spend the afternoon putting ears of wheat into plastic bags.

Amy was in the farmyard labelling zip-lock bags with crop variety, field, location and date. She waved at Sally. "Look at all this – Günter and Darren are still out there doing more."

"Brilliant."

"How are you, anyway?"

"OK. How many samples have you taken?"

"Dunno, lots. Have you recovered from Saturday night?"

"Yes, thanks. Have we got enough bags?" Sally picked up one of the bags and examined it, without looking at Amy.

"Probably, Darren's in charge of that. Did you feel bad on Sunday morning?"

"Why, did you? How are we ever going to process all these? Vangelis wants everything weighed and counted within a couple of weeks."

Amy gave up her labelling and leant on Sally's car. "I just wasn't sure if you were OK."

"Look, we don't have time for this!" Sally was surprised by the harshness of her own voice. "If we're going to get this done we better get on and do it."

Amy flinched, but Sally was too relieved not to have to talk about Paul to feel any guilt. It was like putting unpaid bills into a drawer that would never again be opened.

They walked in silence to where Günter and Darren were standing in the crop. Sally handed Günter the car keys. He frowned. "First you make me to go onto a farmyard and cut food that cannot yet be eaten, and now you make me to drive on the wrong side of the road."

"You love it really. Now go and do something useful with our data."

Günter put his hand on Amy's shoulder and grinned at Sally. "No time for that, I have to write Amy's thesis."

Amy seemed happy to follow him back to the car.

Even if counting the number of grains on each ear would be mind-numbingly boring, the process of picking them was cathartic. The sampling regime was strict and accurate. Samples were taken at regular intervals in each of the fields, in a pattern carefully designed so the results from the GM and conventional varieties could accurately be compared.

Sally and Darren spent the afternoon in neighbouring fields, stopping only to straighten their backs or to bat insects away from their faces. As the light began to fade and her stomach began to rumble, Sally reluctantly put her haul of samples into the back of Darren's car. Darren was already waiting, lying on his back and pretending that the sun was still giving off enough heat to sunbathe.

He patted the grass beside him. "Come and join me."

Obligingly, Sally sat down and began picking at the dandelions. Darren wouldn't be as easy to brush off as Amy had been, and she was already constructing an apology for snapping at Amy that wouldn't invite further questions.

Darren propped his head on his arm and looked at Sally. "Do you ever get the feeling that things are all coming together?" He said this with such calm conviction that Sally felt her insides relax.

"I do, I really do."

"I see all these fields, ready to harvest and I realise that we've made it. This paper is going to be ours; this mutation will genuinely make a difference."

"Such a tiny change in DNA and it can do so much. It's crazy when you think about it."

Still lying down, he turned his head awkwardly to see the fields surrounding them. "We've worked on this for so long, and it's only now I can see this crop that I believe it's for real."

"I feel guilty that you did all this work before I arrived; I've just come along for a share in the glory."

"Don't feel guilty. This is just the start. We've all got so much more to do together. We'll have the Pope advertising GM by the time we've finished."

"Right now you could probably convince me it can be done, but one step at a time."

Their peace was shattered by the thick revving of a tractor. The farmer, Roger, climbed down and came to stand beside them. His bald head glowed shiny red from too much sun.

"When are you kids going to be done out there?"

"Just a few days."

Roger sucked in his breath. "The weather won't wait for you. And we need to get the harvest in."

"The forecast is good, and we have lots of samples."

"You'd be thinking differently if these letters were addressed to you, I can tell you that much."

"Letters?" Sally asked.

"Hate mail, I've been getting. They say I'm going to Hell for messing with God's creation, and I'll have my house burnt down because we're poisoning children."

A weight appeared in the pit of Sally's stomach. "I'm so sorry. We'll do something, we just didn't know, we can…"

She turned to Darren who shrugged.

"It's empty threats, and we'll be done soon. You'll be harvesting by the end of the week."

"That ain't a moment too soon."

"We're working as fast as we can." Sally wished Roger hadn't just caught them lying on the grass.

Roger pointed to the farmhouse. "My wife, she's nervous. It's making her edgy and I can't say as I blame her." He climbed back into the cab of his tractor and the ground shook as he continued past them on the track.

"We can't just let him receive hate mail," Sally said when the noise of the engine had faded.

"There's nothing we can do. Don't let it get to you, worrying won't fix the problem, worrying is the problem. Let's just look at our fields of golden wheat and dream."

They surveyed their realm in silence, listening to a flock of sparrows arguing in the hedgerow. Already the weight in Sally's stomach seemed lighter. "I can't even remember which plots were GM and which were control, they're all looking so good."

Darren rolled over and unfolded some crumpled plans, photocopied maps with green highlighter outlining the fields.

"You were doing GM this afternoon, and the one in front of the farm house is GM, and half the largest field. You couldn't tell, could you?"

Sally shook her head, the corners of her mouth curling into a smile. "It's worked."

Chapter 9

On Wednesday morning it was just getting light when Sally's alarm began its musical ring, set early to make the most of a day in the field. As her dreams morphed into consciousness, her first thoughts were rain. She could hear it running over the top of the blocked gutter and down her window. Two days into their sampling and their plans were thwarted. Their choice was to keep going and soak to the skin in the field or miss a day, and she knew which Vangelis would choose. She stood at the window for a moment trying to gauge how heavy the rain was, then slipped out of her pyjamas and into fieldwork clothes.

Downstairs in the kitchen Mel was eating her cereal, looking pristine in a white blouse and high-waisted skirt. She sniggered at Sally's waterproofs. "You look stunning today."

"Thank you."

When Sally stepped out of the front door the world seemed uniformly grey. But Cambridge rush hour didn't stop for rain, and cars were still nose-to-tail in a chaotic gridlock. Her hood reduced her peripheral vision, and she stepped out in front of a startled cyclist. She raised her hand in an apology, but he had already swerved past her to undertake the stream of cars.

In the office Amy was sitting at her computer, surrounded by empty mugs and piles of paper. It looked like she'd been there a while.

"This wasn't forecast." Sally unzipped her coat, dripping water onto the floor.

"Did you know lots of British forecasts are no better at predicting the weather than if you'd just looked out of the window and said 'tomorrow will be the same as today'?"

"No, but I do know that yesterday wasn't rainy."

There were heavy footsteps down the corridor and Darren walked in. He hadn't been as efficient with his waterproofs as Sally had, and he looked like a bedraggled dog. "This is going to be fun."

"Vangelis said not to go and sample," Amy said.

"How come?"

"I'm not sure. He spent so long telling me that my writing is shambolic and my graphs are formatted all wrong that I'd zoned out by the time he started to talk about the experiment."

"Well you keep writing madness and we'll go and ask him."

Sally hung up her coat and followed Darren to Vangelis's office.

He swivelled his chair round to face them. "Looks like you have a rest day."

"We can't afford that." Darren sounded impatient.

"A day won't hurt and you have piles of samples that haven't been sorted or recorded into lab books."

"We can do that when we've collected them all."

"What proportion have you got already?"

"Amy and I were out there at 7 yesterday morning, and Sally stayed with me until it got dark."

"That's not what I asked."

Darren frowned and looked to Sally for support.

"See," Vangelis said, "that's exactly why you need to take this opportunity to sort out your samples."

Sally thought of their conversation with Roger, and felt obliged to pass on his fretting. "The farmer wasn't happy – he wants it harvested as soon as possible."

"Tough – we're paying him to do this field trial. Now go and do some sorting."

* * * * *

Bin liners full of samples covered the floor of the storeroom, which already had the warm, dusty smell of grain. There was a workbench running down one wall, and Sally laid out cardboard boxes along its length. She labelled each one with a dried-up permanent marker, so samples could be divided up based on where they were collected.

She pulled out her first handful of samples. "I feel guilty about Roger."

"The hate mail?" Darren opened a lab book and laid out the plan of their fields.

"Yes."

"It was probably his ex-wife."

"Does he have an ex-wife? He said his wife was in the farmhouse."

"That's a new one. During our first field trial he slept with Judith and his wife took an intense dislike to GM and scientists."

"God, I didn't know Judith was *that* evil."

"Sally, that was a joke. I've no idea whether he has an ex-wife or not. But you know that GM Freeze send letters to their groupies so they can copy them out and drop them in the letter boxes of the immoral conspirators who want to profit from GM crops, because we all know that if you're into GM crops you only think about the money. But you shouldn't let those psychos get to you."

"I guess it was his choice to do the trial, but you shouldn't joke about his wife."

"OK, but you're right it was his choice and he's been doing it for three years so he knows what it's about."

Reassured by Darren's rationalisation, Sally picked up a new pile of samples. She peered at the labels, trying to decipher Günter's scribbles.

Darren stopped writing and looked at her. "I like it that you worry though."

The small room suddenly seemed far too hot.

The time passed quickly sitting in the storeroom talking and sorting, but too many hours in a room with no windows began to get to them. They allowed themselves a break for labwork and emails.

"Don't get carried away in the lab, let's be back here at 2 pm and not a moment later." Darren said with mock seriousness.

"At your service."

The lights were on in the lab; the day hadn't brightened up. Sally raided the cupboards for chemicals and lined up the clear glass bottles on her bench. She was mixing some Phenol-chloroform when Darren walked in. His expression was grim, and she thought for a moment that something had happened.

"Your friend's here," he said.

"My friend?"

"I don't know his name."

Sally paused, a full measuring cylinder still in her hand.

Darren scowled impatiently. "Well are you coming or not? I can tell him to go away if you like."

"Yes sorry, I just wasn't expecting anyone."

She followed Darren out of the lab.

Paul was waiting for them in the office, still standing in his coat.

"Paul?"

"Hi."

"Are you OK?"

He dug his hands into his pockets and shifted his weight from one leg to the other. "Sorry, I just thought I'd call in and see you, I hope you don't mind."

"It's fine."

"I didn't get much chance to talk to you on Saturday, and I knew where you worked."

"Reception let you up?"

"I've known Jennie on reception since you were still at school." His shoulders relaxed a little as he said this and the hint of a smile appeared, but his glance darted to where Darren was standing in the doorway.

Sally gave Darren a look that she really hoped said 'go away'. But he took a step closer to her, so they were both looking at Paul as if they were an interrogation team daring him to speak. Sally's throat dried up.

Paul was silent for a moment, then addressed Sally as if Darren didn't exist. "It's just, I know you're busy, but I was wondering whether you'd like to come and grab some lunch. But I guess with your work…"

"No, it's OK." Sally thought of the bin liners of samples sprawling over the storeroom floor then turned to Darren. "Do you mind?"

He shrugged. "Up to you."

"Thank you, I'll be back soon and we can keep going with the samples."

"I'll clear up your stuff shall I?"

"No don't worry, I can do that quickly." Then she imagined making up the solution while Darren and Paul looked on, nobody brave enough to speak, all attention focussed on her shaking hands. "Actually Darren, would you mind?"

"Whatever." With a last look at Paul, he walked back to the lab.

Paul smiled with relief as the door closed behind him. "Do you want to go into town or shall we avoid the rain?"

"Well I dressed for the field today, so I can deal with some rain." Sally reached for her coat, wishing that she was wearing something other than muddy combat trousers.

"There's a good cafe on Trumpington Street."

"Let's go," Sally said, keen to be as far away as possible from the watchful eyes of the department.

They walked through the corridors in silence, every step away from the lab making them a little more relaxed. Sally concentrated on the research posters that lined the walls to keep her mind from wondering why Paul was there. They would once have attracted admiration at conferences around the world, but now their corners were curling and graphs beginning to fade. When she was feeling uninspired she liked to read them, just to remind herself of the world she was privileged to understand. When a cell divides how does it ensure that the right number of chromosomes goes into each of its daughters? How does it lead to cancer when they get this wrong?

Suddenly Paul pointed at one and laughed. "How do bacteria affect the reproduction of the insects they live on? That's James's work. Bacteria control your sex life. Do you remember? Nothing's changed for him then."

Sally took a step closer and read the date on the poster. "2009, it's the same poster as when we were here!"

Paul smiled. "They never kept any of mine up. Still, it's good to think that we can't have been gone too long."

They continued their walk. The feeling began to spread over Sally that their silence was because there were so many places they could start, not because there was nothing to start on. She glanced over at Paul. Sometimes the more effort you put into remembering something the more time the memory has to mutate into something else. But he was no less attractive walking along beside her than she'd remembered. He caught her eye and smiled.

The cafe was packed, and condensation covered the huge windows. When they'd pushed their way to the counter Sally pointed at a goat's cheese Panini.

Paul looked amused. "Do you think we've gone up in the world?"

"I'll still have beans on toast for supper."

They queued alongside mothers with oversized pushchairs until they reached the till. As Sally reached for her wallet he gently pushed her hand away.

"I'll get these."

"Are you sure?" Her hands burned at his touch.

"It's the least I can do."

"Thank you."

The cashier tutted impatiently, and Paul turned to her before Sally had the chance to ask what he needed to make up for.

When they were sitting at their table he said, "So, tell me everything."

"I did a PhD. It was hard work, but I don't need to tell you that."

"I always knew you would, I could see you were good right from your first day in the lab."

Colour began to rise in Sally's cheeks. "I guess it did suit me well, and it's landed me a pretty good job."

"What's your research?"

"Insect resistance genes, building on the success of Bt crops."

"Well, well Sally. What's happened to turn you away from being an idealist?"

"I like to think I still am, but I tell myself I'm now into things that might actually work."

"I distinctly remember you saying that GM was just people looking for an easy fix."

"I hoped you'd forgotten that."

"Don't worry, if that's all you want forgotten from your student days you're doing pretty well."

It wasn't all that she wanted forgotten. The night she spent with him may have been one of her most vivid memories from Cambridge, but it wasn't one of her proudest. By rights, it ought to be forgotten. Perhaps he was thinking about it too, because his smile had faded and he sipped dispassionately at his tea.

She fought to lighten the mood. "I'd still love to be hugging trees and fighting against everything new. And I know I said we should be scared when there are so many people we need GM to feed them. I guess I still am but I realised I can't do anything about the people or what they choose to eat, but I can do something about the food."

Paul nodded, still not looking her in the eye.

"At some point I noticed that modern GM scientists, well the academic ones at least, seemed to have a similar agenda to me: growing more food, using less pesticide. Anyway you haven't totally caught me out – I was never against research into GM, just sceptical about whether it would work."

"And is it working?"

"Oh yes."

It was a relief to have someone she didn't work with take an interest in her field trial and she found it hard to stop herself from talking. But that didn't seem to be why Paul was holding back. Whenever conversation strayed towards him he froze up, and somehow they were talking about her again, or about the times they'd shared. He kept his life since they parted locked away from her.

They'd been talking for nearly an hour when she felt comfortable enough to ask him about himself outright. "Where do you work?"

"In Cambridge."

Sally waited for him to say more but he stayed resolutely silent. She opened her mouth to push him, to ask what had happened to America, but at that moment a toddler began to bawl behind them.

"Brat child," she mumbled.

They both laughed until long after the child had ceased its wailing.

Eventually Sally looked at her watch. It was already 2 o'clock.

"I guess you need to be getting back," Paul said.

She nodded reluctantly.

"I'll walk back with you."

"Don't you need to be in work?"

"I took the day off." His smile looked sheepish.

The rain was easing as they walked towards the lab. Outside the department they paused, both of them reluctant to say goodbye, but too unsure to propose another meeting. Sally was aware of watchful eyes on her, but nobody seemed to recognise Paul.

Eventually Paul pulled out his wallet and opened it to reveal his business cards. Sally strained to see the logos on them, but instead he took a crumpled receipt and wrote his number on that. "Here, if you ever feel like getting in touch again then I'm always around."

"I will."

It was gone two thirty by the time Sally returned to the lab. She made two mugs of black coffee then went to the storeroom to see Darren. He was focussed on sorting samples, already reaching for the next one with his left hand as he recorded notes with his right. He didn't break his flow when Sally entered. She stood in the doorway looking at the piles of bags that now reached the top of each box.

"Haven't you got anything better to do than stand and watch me?"

"I brought you some coffee." Sally stepped into the room and placed a steaming mug on the bench next to him. She didn't sit down.

"Thanks."

"Do you need any help?"

"Actually I've worked out a system."

"I can join in."

"I'm sure there's something else you need to do."

Sally lingered, staring at his back as he carefully straightened out a sample bag. "I'll be in the lab. Come and get me if you need anything."

"Will do."

Chapter 10

When the next day dawned sunny, Sally pulled on the same clothes as the day before and left without breakfast. She was still the last to arrive in the office; they had all arrived early to make up for lost sampling time. Darren's mood hadn't lightened and he packed their equipment with determined efficiency. Sally neatened up their boxes of samples, for the sake of feeling busy, and tried to gauge whether she needed to apologise.

They were interrupted by the office phone ringing. Sally picked it up, relieved to have something else to do.

"Do you have a statement?" a man's voice demanded.

"Sorry?"

"Do you have a statement?"

"I'm sorry, I think you have the wrong number."

"Am I through to Vangelis Papadakis's lab?"

"Yes."

"Look, don't mess with me. I just want a statement. It's easier for us all."

"I'm sorry, I really don't understand." Sally could feel colour rising in her cheeks.

"You're wasting everyone's time."

The line went dead.

"What was that?" Darren clipped his backpack closed.

"I've no idea, but whatever he was after he was really aggressive about it." Sally's brain kept searching for something she might have done wrong. "It was us he wanted though."

Darren shrugged. "Probably a salesman."

"But he asked for a statement."

The phone rang again. This time Amy reached for it.

"Good morning, crop genetics lab." There was a pause, then Amy frowned and said sweetly, "that's no problem. It's near Wilbraham."

Sally and Darren looked at each other, Darren's anger forgotten in a moment of shared fear.

"C B six, eight F D…"

Darren grabbed her arm. "What are you doing?"

Amy turned round, shocked at the anger on Darren's face.

"He asked for the postcode of the field trial."

"You idiot!"

"Calm down won't you." Amy folded her arms defensively, clearly scared by Darren's intensity.

"Did he hang up on you?" Sally kept her voice calm.

"Yes, when I'd given him the postcode."

Darren banged his fist on the desk. "Someone asks Sally for a statement, someone else wants the postcode of our field trial and then puts the phone down. That's not normal, Amy!"

"I didn't tell him anything he couldn't have found for himself."

"I will go and get Vangelis." Günter stood up. More than the phone calls, it was the grim look on Günter's face that made Sally's heart pound in her ears.

"I'm going to the field trial." Darren snatched his backpack and left. The door slammed behind him.

"Go with him," Günter said to Sally, "and do not let him go anywhere without you. Anywhere. I don't know what has happened, but he won't do sensible things when he is so mad."

Darren was in the car park by the time Sally caught up with him. They climbed into the car and settled themselves amongst the mud and crisp packets that charted the biology department's journey since the car's last annual clean.

It started on the second attempt and they eased out of the car park. As they turned onto the road the left wing mirror whacked against a parked car. Darren didn't react and Sally wound down her window to click it back into place. Darren revved his engine at every junction but his impatience was just rewarded with red lights and traffic jams. As soon as they were out of the city and onto the lanes he put his foot down. Sally concentrated intently on the view outside the window. It was a glorious day. A combine harvester was making the most of it, and grain poured out of its extended arm. Half of the field was already shaved down to stubble.

Without warning Darren swerved to overtake a Land Rover, throwing Sally sideways into the door. She turned to tell him gently that it wouldn't make any difference, whatever had happened couldn't be changed, but then she saw his expression and returned her attention to the passing hedgerow.

The smell of burning reached them before they could even see the farm. It reminded Sally of the last summer of stubble burning she'd experienced as a child, an acrid smell she associated with environmental damage and junior school. Darren turned down the pot-holed track which led to the farmhouse and stopped the car. Only as Sally stood up and looked over the hedgerow did the extent of the destruction hit her. Where earlier in the week they had collected samples of healthy, ripe grain, all that remained were green islands within a blackened landscape.

Further down the track, the BBC radio Cambridgeshire van was waiting for them, plastered in logos and with a large aerial extending above it. A young journalist leant against the bonnet, his attention focussed on his mobile phone. Darren ignored him, instead striding from one side of the track to the other to look out over what remained of both the fields. "How much has gone?"

Sally wanted to point out she knew no more than he did, but at that moment she only dared pacify him. "We can't see all of the trial; the rest could be totally fine."

"It's trashed, totally trashed, look right over there."

On the horizon a hedgerow had been burnt, and a tree emerging from it had been reduced to a skeleton. Suddenly that seemed to be the tragedy; Sally thought of the birds which could have been nesting in the hedgerow, chicks burnt to death before they could even fly. For a moment she would have been happy to sacrifice the whole field trial if the hedgerow wildlife could have survived.

The journalist left his van and came up to where they were standing. "I'm really sorry to interrupt but the show's on air and we're running a little bit late." He looked at his watch then smiled at Darren. "Now you must be Vangelis? Now don't worry the interview won't be live; there will be a time delay of a few minutes, so there's no pressure at all." He began to untangle the cord for a lapel microphone. "It's a bit windy so if we could stand in the shelter of the car that would be fantastic, and I'll just put this on you…"

Darren pushed the microphone back towards the startled journalist. "I'm not Vangelis and I don't have a bloody clue what's going on. Sorry to deny you some voyeurism, but we need to see what can be salvaged from this mess."

Without even a look back for Sally, he began pacing towards the farmhouse. For some reason Sally felt obliged to give the journalist an apologetic smile before hurrying after him. They walked in determined silence until a horn sounded from behind them and they turned to see a police car with sunlight glaring off its silver bonnet. The driver wound down his window and leant out.

"Who did this?" Darren demanded.

"Sorry sir, you are? This is private property."

"Don't tell me I'm trespassing! I'm the scientist for God's sake. This was my field trial; these bastards are the ones you need to get for trespassing."

The policeman didn't react to Darren's outburst. "It's not yet clear who's responsible. Sometimes people own up to these things as part of their campaign, but not this one, or not yet anyway."

"Do you need details of what's been destroyed?" Sally's voice shook, but she hoped being practical would snap Darren back into acting reasonably.

"Thank you, we will come on to all that, and we'd appreciate your help later, but for now we've got more urgent things to deal with." He sat back into his car and pointed through the windscreen. Darren and Sally followed his gaze to the farmhouse ahead of them.

They stood in silence as a thin column of smoke rose from a jagged hole in the roof.

The policeman gave them a moment to absorb the situation then turned to them once again. "I'll give you a lift."

Sally and Darren squeezed into the back of the police car and they continued down the track, every jolt bringing Sally's stomach closer to her mouth. As they emerged in front of the house to a waiting group of journalists, Sally feared a paparazzi moment, but their arrival didn't even turn heads. A couple of photographers stood slightly apart from the pack but both were staring at the screens on the back of over-sized cameras.

"Thank you," she said to the policeman and then stood by Darren's side to examine the house. From this close the roof was hidden and, beyond the column of smoke, the only indications of the destruction inside were missing upstairs windows and charred patches of wisteria. A faint smell of burnt timber filled the air.

A fire engine was parked next to a brick outbuilding, and two firemen stood tidying away the hose. One of them smiled at Darren and Sally.

"What happened?" Sally asked.

"Wife went to get herself a glass of water about 5 am and thought she smelt smoke. Opened the dining room door to see flames licking the curtains. Called her husband and they left pretty quick after that. These old houses, they're full of wood, held up by great beams. By the time we got here there wasn't much to be saved. Pretty much done now, just need to wait until this smoke's gone. Don't want it catching again."

Sally's knees gave a sudden wobble and she nearly grabbed on to Darren, but she was determined to give off the illusion of control. "Where's the farmer?"

"He's OK, gone with his wife to stay with a brother further down the road. Bit shaken, but no harm done."

Sally shuddered at the thought of the farmer returning to claim the charred remains of his life.

"How did it start?" The edge had gone from Darren's voice.

"No doubt at all that it was deliberate, and we'll find out exactly how. Are you the scientists?"

Darren nodded and ran his hand along the shining fire engine. "I can't believe we did this."

The fireman paused his tidying to look straight at Darren. "Don't think like that; it sure wasn't you. And I've seen buildings burnt to the ground and they still found the evidence to convict whoever had done it. So don't you go taking any blame, alright?"

At this point one of the journalists made the first move and came to question them. He looked younger than Sally and she suspected this was one of the more interesting events the local paper had sent him to report on.

"Are you the scientists?"

"Yes," Sally said cautiously.

"Can I ask you some questions about your trial?"

They both nodded and took it in turns to answer his questions, Darren temporarily calmer. Most of the questions seemed to miss the point, but he gave the impression of being genuine and interested. None of the other journalists came over to join them. When Sally saw they were interviewing someone else, she remembered that the newspapers had the power to carry whichever story they chose, and she didn't want to let someone else help them make that choice. Darren followed her to where the small group was standing near the farmhouse door.

The lady being interviewed was middle-aged and managed to look smart in her waxed jacket. She spoke as if she'd practised her lines. "I regret damage to an individual property, and my heart goes out to the farmer, but I think this is sending a clear message that nobody wants their countryside polluted with plants straight out of a high-security lab."

"You did this?" Darren stood squarely in front of the lady, and Sally glanced frantically to where the policemen stood, aware of her middle-class belief that nothing bad could happen when a policeman was present.

"No," the woman said. "I don't know who is responsible for this decontamination of the countryside, but I am a spokesperson for GM Sense."

"You don't have a clue what you're talking about." Darren shook his head slowly but thankfully took a step back from the lady.

"This isn't contamination of the countryside," Sally said. "It's safe. There's no way we'd be allowed to do a trial which genes could escape from." She looked around the journalists, trying to gauge whose side they were on.

"The very idea that genes could escape shows how entirely unnatural genetic modification is."

Sally suddenly realised this was a game of words not of evidence, and she was totally unequipped to play it.

The woman continued to speak, gesturing to the burnt fields. "This is a message to you from the British public."

"Unless 'The British Public' are all arsonists and vandals, don't try and say this is everyone's view." Darren's hands clenched in his pocket as he spoke.

Before the lady could respond, a blonde journalist turned to Sally. "And how do you feel about the events of last night?"

"We were nearing the end of a valuable and safe trial, which is now impossible to complete. This experiment showed real promise. We've found a tiny modification to the genetic code of these plants which protects against pests – species of beetle and sucking bugs that until now we've only controlled by spraying insecticide."

Darren turned and walked away from the group. Sally found that words came slightly easier; she had feared what

Darren might say far more than anything the journalists could come up with.

The blonde journalist looked up from her shorthand, her make-up and painted nails incongruous on the farm. "And what do you say to the protesters who have caused this damage?"

"We are appalled at the way the farmer has been targeted. We are always happy to engage in conversations with anyone who is unsure of the benefits or safety of GM crops. This is not a constructive way of expressing those views."

The woman from GM Sense spoke up again, still sounding as if she was reciting her campaign slogans for the BBC news. "I spoke to Vangelis Papadakis this morning and was told quite clearly that he had nothing to say to me. That's not engaging in conversation, it's withholding information."

At this point one journalist checked his voice recorder and the other three scribbled frantically. If Vangelis was provoked, Sally could easily imagine him telling an anti where to go. But Vangelis wasn't here, and she had the presence of mind to protect the moral high ground. "When I left the office this morning we were already getting demands for information before we knew what was going on ourselves. I'm not aware of a single request for scientific information about these trials this morning. But if you have any questions I'd be only too happy to answer them." She looked around her captive audience, making eye contact with each of them, challenging them to find a question she couldn't answer. As they stood, momentarily silenced, she almost began to enjoy her power.

When her heart rate eventually returned to normal, she recognised this glimmer of pleasure as adrenalin and not a morbid desire to benefit from someone else's pain. But now it was enough to make her retreat to where Darren was standing kicking at the dirt. That was the photo which would make the front cover of Friday's papers: Darren and Sally against the backdrop of the smouldering farmhouse, their heads bent together conspiratorially.

"I can't believe this," Darren said when the journalists had turned their attention to the policeman.

"Nor me."

"One night of partying for them. Three years lost work for us."

"It's not three years, just this one season. This time next year…" She trailed off, unable to convince either of them that a year didn't matter. If you didn't get results you didn't get funding. If you didn't get funding none of you had a job.

Her phone rang in her back pocket. It was Amy.

"Sally, I'm so glad you answered. Darren's phone's off. We keep getting calls and Vangelis has disappeared somewhere. What's going on?"

"Sorry Amy, it's not good."

"Just tell me."

She had no idea what to say. Somehow it had been easier to take everything in seeing it one piece at a time, rather than sitting in a lab and hearing the whole story in one heavy hit. She looked at Darren in panic, trying fruitlessly to make sentences form in her head.

"It's OK, let me." He smiled and gestured for her to hand over the phone.

"Hi Amy, sorry to keep you waiting. We would have called but Sally's turned into a bit of a celebrity here…"

Sally followed Darren round the side of the house to where a wooden bench looked out over a murky fishpond. It was a relief to be out of sight of the journalists, and she could be free of the feeling that her thoughts were constantly being invaded. They were in the shade of the house and goose pimples rose on

Sally's arms. She sat close to Darren and listened as he recounted the story to Amy. It was strangely reassuring to listen to his summary of events. All the facts were accurate, but said in a dismissive way which was completely contradictory to his earlier anger. "And you should have seen the BBC man's face when we walked away – like it was the first time anyone had ever said 'no' to him. Bet he's telling his mother about it already."

"How was she?" Sally asked when Darren had hung up.

His tone was serious again. "A lot to take in I guess. I said not to worry, and we'll keep her up to date whenever we get more news."

"Thanks for telling her. I just couldn't think how to put it."

Darren ran his fingers through his hair. "I'll talk to Amy any day. I even feel better having spoken to her. It's the hacks I just can't deal with. Sorry I left you rather stranded out there."

"That's fine. It was almost satisfying."

"You were great." He smiled at Sally. "Thanks for protecting me from myself."

Sally squeezed his hand, relieved she now had a supporter rather than a threat to the world's perception of scientists. "It's not over yet. I think we should go back out there."

"OK, I'm ready."

The policeman was taking questions, while the journalists stood listening like students on a school trip. Darren and Sally stood behind them, trying to glean more information. Sally ignored the repeated ringing of her phone.

When it rang for a fourth time the lab number once again flashed up on her screen. This time she answered it.

"Amy stop calling – there's nothing more to know."

"Sally?" It was Vangelis.

"I'm sorry, have you been trying before?"

"It doesn't matter. Have the journalists found you?"

"Yes, a few of them."

"Well give them my number and refuse to answer any more questions." Vangelis's voice was matter of fact. "I hear that not everything's been touched?"

"I haven't seen any that's OK, but there might be."

"OK, I want you to go with Darren, drive the car round the corner and wait until the press have cleared off. Then come back on foot and keep sampling. If anyone tries to talk to you don't say anything – you don't know who they could be."

Strangely it hadn't crossed Sally's mind to try and salvage the situation. Damage limitation on their image was all she'd hoped for. The morning had been too intense for her to recover quickly, and at the idea of picking up the pieces of the experiment she felt only exhaustion. But she reassured Vangelis it was fine and went to tell Darren.

The policeman gave them a reference number and instructions to call the station that afternoon. The firemen again reassured them that it wasn't their fault and, their feelings of guilt unaltered, they said polite thank yous and returned to their car. Collecting samples from patches of untouched crop while the emergency services cleared off home was almost more than she could deal with, but together she and Darren picked their way across burnt field to the remaining patches of wheat. Sally forced herself to keep collecting ears of grain, though more than once she had to take a second sample because she'd forgotten to label the first. They stayed sampling until the sky clouded over and they had the excuse to return to the office.

* * * * *

When they had gone through post-mortems with Vangelis, Amy and Günter, Sally couldn't face any more circular discussions about who and how and why, but they still had the police to deal with. Darren fumbled in his pockets for the crime reference number and dialled the police station. "Hi, I'm Darren, I wanted to give details regarding the crop trial that was destroyed last night."

Sally pulled up a chair and sat next to him, offering her silent support. She leant forward on his desk, close enough to hear the policeman's muffled voice.

"Is there any news on who's responsible?" Darren fiddled with the telephone's coiled flex.

"Not yet, but we are taking the matter very seriously and will keep you updated with all the developments as they arise," he said with practised patience. "We're trying to determine the exact time of the incident. Were you at the site yesterday?"

"No, it was raining. We were there on Tuesday until 7 pm."

"I have spoken to the farmer. He was there yesterday, but can I confirm that you were not?"

"Indeed."

"And you were the last of your team to visit the farm?"

"Yes, along with my colleague Sally Jones."

"Sally, is that Miss or Mrs?"

"Doctor." The patience was starting to leave Darren's voice.

"So you and Dr Jones were at the Farm in question on Tuesday until 7 pm…"

Sally couldn't bring herself to follow the rest of the conversation. She ignored the painstaking details and listened only to the frustration in Darren's voice. Darren shook his head when he finally put the phone down but seemed to have run out of insults.

Police statements were followed by statements for the press and statements for the university, all worded in such artificial language that Sally's tired brain began to wonder if they'd been computer generated.

When at last they had finished, Sally left by the back door, hoping not to bump into anyone who might want the story recounted to them. She kicked the ground as she walked, trying to rid herself of her frustration. But movement and fresh air made her body at least feel better. A gentle breeze cooled her, relieving the mugginess of the afternoon.

Not ready to go home, Sally walked along the river bank. Students on bikes dodged her, only swerving at the last moment. She watched a mother duck waddle along with a trail of ducklings in tow, one lagging behind. It stopped, stood as tall as it could and flapped its stubby wings, quacking gently to announce its newfound skill. The duckling's evident delight was endearing, and Sally crouched down next to the mother.

She was startled by a voice behind her. "Them's her fourth brood, 8 of them."

Sally instantly recognised the hunched figure on the bench – it was the bag lady who she had met on the night of her interview.

"How do you know how many broods she's had?"

"Don't you know that kind o' thing about your friends? I fed her when she was just a wee baby, and I've been feeding her ducklings every year since."

Sally surveyed the bag lady and wondered whether she'd been on the streets for four years of ducklings, if indeed she lived on the streets at all. She was wearing a baggy knitted jumper which had faded to grey. The number of holes in it suggested it might not have been taken off for all those years.

Unsure of what to say, Sally turned back to admire the ducks, but the lady interrupted her.

"Now I know you haven't come to talk to my wee ones for nothing – come over here and tell me what's up."

Sally's knees cracked as she stood up a little too sharply. She crossed the towpath and sat rigidly on the bench next to the lady, wondering what about her body language had given her mood away. They sat in silence while the ducks came to peck around their feet. When it became clear that she wasn't going to get any more prompting, Sally began.

"I'm a scientist, and we've been doing this experiment, all about wheat that doesn't get eaten by as many insects. It was looking so good, and I really thought it was going to work." Sally was horrified to feel her voice begin to shake and glanced over at the lady to see if she'd noticed. But her wrinkled face was impassive, and there was no way of telling if she had any interest at all in what Sally was saying. Unwilling to stop now she'd started, Sally ploughed on. "If it works we can publish the results, and what we discovered can go on to help people use less pesticide yet still lose less of their harvest. But the trouble is it's GM." Did the bag lady have any idea what GM meant? She gave no indication either way. "And lots of people don't like it. Well, last night activists found out where the trial was and burnt it to the ground."

The lady didn't speak and Sally began to think she'd understood nothing. But then she slowly shook her head and turned to focus her cloudy eyes on Sally.

"When you've seen as much violence as me you'll learn that sometimes it feels like it's the only way. Without violence ain't no one going to listen."

"But burning things, surely that can't be the way to change things."

"They standing up for what they believe in and, right o' wrong, maybe it's better than doing nothin' at all."

"I would have listened." Sally said this quietly, not sure whether the lady would hear, but her ears seemed as sharp as her eyes were cloudy.

"Would you really, pet? Sometimes when people believe things they get all blind to everythin' else."

Sally considered this, wondered if she took all the evidence seriously enough, good and bad. Maybe she would have listened to the activists, who knows, but she would never do any work if all she did was listen to people who wouldn't change their minds. She did listen to other points of view, even if she didn't respond, she noticed. Then she tried to imagine Darren listening calmly to the views of would-be activists. He simply wanted to be right.

"No," she said eventually. "Darren wouldn't. But I would. I think things through, when Vangelis and Darren get blinkered, I still think."

With a loud quack the mother duck launched herself into the river then shook her tail to rearrange the feathers. Sally thought about Darren's desire to be right, but their motivations seemed irrelevant now they had no trial.

The lady was still looking at her. "Tell me, m'love, you feeling better about that man o' yours?"

Sally looked at the lady slumped on the bench, shocked that she remembered her.

"Yes, thank you, much better."

"Good girl."

For the first time that day Sally was tempted to smile. She was feeling far better about Paul, and she'd happily let the lady think it was because she'd forgotten him. Then she remembered her lunch, still in her bag. The morning had left her without an appetite, and Darren had bought packets of crisps for them all to share.

"Do you like cheese?"

The lady's eyes widened as Sally pulled out her lunchbox and handed over the contents. "Thanks for talking to me, I feel better." But the lady didn't hear; she was devouring the sandwiches as if Sally didn't exist.

Chapter 11

Exhausted, Sally collapsed on the sofa and flicked through the TV channels. On one an overweight woman was sobbing because it was raining on her wedding day, on another a man dramatically wiped away tears because the judges hadn't liked his pomegranate mousse and chocolate sauce.

Normally this would entertain her, but today their inability to keep things in proportion left her bitter, she just didn't have the energy to do anything else. It was a relief when Mel came home. She turned off the TV then perched on the chair opposite Sally.

"What happened to you? Even dancing celebrities aren't that depressing."

"You could say we had a bad day."

Mel gave a mocking smile. "Try coming to work with me."

"No, seriously, a bad day."

"Don't tell me one of your plants is sick."

Sally scowled. "All of them actually. Burnt to the ground by activists, along with the farmer's house."

"Guess that counts as a bad day." Mel's tone was casual, as if Sally had announced the demise of the coffee machine.

"He could have died, Mel!"

"Yes, but he didn't, and it wasn't you."

"I don't think we can finish this experiment."

"Do it again then."

"Oh, no problem. I'll grow some fields of wheat tomorrow. I wonder why I didn't think of that."

Mel gave a sympathetic sigh, making Sally feel guilty for snapping. "I know it's not easy, but these things happen."

"We've wasted all this time, it delays our results being published. We think this gene is going to work, and now we have to wait another year to prove it."

Mel shrugged. "It's just a matter of time. Anyway, you get paid to work not to get results."

"I don't do this to get paid. I'd be a lawyer if that's what I wanted. But I don't, I want to make a difference." As soon as she said it, Sally regretted the gibe at lawyers, but Mel didn't seem to react.

"Sally, you care too much. You wind yourself up over what results you get, then you come home and make yourself miserable. It doesn't even help your work."

Attracted by their voices, Liz walked in. She joined Sally on the sofa and looked at them expectantly. Sally searched for something to say, fearing that Liz might side with the activists if she knew what they were really talking about. Mel seemed to have the same thought and instantly snapped into joking with Liz, and the two of them filled the room with cheery banter. Sally turned the TV back on and convinced herself that if she listened to them for long enough their mood would lighten hers. But it didn't, it just made her feel distant from their world and pushed her thoughts back to her labmates. Presumably they were no better company than she was, but now the shock was over, was it anger they felt? Or determination to continue, or disappointment about lost work, or fear of how this could affect their future? She had committed too much emotion to the day's failure, and exhaustion dulled her disappointment. Mel's idea of going to work, having a good time, getting paid but not caring whether any of the experiments worked was an appealing one. She knew Mel managed to pull it off, the not caring at least, even if not the having a good time.

When Liz and Mel started discussing celebrity chefs, Sally couldn't take any more and escaped to her room. Lying on her bed she flicked through the contacts on her phone, looking for someone who would listen. She passed the names of everyone she'd worked with her during her PhD. They were fun labmates and she missed their company, but she couldn't face speaking to them. They'd understand, they'd be sympathetic, but ultimately they'd be glad it wasn't their experiment.

Out of options, she reached for her handbag and pulled out the receipt on which Paul had written his number. You could tell he'd only had his hand to lean on because the writing was faint and he'd nearly pressed through the paper. She straightened it out and laid it on her bedside table, trapped down by her alarm clock. Reassured by its presence, she fell asleep still debating whether or not to call.

* * * * *

"You look better," Mel said when Sally came down for breakfast.

Sally avoided looking her in the eye but said casually, "I'd be even better if I was still in bed."

"Wouldn't we all."

Sally walked slowly on her way to work, dreading the verdict on how totally their experiment had failed. There was still a chance they had collected enough samples, that yesterday was a blip that might taint their reputation but wouldn't touch their data. She tried to ignore the voice in her head which knew really they had not, that yesterday's emergency sampling had been too little too late. But what she feared the most was that they had almost enough. That in half an hour's time she would still have to sit down in the windowless prep room and begin the task of weighing every single grain from every single sample. That it wouldn't be worth delaying publication, but instead they would be forced to publish data where the sample size was too small – data that wouldn't interest the top journals. The kind of incomplete data which meant that, when she spoke at conferences, people would say over dinner "*I thought they would have been more thorough than that, I would have wanted something rather more convincing myself*" and then pour more glasses of free wine and feel the warm glow of superiority.

Outside the newsagent a billboard read 'Farmer targeted in GM crop scandal'. Sally was almost amused by the ambiguity of whether the scandal was the crops or the targeting. She wondered about going in, but decided she'd rather assess the damage with Darren there to laugh it off. Curiosity nearly got the better of her as she passed the shops next to the department, but by that time she was already running late.

Amy was at her computer when Sally arrived. She quickly closed the window she'd been looking at. "Sally, how are you?"

"I guess I'm about to find out."

"Do you want some tea?"

"Actually I think I could do with some coffee to face this morning, so if you're making…"

"Sure." Amy got up then saw Sally lean over to turn on her PC. "Why don't you come with me?"

"You're scared of the kitchen?"

She didn't answer, so Sally followed her and listened to Amy's incessant stream of chatter, clearly planned to ensure Sally couldn't ask about the newspapers or the samples.

Sally carried her steaming coffee back to the office and opened up Internet Explorer. "This doesn't make any sense. Someone destroys our experiment and I'm scared what the papers will say about us."

Amy jerked her mouse so her screensaver was replaced with the headline 'Cambridge genetic scientists condemn the behaviour of activists'. "Look, read what it says on the BBC. There's a quote from GM Freeze about how they regret what happened to the farmer but that it was right to end the trial by whatever means possible. They should have kept out of it I say. They claim not to have done it, but with quotes like that everyone will wonder."

Sally read the article on Amy's screen. It was fair and accurate, and was supported by a dramatic photo of the singed farmhouse.

"Well, good to see I get a quote about my own experiment, not just GM activists."

"You're quoted quite a lot saying something about being appalled by the attack. You sound quite impressive…"

Amy next showed Sally coverage in *The Guardian* and gradually worked down to the *Daily Mail*, in which the photo of Sally and Darren looked impressively sinister. It wasn't long before Sally had read as much as she could take in one sitting. She wanted to go and speak to Vangelis, but it didn't seem fair before Darren arrived and there was still no sign of him.

Sally thought back to the night before, and how appealing it had been to give up caring. There was a certain attraction to not worrying about turning up on time or working hard or being bothered about her results, and there had even been the distant attraction of quitting totally. She was embarrassed by it now, but knew from experience that Darren's mood swings were far more extreme than hers.

The clock turned to 10am and, unable to wait any longer, Sally decided to call him. She reached for the phone, but there was no dial tone.

Amy glanced over from the computer. "Sorry, I forgot to tell you, they've diverted our phones to the press office."

"That's probably wise." Sally used her mobile instead. The ring on her phone was matched by a ringing from Darren's coat hung behind the door.

"Did Darren leave his phone here overnight?" Sally asked, not sure if this was a good sign that he had to come back for it or a bad sign that she now had no way of reaching him.

"No, he's already here."

"Where?"

"I dunno, probably with Vangelis or playing with the samples."

"Why didn't you tell me? And how come you're here, didn't you want to find out how much we have?"

"You're the same as Darren, you arrived this morning suddenly believing it might all be OK. I admire your optimism but sadly I don't share it. Hence I'm reading idiotic blogs about evil scientists rather than writing my thesis."

"That doesn't quite follow. And am I the evil scientist being blogged about?"

"It's no paper for us, no grant proposal for me, so a PhD is kind of redundant if it doesn't get me a job. Makes a thesis rather pointless."

"Sounds like an excuse to me." Sally sounded worryingly like her mother.

"That's all very well for you to say. You know you have another chance. You've got two more years of funding. I haven't been paid for six months while I finish writing my thesis, and you know as well as I do that my grant proposal needed that paper, and that it was by far my best chance to stay in this rat race called academia."

Sally gave her a hug. "It's not a waste, it's an amazing achievement and there are so many things you can do with it." Her words, meant to be reassuring, sounded very much like admitting defeat.

"I know really that most grant proposals go straight in the bin, so it might not have made the blindest bit of difference. But I can allow myself one day of feeling sorry for myself instead of fighting with my thesis."

"OK, you get one day of sympathy." Sally pushed her chair back under her desk. "I'm off to find Darren."

Darren was alone in the prep room. He smiled as Sally entered and looked at his watch. "What time do you call this?"

"I was waiting for you in the office. I thought you couldn't face coming in today so you'd stayed in bed, or left the country or something." Sally almost giggled with relief that he hadn't.

"Thank you very much! Actually I came in early to see what we have, and Vangelis and I have just been talking about things."

"And?"

"And." He paused with the attempted the drama of a games show host, but his poker face was ruined by a smile. "We've got enough!"

"Enough? For what?"

"What do you think? For our paper."

"What, how, really?"

Darren laughed at her. "Be happy Sally, we worked hard enough. I hadn't quite realised how much we'd got earlier in the week. So many of us were out there I'd kind of lost track, and Amy had a load she hadn't given me, and we got some more yesterday afternoon."

Sally felt her clenched stomach relax and sat down in a chair with a thump. "I can't believe it, I feel an idiot for taking it so badly."

"Don't worry – I think I'm the one who over reacted. Anyway, get to it, we've got work to do!"

Sally reached for Darren's lab book in which he had written an immaculate chart of exactly what samples had been collected. He was right; it was almost as many as they'd been hoping for.

"You've sorted out all these samples already?"

Sally hadn't meant this as a challenge, but Darren's answer was defensive. "Yes."

"I'm impressed."

Thankfully this compliment lightened Darren's mood. "And you thought I couldn't be bothered to get out of bed."

"I didn't really."

Darren raised his eyebrows at her, and his smile suggested he knew full well that she was lying.

"How come you didn't wait for me to speak to Vangelis with you?"

"Never satisfied. Isn't the fact we can do the experiment enough for you?"

Her question had been innocent but she wasn't sure whether or not the answer was a joke. Deciding to ignore it she wrote the date in her lab book and began a summary of the sampling.

* * * * *

When Sally left at 7pm that evening her eyes were fuzzy from intense hours of weighing grain and her phone was full of messages. Some offered their sympathy, some complimented her on how impressive her quotes sounded, and her mother congratulated her. Happy to have even misguided congratulations, Sally called her mother back.

"Hi Mum, thanks for your message."

"You're welcome dear, but I must say that next time you pose for the papers you really should choose something a little more flattering to wear."

"I can assure you that if I'd known I would be hounded by journalists I would have worn some lipstick and not had holes in my trousers. In fact no, if I'd known what was going to happen I would probably have stayed in bed."

"Nonsense, you've got to make the most of these things. Not everyone gets their photos in the paper."

Sally could imagine her mother spending a happy morning showing the *Daily Mail* photo to anyone and everyone who would listen, for once proud of her daughter's achievements. "I'll grant you that one," she said. "And I suppose almost no one gets their photos plastered everywhere for doing something good."

"Don't forget, all publicity is good publicity."

The closest Sally's mother came to fame was reading *Hello!* magazine, but Sally didn't like to point out that she was poorly qualified to discuss publicity. "I'm afraid it isn't, and good publicity is probably poor consolation for the farmer. But we're lucky, our experiment's OK. We needed to collect enough wheat from lots of different places in each field, and we did it."

As Sally explained the good news to her mother it seemed like a hollow victory. Darren may still be smiling, but even a paper in *Nature* couldn't bring back the farmer's house. Even the most promising results were meaningless if the general attitude to GM crops really was 'burn them'.

Her mother quickly moved on to gossip, stories gained as a result of a day spent hanging round the village hoping to bump into new people to show the papers to. Sally half listened to tales of how the Barfoot-Saunts had run out of money to put windows into their extension and of Gillian's granddaughter who had the measles. It was vaguely reassuring to listen to her mother's contented wittering about mundane events and, by the time she arrived home, her relief about the experiment had once again pushed aside fear for the farmer.

Later that evening she cooked supper for Mel and Liz, forcing any thoughts of the day's highs and lows out of her head, pouring someone a glass of wine whenever her thoughts slipped back to the samples they'd collected or the work they still had to do.

When she lay in bed, her head swimming from far more wine than she'd usually permit herself on a weeknight, she wondered whether Paul had seen the papers. Had he Googled the coverage in his lunch break? Did he read it with fascination, disapproval at what her work had led to, righteous anger at what the protesters had done? Would he call and offer his sympathy?

Then she remembered that he didn't have her number.

* * * * *

Processing the samples was as mind-numbing as Sally had expected.

On the face of it the task was extremely simple – weigh the grain and record the result. But mistakes would threaten to creep in; the right number so easily slipped into the wrong place or she would simply write the wrong number.

Sally's eyes almost blurred from staring at the balance, and her hands threatened to bypass her brain as they followed the same incessant routine. Her fingers began to hurt from pinching off each grain of wheat. When she ever caught herself making a mistake she would instantly leave the prep room and force her brain to focus on labwork for their new experiments or on writing up the paper. Only when she was satisfied with her concentration would she return. Darren, however, never left his bench. When Sally pushed him he brushed her off claiming mistakes were for the weak. She tended his plants in the glasshouse, conscious he would happily leave them to shrivel rather than delay their results.

Left alone in the dingy prep room to weigh thousands of grains, Sally would no doubt be driven to insanity. But Darren managed to turn it in to a social event. A shared focus, which had already defied the odds, helped spread the feeling they were invincible. Darren talked endlessly about plans for their next experiments, which became more ambitious and more monumental by the day. Each one was designed for publication in the top journals for advancing their careers. Sally was happy to indulge his fantasies and soon became sucked into them. Somehow these discussions always stopped if anyone else was in the room; there seemed no need to dampen their ideas with realism.

Darren delighted in online coverage of their experiment, mainly on obscure blogs or websites for dysfunctional campaigning groups. He'd even grown to like photos of him and the fire engine. Multiple anti-GM bloggers claimed that

Vangelis had paid Darren and Sally to keep quiet about previous findings. He both lived in a £400,000 pound house paid for by one multinational biotech company, and a house worth half a million thanks to a deal with another. Sally and Darren were regularly lovers, though Darren was particularly pleased to read that they also owned a patent set to make them rich.

He was happy to ignore sensible coverage: "I know what happened – I was there, and I've heard every argument for or against our field trial. In fact, I probably thought them up." But Sally felt guilty, knowing she could be listening, commenting, dispelling rumours before they morphed like Chinese whispers. Instead she hid away with just grain and Darren for company, distracting herself with counting, weighing and recording results. Sally avoided the Internet as if insults from anti-GM lobbyists would search for her, rather than the other way round. When she heard the stories from Darren they made her laugh, but when he wasn't there they got to her. Phrases like '… trials performed just fields away from the unsuspecting public…' haunted her. She wanted to contract into her scientific world, ignore the curious focus from everyone outside it, yet knew she'd have to face up to the consequences.

Chapter 12

Sally was sitting in her room reading when there was a knock on her bedroom door and Mel's head appeared.

"You busy?"

It was early for Mel to be home, not even 7 o'clock. And she had broken house protocol, the unspoken agreement that rooms were sacred, to be entered by invitation only.

Sally put her book down on her chest of drawers, amidst a pile of jewellery and dust. "Come on in."

Mel collapsed on Sally's bed and lay staring at the cobwebs on her ceiling. "You really should clean occasionally you know."

"I've got better things to do, thank you very much. Like ask you what's up?"

"Maybe the gods wanted me to sympathise with you for once, because I had a bad day at work too."

"Activists burnt your office down?"

"God, no, that would be the best day of my career so far. Redundancies at the end of the month – eight at risk notices were handed out today."

"And you were one of them?" Sally suppressed the guilty fear that without Mel's job they couldn't pay the rent.

"No I wasn't."

"That's good."

"Barely. It's got to everyone. We watched and waited as one by one people were called into the partner's office. My boss included."

"But you hate your boss."

"Not as much as I hate the guy who'd be my boss if she goes, and if I have to answer to him you might as well say goodbye, because you'll never see me home before midnight."

Sally tried to sound soothing. "I guess she might not be the one to go, and you just have to wait to find out."

"It's not just that. You can't imagine the atmosphere in the office. It was cutthroat anyway, but now I hardly dare accept a coffee from anyone in case it's poisoned."

Sally tried to imagine and knew she couldn't. Insecure jobs were second nature in academia, but she'd never felt that her colleagues could become enemies. "I'm sorry, it sounds tough."

Mel sighed. "I guess if I tell you not to take things to heart I'd better do the same myself."

"There are always other jobs, you're not stuck with this one."

Mel didn't respond and continued to examine the ceiling. Finally she changed the subject. "So who do you call before you go to sleep then?"

"Mel you know you're the one I wish goodnight to."

"Who's number is this then?" She pointed to the receipt carefully laid out on Sally's bedside table.

"Oh, that's Paul's."

Mel propped her head on her elbow and looked at Sally. "Tell all. How did you get it?"

"I didn't get it, he gave it to me. He came to my lab and then we went for lunch. At the end he said I could call him if I wanted and gave me his number."

"Last time we talked about it you never wanted to see him again. Now you call him to say goodnight and you didn't even tell me?"

"Actually, I haven't called."

"At all?"

Sally shook her head.

"Why not?"

"I'm not really sure."

"That's a feeble answer. Because you don't like him, because you don't want to like him, because you're scared of calling, because you're scared things won't be the same?"

"I don't know." Sally fiddled with her necklaces, carefully straightening out chains that had been abandoned in tangled piles, but she could feel Mel's expectant gaze. She wasn't going to get away with not answering. "I like him, I admit that. When we went for lunch it was easy, not like we'd been apart for so long."

"At least you admit that. But why didn't you call?"

"I think I don't want to seem too keen."

"How long ago was this?"

"About a week."

"About?"

Sally looked at the red numbers on her alarm clock. "OK, 6 days, 6 hours and roughly 26 minutes."

"Sally, swallow your pride and stop playing games of *You're Not Important To Me*."

"I am planning to call."

"Call tonight." Mel picked up the receipt and held it out to Sally, who ignored it.

"He's married."

"I don't care. Call."

Mel lay there in silence with an expression that suggested she knew she had won. Eventually she sat up, declared she was going to cook couscous for them both and left. When the door had closed behind her Sally rehearsed in her head what she'd say when Paul answered her call. Was it too soon to suggest they meet again? She tried to imagine calmly talking about her experiment. It seemed wrong just to say 'we've got the samples, everything's fine' after all he'd read in the papers. Billboards around Cambridge had announced the news, and it was hardly likely that he had walked passed and ignored them.

When Mel called her for supper she was still holding the receipt and her phone. Reluctantly, she returned them both to the bedside table. It was late anyway, and she pictured Paul on the sofa with Katie, his arm around her delicate shoulders, not exactly waiting for her call.

* * * * *

By Friday Sally's concentration span had reduced dramatically, and she could barely spend an hour weighing samples without getting fidgety. Darren was in charge of storing the samples, and every time they seemed to be getting somewhere he would go to the freezers and return with bags of wheat ears. But as the afternoon dragged on she got a second wind, and at 5 o'clock she and Darren were two hours into a productive session.

"What are you up to for the weekend?"

"It's Mel's birthday tonight, we're heading to the pub."

"Sounds good. Why don't you head off now?"

"We seem to be on a roll." Sally pointed to the pile of samples that were now in bags with large black scribbles on – a simple way to identify which ones had already been weighed. The pile was growing precariously tall, and each new bag they added threatened to alter the delicate balance. "I'll just do a bit more."

"It looks like a pretty good effort for one afternoon, why don't you call it a night."

"Are you going somewhere you don't want to tell me about?" Sally nudged him, hoping he was about to reveal an interesting secret about his life beyond the lab.

"No don't worry about me, I'm fine here."

"I'm not going to the pub while you work. You've been here late every night of the week."

"I've had Vangelis with me some of the time."

"You've both got lives too. And Vangelis has children and a wife, surely he should be with them."

"He's not staying tonight, and anyway his time isn't more important than yours just because he has a family."

"Or yours, so let's do a bit more together and then both go."

Darren didn't seem to appreciate the camaraderie. "This is stupid. You should go home."

Sally stopped sampling and sat back in her chair. The only thing that had made it bearable to stay weighing and recording until they were cross-eyed was their constant talking and joking. Could she really be just an annoyance he'd rather be without? She waited, hoping he would say more, explain what was wrong.

But he placed a sample on the balance then turned to her. "You going?" His smile was friendly but his point was clear.

She closed her lab book, neatened up the samples, then turned to leave. "Have a good weekend then."

Back in the empty office she began to gather her belongings. The cardboard box they used as a temporary recycling bin was overflowing with paper, so she picked it up and carried it down the corridor. On the way back past empty offices she glanced through the glass on Vangelis's door. What she saw made her pause and stare. He was standing close to Judith, smoothing her wiry hair behind her ear. So this was the woman he'd chosen to spend his Friday night with. At that moment Vangelis glanced over to the door and his eyes met Sally's. She didn't stay long enough to see his expression, but there was no doubt he'd seen her watching. She hurried back to her office, colour rising in her face.

Sitting in front of her computer she propped her head on her hand. She defaced a piece of scrap paper with scribbled patterns. She wasn't going to risk walking down the corridor until she could be sure of not meeting Vangelis and Judith.

Darren was spending Friday night working overtime to get their data recorded, while Vangelis went off with his mistress. Presumably his wife imagined that it was Vangelis who was alone in the dingy prep room while his employees headed to see their friends, partners, families. There was nothing Sally could do to change Vangelis's evening, but she could at least stop Darren being enough of a sucker to waste his. If she invited him to the pub for Mel's birthday he would have something better to do than write numbers in a lab book.

When enough time had passed to be confident that Vangelis and Judith had left, Sally headed over to find Darren. Outside, the sky had turned grey so the lab's automatic lights flicked on as she walked through. A pile of microtitre plates was sitting on the draining board. She pulled off a sheet of blue tissue and began to dry them. She scrunched up the corner of the paper and dipped it into each of the 96 wells in the plastic plate, all designed to contain just a few millilitres of liquid. She knew she was only stalling. She could hear Mel's voice teasing her for worrying '*someone's being friendly and telling you to go home early, and you decide it's because he doesn't like you. That makes sense…'* But still she didn't know if Darren would welcome her offer or just brush her off again. She knew little of his friends; he lived alone, had no siblings, had little contact with his mother and even less with his father. But she was constantly entertaining him with anecdotes about her housemates and he was fascinated by the strange household of a scientist, a poet and a lawyer.

When she made it to the prep room she opened the door to find Vangelis there too. The pile of processed samples had been removed and the room had clearly been tidied for the weekend. Neither man spoke, just looked at her. Remembering her last encounter with Vangelis, she dipped her eyes and hoped Darren would say something. But he seemed awkward too, and shifted his weight nervously from one foot to the other. In the end it was Vangelis who spoke first.

"I'm impressed with how much you and Darren have done." His tone was flat, and Sally wasn't sure whether he expected a response. But she wasn't going to say what she really came for, so this was a chance to at least say something.

She picked up Darren's lab book and flicked through the pages to the correct date. "Look, we've done nearly half of what we have to do, and from what I can see so far it's looking perfect…" Darren reached out to take the lab book from her. But it wasn't Darren's lab book, it was Vangelis's. The table was neat, too neat, and the label indicated he'd done a whole new batch of sampling in the last 15 minutes. Slowly Sally looked from the book to Vangelis and Darren.

She shook her head. "God, I've been stupid."

"There's nothing here that should worry you Sally." Vangelis reached out for the lab book and Sally let him take it.

"Nothing to worry me?" Sally hoped her tone was as mocking as Vangelis's had been patronising. She looked at Darren, trying to fathom his betrayal.

He turned up his hands in a gesture of helplessness, as if explaining events beyond his control. "I'm sorry we didn't tell you what we had to do. But we had no choice and I just didn't want to worry you with it too." He stepped forward, to try and comfort her. But she shook him off and he retreated.

"So you're happy with this?" Sally addressed them both.

"Now don't get me wrong," Vangelis said. "This is far from ideal, and if there was any alternative I can assure you we would have taken it. But we just have to work with what we've got."

"It's fabrication, it's fraud! You're telling me there's no alternative to a criminal offence?"

"Now I'm going to leave you to calm down and we can have a chat on Monday. Have a good weekend both of you." Without a look back Vangelis left.

Sally stared after him. "I'm overreacting? I'm a woman, I can't think straight when I'm angry? I can't believe him!" His attitude stung as much as the lies.

Darren again reached out his hand to touch her arm, and this time she didn't move away. He sat down on the workbench, still looking at the closed door. Sally came to stand beside him.

"I really didn't want you to find out like this," he said.

"You didn't want me to find out at all."

"I know, but if I'd had any idea I'd be having this conversation with you now I promise I'd have told you from the start."

"You'd have told me to make it easier, not because you wanted my opinion."

"We made the decision that those bastards could burn what they liked but they weren't going to destroy our experiment."

Sally looked at him. "No, you didn't. It wasn't your decision to make. I'm not going through with it."

Darren's eyes widened, and Sally was pleased to see a glimmer of fear for the first time.

"But we have to."

"Darren, we don't."

He was silent for a moment then his look turned triumphant. "If you're not going through with it, why didn't you tell Vangelis?"

Sally realised what Darren meant; he was much easier to stand up to than Vangelis was. "He left before I had the chance. But I will." She didn't sound convincing even to herself.

"We should talk about this on Monday. I don't know about you but I'm too tired to think straight."

He was right, and Sally stood up to leave, suddenly keen to be as far away from the university as possible.

Darren didn't move though. "What had you really come in to say?"

"I was going to invite you to the pub with Mel, but I think the moment's passed."

"I'm sorry, I'd like to have come."

"You can still go if you like. They're in The Boathouse. Send my apologies."

"You're not going? But it's her birthday."

"Thank you for reminding me, but I'm not in a birthday mood."

"Sally, don't. Please don't make us both go home and spend the evening stewing. Let me take you to Mel's, nothing good is going to come of sitting by ourselves to worry."

Much as she didn't want him to be, she knew he was right. "I'm not exactly dressed for it."

"That makes two of us. Come on."

* * * * *

A dozen of Mel's friends were sitting round a large oak table near the bar. Liz was the only one Sally recognised. She and Darren sat on the opposite end of the table to Mel – Sally knew that Mel would see right through her, but she could keep up a comfortable act speaking to strangers. The nervous glances she and Darren kept throwing at each other were the only outward signs that anything was wrong. But as everyone got merrier and the only effect Sally's wine had was to dry out her mouth, she began to feel that she couldn't last much longer. When Liz started telling Darren about the dangers of capitalism, Sally took the chance to slip outside.

The wind was cold and she wrapped her arms around herself. A small group of smokers crowded around the door, seemingly unconcerned by the cold or by the stale smell that engulfed them. They took no notice of Sally, standing alone amongst them.

"What's wrong?" Darren's voice came from behind her.

"What do you think?"

He looked slightly defeated, so Sally relented. "I'm sorry, I know it's not your fault." She looked beyond the haze of cigarette smoke to the river, which was still visible in the fading light. "I just came out to get some fresh air."

"I know what you mean. It can be a bit stifling in there."

"If I tried any harder to fix a smile it would take surgery to remove it."

"I'm glad we came though, it was nice to meet your friends."

Sally didn't have the brain power left to work out what that meant, so she turned back to look into the bar. Inside the pub Mel carried a tray of shot glasses back from the bar. She was wearing four-inch heels and had been drinking for the last five hours, but the tray didn't wobble. Sally watched her with respect. "Sometimes I wish I was Mel."

"Why? There are so many reasons not to."

"She's so perfect – she's elegant, clever, funny and everything always seems to work for her."

"Just because she can work 12 hours a day then get drunk on Friday night and still look stunning that doesn't make her life perfect."

Sally turned to him. "You think she's stunning?"

Darren looked as if he was trying to work out the right answer.

Sally didn't make him suffer. "OK, I know she hates her job, but she's good at it, and she pulls everything off with this air of complete control. It just seems effortless."

"I'd choose a job I care about over that. What's the point in impressing people when you don't impress yourself."

"Maybe it's not a job that means anything that she would impress herself with, maybe looking good is enough."

Darren didn't contradict her, but his silence confirmed they were empty words. No doubt it was enough for some people, but Sally was starting to realise that it wasn't for Mel.

Inside the pub Mel put two shot glasses in front of Sally and Darren's empty chairs. As she looked around to see where they'd gone, the sequins on her dress caught the light.

"You're right, she is stunning," Sally said.

"Come on, our tequilas are waiting. People will start to talk." Darren placed his hand on the small of Sally's back and gently but firmly guided her back into the pub.

Mel was the first to return her empty tequila glass to the table, grinning through her grimace. The cheers that followed sucked Sally in and, before she knew it, she was at the bar with Darren ordering another round.

When the bell rang for last orders the party began to disperse. Mel stood near the doorway hugging each of her friends as they passed. Liz and Sally waited for her, aware the taxi was sitting outside, but not wanting to spoil Mel's goodbyes. Eventually she was free and beckoned for Liz and Sally to join her.

Just as Sally was about to follow, Darren bent down and said in her ear, "Don't worry, we'll work things out." Then Liz caught her arm and the three housemates were heading for the taxi.

Chapter 13

Sally wasted her weekend, her head filled with ways to confront Vangelis. To keep herself occupied she walked along the river, listening to the rhythmical splash of blades as each rowing crew came past. Replaying their last conversation, Vangelis derisive about her reaction, made Sally bitter. His exact words and his tone of voice were more offensive every time she remembered it. So she practised what she would say when they spoke, prepared herself for every counter-argument he could come up with. Each of these imagined conversations ended the same way, with Vangelis relenting, persuaded round to Sally's point of view.

Back at home she even wrote out scripts on the back of discarded envelopes, just as Liz decorated their junk mail with inspired metaphors or phrases, unintelligible to Sally but apparently insightful. The only difference was that Liz's words would be crafted into poetry, while Sally's were destined for the recycling bin.

In the evenings she sat with Liz and ate popcorn in front of the TV. It was a relief to have company, particularly from someone who wouldn't question her. They could inhabit the separate worlds in their heads while enjoying the same Sunday night game show.

This was the kind of time when she used to imagine a conversation she could have with Paul, explaining the facts until somehow they made sense. But now she had seen him again, the thought brought no comfort. He was no longer just a concept, but a real man who could be contacted via 11 digits written on the scrap of paper by her bed. Where once he'd been someone she could have shared this with, if only she knew where he was, he was now another person to hide it from. She wondered again whether she should call him, but the facts had realigned since Mel had lain on her bed and given instructions that Sally had fully intended to obey.

On Sunday evening, before she went to bed, Sally picked up Paul's number, folded it into a neat square and tucked it into her wallet. She knew she wouldn't lose it, but it would no longer be taunting her by her bedside. Now she knew herself to be a fraudster she wasn't planning to call.

* * * * *

When her Monday morning alarm aroused her from chaotic dreams, Sally tried to remember what enthusiasm had felt like. Enthusiasm for anything. Just two weeks ago she had suppressed a grin as she returned to the biology department with Paul's number in her pocket, ready to do the experiment that would take her from obscurity to respected geneticist. Now, as she stood in front of her open wardrobe waiting for inspiration about what to wear, any excitement she had felt for science or Paul seemed pathetic.

When she arrived in the office Amy, Günter and Darren were clustered round a computer, laughing at photos on Amy's Facebook page.

"Hey Sally, how did you feel on Saturday morning?"

Darren seemed oblivious to the fact that within seconds of Sally arriving he had forced her into her first lie. The look of openness that had been on his face when he whispered reassurances before she joined Mel in the taxi had gone.

"Perfect, thank you. Why, didn't you feel too good then?"

"How would he know?" Amy asked, "He never wakes up on Saturday mornings."

"That's not true, and you know it." Darren gave Amy's ponytail an affectionate tug.

Sally decided not to follow any train of thought that would question how Amy might know this. She dumped her bag and went to sit at her lab bench, waiting until she could speak to Darren on his own. She sorted through conical flasks of solutions, picking out the ones that had been left too long and needed to go down the sink. She was tipping them away when Darren walked in, the potent smell of acid already making her feel sick.

She felt no need for pleasantries. "What's going on?"

"What do you mean?" Darren sounded innocent.

"Don't give me that."

"Sally, please, let's not start like this. Put this down and let's talk." He removed the flask from her hand and waited while she took off her lab coat. They walked in silence to the storeroom, Sally's heart pounding at the thought of having the arguments she'd so carefully rehearsed, even if it was only with Darren.

When the door was closed behind them Darren stood close to her, with a look of concern that almost made her weaken. But she didn't.

"Where's Vangelis?" She demanded.

"In a meeting."

"When's he out?"

"Lunchtime. Why?"

"You know why. He gave me 'oh calm down Sally we'll talk about it like adults on Monday' and now he's not even here."

"The meetings are with the head of department about the new building."

"The meetings are a load of self-important people talking about architects' plans drawn up for hundreds of pounds that could be spent on science."

"Look, let's just get through some samples and wait until he's free."

"I'm not doing any samples."

Darren shook his head and sat down with his back to her. He opened his lab book and wrote the date.

Sally wasn't going to be brushed off that easily. She sat on the desk next to him, blocking out his light. "Darren, some psychos destroyed our trial, we didn't get enough samples. That means we don't have an experiment anymore. End of story."

Darren looked up to where Sally was sitting. "What are you going to do now while I get our work done? Go and pour all your solutions down the sink? In fact, I've got a better idea, why don't you help Amy."

Sally let the door slam behind her. In the lab she collected the dirty glassware and, hands trembling, carried it to the autoclave room. She bent down to stack the shelves in the autoclave's drum and closed it up. Children suffocate in washing machines, and a room full of autoclaves gave the same feeling. It made her queasy at the best of times to think of the heat and pressure needed to sterilise their equipment, but as she looked around at the open chambers of five empty autoclaves she could imagine the pressure closing in on her.

She quickly left the room and headed to Vangelis's office. His chair was empty and his computer was off; there was no sign he had been there so far that day. But Sally had nothing better to do than wait, so she stared at the poster next to his office – a diagram of a cell-signalling pathway. The tangled flow diagram was decorated with protein names, no more intelligible than the random letters and numbers on her student loan statements. Behind her the same technicians wheeled trolleys of glassware or plants up and down the corridor. When they started to give her strange looks she retreated to her office and sent Vangelis an email asking to meet. Within 10 minutes she had a reply.

> *in meeting with directors, running workshops rest of week free 5.30 if urgent wait me in ur office*

The signature underneath it announced in perfect English that it was sent from his mobile device so please excuse brevity or spelling errors…

She looked at her watch – 6 hours to waste before she could confront him. A long lunch break, a detailed email to her mother about nothing in particular and multiple trips to water plants in the greenhouse couldn't distract her. Bored in the office, she picked at her nails until the cuticles were outlined in blood. Günter and Amy tried to cheer her up and gently probed about what was wrong, but she deflected them. She had no intention of cheering up.

Thankfully Amy and Günter left as soon as was vaguely respectable, perhaps to be free of Sally. By 5.20 she was alone and could think about what to say. The phrases in her head were sounding increasingly contrived: 'violation of codes we have signed up to as a profession' … 'distortion of the truth we are searching for'…

She was sinking deeper into panic and clichés when there was a bang behind her. The office door swung open, and she jumped up to face it, but it was Darren not Vangelis who stood in the doorway.

"Amy's just gone." Sally hoped her eyes gave away some of the anger she still felt.

"How do you know that isn't exactly what I was waiting for?"

Sally shrugged; the hope that he would see his position and leave was fading.

He came to stand in front of her. "It was lonely sampling without you."

"It was also pretty pointless given that the numbers you produced are part of a scam."

"Did you speak to Vangelis then?" Darren suddenly lost his smile.

"No, he's been in meetings and he said he'd come to see me."

"When's he coming?"

Sally glanced at the wall clock and watched as the minute hand settled over the number six. "Now."

"I'm just in time then."

"Just in time to get your stuff and go."

"This is my decision too you know."

"I think you forfeited the right to be part of this conversation when you tried to make the decision without me."

In many ways she wanted him there when she spoke to Vangelis; her well-rehearsed arguments deserved an audience. But it was an eye for an eye as far as withholding information went, and she had to show him that his opinion was irrelevant.

"You're shaking." Darren pointed to her hands.

"I'm not." Sally gripped the edge of the desk she was leaning against in an attempt to immobilise them.

"Sally, all this needs to be is the three of us having a discussion we admittedly should have had a week ago. It's not each of us against the other in a battle of wills. That's only in your head."

Sally looked away, trying to think of something to say that sounded rational when the thoughts spinning in her head were neurotic. Darren took a step closer to her. Slowly he reached out to put his arms around her until his hands were flat against her back. She kept her arms clamped by her side, fearing she would be weakened by accepting comfort from Darren but couldn't bring herself to push him away.

"There are options you know; we can talk things through," he said gently, his mouth just inches from her ear.

For a moment she believed him, and fraudulent data felt no different to the challenges that face anyone who has ever worked with children, animals or PCR machines. She let her head rest on his shoulder and for the first time since she'd stumbled upon the make-believe data her body relaxed. But the feeling was short lived. She pulled herself backwards so they were once again facing each other, his look one disappointment.

"There are some things I need to tell Vangelis alone," she said quietly. "I'm afraid this isn't going to be a 'ways to be slightly less dishonest' meeting."

"I don't care if it's a 'you can rot in hell with my mother-in-law' kind of meeting, I still want to be there."

Sally shook her head, and Darren finally looked defeated.

"OK, if I wait in the lab will you at least find me afterwards to tell me what happens?"

"There will be nothing I haven't told you already. There is going to be no fabrication; we're going to keep our careers and our morals intact. I'm not going to have everything I've been working for undermined by lies."

With a long look at her he turned to leave. "Good luck."

Sally waited for Vangelis until hunger and emotional exhaustion over took her. When her confidence in how she would deliver her arguments disappeared entirely, she decided it was wise to admit defeat. As she walked home she began to wonder if Vangelis had come to her office at 5.30 after all. She thought about what he would have seen through the glass panel in the door, and of all the assumptions she had made when she'd seen him alone in his office with Judith. Maybe he'd seen her and Darren and decided to walk away.

Darren texted her later asking for news, but she deleted it. They could go to bed without saying any of what needed to be said, and Sally was confident she could keep it that way the next day. She had no intention of listening to any of Darren's arguments.

Chapter 14

"They say that to get anywhere in science you need a theory that's controversial enough for everyone to want to prove you wrong, but not so wacky they think you're mental. I'm not so sure." Darren paused for another mouthful of cake before explaining. "I've never felt as popular as today. Everyone's heard about what happened to our experiment, who needs theories to achieve fame?"

"True, but it would be good to have been able to eat my lunch without a stream of well- wishers telling me how wrong activists are. The state of the farmhouse had kind of convinced me of that already," Sally replied.

"Oh Sally, you're too modest. You need to get used to the limelight, whenever we go anywhere with Vangelis his fan club flock around us."

"Flock around him you mean."

Darren shrugged and looked around for another plate of cake. They were in London for a symposium on herbicide resistance, and the lunch, at least, had been worth coming for. Vangelis had deemed the delegate list to be sufficiently important to make it worth sending them, so Sally had endured a morning of presentations and small talk. During every break she had listened attentively to academics keen to voice their opinion on 'misguided extremism' and 'popular perception'. The effort of smiling and nodding was beginning to wear her out.

When even Darren had to refuse the canapés offered round by scowling waitresses and they had freed themselves from networkers, they began collecting free pens and sweets from the trade stands.

Sally was helping herself to the latest journal issues when Darren stopped her.

"I didn't know your friend was in league with the enemy."

Sally followed Darren's gaze to the next stand along, above which a huge banner announced that it was the Food and Environment Research Agency, the body in charge of regulating GM crops. It took her a moment to work out what Darren meant, then she realised the man in a suit standing below the banner was Paul. He was engrossed in conversation with a blonde girl not much older than Sally, their heads bent over a form which Paul was explaining. She'd never seen him in a shirt and tie before, and she hadn't expected him to look so natural. She watched him with fascination, her mind trying to come to grips with his transformation from scruffy scientist to suited regulator. Darren was looking at her.

"They're not the enemy, Darren."

"Whatever you say. You're going to speak to him?"

"He's busy." It had been three weeks since Paul had given her his number, long enough for him to think she had casually dropped it into the bin as soon as his back had been turned. If she couldn't summon the courage to call him from the safety of her own bedroom, she had no intention of speaking to him somewhere that her misfortunes made her a minor celebrity and Darren would monitor her every move.

"So, how many applications for trials did he decorate with rejected stamps this week?" Darren asked.

"You know it's not that simple."

"You don't have to pretend to me that it's all in the name of science. So what does he do?"

"He supports agricultural research."

"I know what FERA's for. But what are honest British tax payers paying him to actually do?"

Darren's look was challenging; he was expecting an answer. Sally's desire not to let Paul see her was rapidly surpassed by a determination not to let on that she had no idea what he was doing here. She'd slept with him, then spent nearly five years wondering what his life was like. Surely she had more to show for it than explaining what he did base on the posters on his trade stand. Seeing no way out if she stayed talking to Darren, she picked up her handful of journals and walked over to where Paul was standing.

He didn't notice them immediately, and Sally began to wonder if she'd got away with it. She busied herself reading a leaflet from his stand, keeping her gaze low. But Darren was determined. He loitered behind the blonde girl Paul was talking to, unashamedly listening in to their conversation.

Sally flicked through the leaflet too fast to be convincingly reading it. The stand was busy and she kept having to side step to avoid people. Then the blonde girl Paul had been talking to walked past. Although she couldn't make out the words, she could hear that behind her Darren had taken her place. She tried to convince herself that Paul wouldn't recognise him. But her feeble hopes were destroyed when Darren called across to her.

"Isn't that right Sally?"

She turned to see both Darren and Paul waiting for her answer. "Sorry, I didn't hear what you were talking about."

If Paul was in any way interested to see her, his expression didn't show it. Sally tried to keep her gaze on Darren.

"You know the lab that put genes for antioxidants in tomatoes and they protected against cancer?"

So Darren had called her in to be the judge of an unofficial scientific competition. It wasn't a role she wanted to play. "They protected against cancer in mice," she said.

"That's the point. The trials in mice showed clear benefits, but they couldn't get approval for trials in people."

"I guess there are lots of issues with it all that we don't know about."

"But am I right that they were stopped from human trials? Paul didn't think so."

"I'm afraid I don't remember." She did remember, and Darren was right, but she wasn't going to be played like that. "You can look it up when we get back to the lab."

Darren's expression turned to annoyance and Sally suspected he had seen through her lie. The three of them stood in silence, until a lady wearing a tailored jacket and too much makeup held a form up to Paul.

"Sorry to interrupt, but can I ask you something?"

"Yes, certainly." Paul's tone was polite, but the enthusiasm she'd seen when he'd been talking earlier had vanished. Only when the lady launched into a convoluted description of EU Code 11.7a did his gaze leave Sally.

An academic whose name Sally didn't quite catch collared them and offered an energetic handshake. "I worked with Vangelis back when he was a grad student, always ambitious, even then, and quite a hit with the ladies." He winked at Sally, who wished she was the kind of person to give a feminist's reply. "So tell me," he continued, "what's this about the Bt strain you're working on?"

Darren began his explanation, adding ambitious predictions about the experiments they would do next. He tried to bring Sally into the conversation, but the stuffy room was making her feel sick. She answered his questions in monosyllables and, when he was in the depths of a description of Amy's grant proposal, she smiled politely and fled.

Safely in the toilets, she splashed cold water on her face. Her mind began to clear and she thought through what had just happened. Darren had seen her discomfort and pushed her, and she'd given in. Paul wasn't the neutral bystander she'd imagined. He was the man who passed judgement on applications for trials, patents and permissions, the person who controlled which research would make it onto the market and change things, for better or worse, and which was committed to a dusty shelf of 'could have been good, but we will never know'.

A lady who looked the same kind of age as Sally's mother walked in and gave a sympathetic smile. Sally returned it gratefully but pulled herself together; she was there to network with scientists not to receive mothering in the toilets. Straightening up her hair, she returned to the conference and to Darren.

She sat through the afternoon talks with Darren beside her scribbling illegible notes that would be in the recycling bin by the end of the week. Her thoughts were swirling, and 'pest-resistant cultivars' were only on the edge of her consciousness. Images of Paul, smart and engaging as he spoke to a stream of confused scientists, pushed their way into her head, along with what he must think of her for not calling. These thoughts were interspersed with the increasingly dull answers she'd given to everyone who had asked what she was going to do about their burnt-out field trial. None of them, of course, alluded to what she really was going to do about it, whatever that might be. But the thought that she was trying to block out, the one that made the least sense, was of how she felt when she'd seen Paul, of how she wanted him as much now as when she had fallen asleep in the warmth of his bed.

* * * * *

It was Friday before Sally found Vangelis to speak to. They sat facing each other at the table in his office; Sally had carefully positioned herself so she was hidden from spying eyes in the corridor. She wasn't offered a cup of tea.

"Sally, sorry I didn't manage to speak to you earlier in the week." His words were ambiguous, there was no way of telling whether he had come on Monday and walked away when he saw her and Darren. She nodded her forgiveness and he continued. "So tell me, how have this week's samples been?"

"I haven't processed any of them."

Vangelis sighed. "How much has Darren told you about exactly how this is going to work?"

"Approximately nothing."

"Well, I hope I can allay your fears. You collected an impressive number of samples in a short space of time, and we'll get data from every one of those. So for each field we will get the information we need, it will just be based on a small sample size. We will keep that exact value as the average and simply add in more values to increase the sample size."

"Fabricate the results so it appears we have a large-enough sample size."

"Let's not split hairs."

"Sample sizes are large for a reason. When your results are used for global food security you have to be confident in them, and that needs enough samples."

"I'm glad you were listening in your first-year stats lectures, but this isn't an undergraduate textbook, this is real life. I don't know whether you read the opinion piece in *Nature* recently saying our obsession with sample size has lost its logic? Papers are rejected because of low sample sizes – good research goes unpublished or money is wasted on sample sizes that are simply unnecessary."

Every research paper is reviewed anonymously by at least two independent scientists, and Sally was always flattered when she was asked to be one of them, even if it was because someone more senior was bored of reviewing and handed it down to her. But she always felt pressure, the responsibility of being the gatekeeper for what research gets published, and to prove her worth had to think of something to say.

"Well that's a debate that should be had in the open, not one that we should make our own rules for."

"That's all very noble, but did you write in to support the article, have you joined the debate?"

Sally looked down at her hands, the blood cleaned off her cuticles but her nails still bitten down to the skin.

"I see not. Anyway, it will be too late for us if there's a move to smaller sample sizes. While I agree with you entirely, that doesn't change what the right course of action is for this experiment."

"I just don't think there is ever a case for publishing fraud."

"Sally, let me ask you one thing. You saw the field trial, you've worked on the samples. Do you think the results would be any different if you had the sample size we hoped for?"

For some reason Sally had been so engrossed with the desire not to lie that she hadn't stopped to ask herself that question. Slowly she shook her head.

"It strikes me that you have your answer."

Sally was relieved when there was a knock on the door and Vangelis called to allow a student to enter. She stood up to leave, smiling at the student but not saying a word to Vangelis. She wanted to think about this when she had some space, away from Vangelis's disapproval.

* * * * *

Sally began the next day by avoiding work and avoiding Darren. She helped Amy with her thesis. Having not been paid since her PhD grant ended, Amy had taken a job in a bar. It eased her worry about where her rent was going to come from and strengthened her determination to be a scientist not a barmaid, but hopefully meant that she had no less brain power to dedicate to writing about single nucleotide polymorphisms. Sleep deprivation, an inevitable side effect of writing a thesis during the day and pulling pints during the evenings, was getting to her. This meant Sally's help was more offering encouragement than scientific advice. But she couldn't spend her entire working day helping Amy, and if she didn't spend most of her time processing samples with Darren it would be noticed. When she sat down in the prep room next to him and reached for a bag of wheat grains to weigh, it wasn't because she had decided to go along with the fabricated results, but more because she hadn't got round to deciding not to. Darren, to his credit, didn't say a word.

Amy, driven mad by dull nights behind the bar, had persuaded them to spend the evening there to keep her company. Drinking on weeknights wasn't normally Sally's style, but as things stood she accepted the invitation willingly. Amy left early, and when 5.30 came a group of people knocked on the door to say it was pub time. Sally and Darren turned off their computers, but Günter didn't stir.

"You're not coming?" Sally asked.

"No."

"Let's go." Darren held open the door so Sally would leave.

As they dodged pushchairs and cyclists on the way to the pub Sally and Darren fell behind the main group.

"What's up with Günter?" Sally asked.

"Oh he's OK," Darren replied, "but his ex is going to be there, and he still refuses to be in the same room as her."

"That's crazy, what happened? I didn't even know he had an ex."

"They were just getting together when I arrived. She's Swedish and had come over to do some work on genetic links with Alzheimer's, actually pretty interesting. But anyway, the pair of them were awful, flirting like you never thought Günter could. I don't know how she did any work, she was always in our office."

"You're right I can't imagine it, but it sounds cute."

"I won't tell Günter you find him cute. Anyway they moved in together pretty fast once they'd finally got together. And they made a pretty good pair – he spent less time at his computer and he could just make her laugh."

"So what went wrong?"

"Nobody really knows, don't think even Günter does to be honest. All I know is that one day he came home and she was gone. She went back to Sweden for a couple of weeks, and when she returned to England it was like Günter never existed."

"How could he deal with that?"

"I dunno, he was pretty down. He never really said much, but one evening we were both at work a bit late, a few days after she came back, and he told me how he'd been texting, calling, emailing and she hadn't even acknowledged it. He'd been to her lab to see her and some guy she works with told him to keep away. He didn't even know where she was living."

The pub was crowded when they arrived but they quickly spotted people they knew. Their friends from the department had pushed two tables together and Amy was behind the bar. A carton of orange juice in one hand, she waved at them with the other. As she served their drinks she seemed brighter and happier than Sally had seen her since the field trial was destroyed. They sat on bar stools and chatted to her, listening to stories about the regulars. When a group of older men came to the bar Sally and Darren left Amy to deal with them and carried their drinks to the table of friends. They were soon absorbed into conversation, with Günter's ex, blonde and beautiful, as a centre of attention.

Sally knew she would be seeing Paul again; Cambridge was a small place and Cambridge scientists an even smaller community. She thought of Günter, abandoned in the office while they went out and had fun. She knew she didn't want to be the one people whispered about, with friends tactfully helping her avoid situations where she and Paul would have to speak. When her glass was empty she didn't return to the bar but instead went outside to a picnic bench overlooking the car park.

The sun had just dipped below the trees, and Sally wrapped her cardigan more tightly round herself. She pulled the folded receipt out of her wallet and dialled the number before she had the chance for second thoughts. It rang once, twice, three times, and she started to think he wasn't going to answer. Then a woman's voice said, "Hello?"

"Oh, I'm sorry, I was trying to call Paul."

"Don't worry, he's just in the shower, I can get him to call you back." The voice on the other end was smooth and friendly.

The image of Katie's photograph, burned onto her blurry eyes as she left Paul's bedroom, came back to Sally. She shuddered. "No, it's OK, thank you."

"You sure? His phone didn't have your number in, shall I tell him who it was?"

"No, don't worry."

There was an awkward silence before they both said goodbye.

Sally watched a young couple leave the pub arm in arm. The woman, who had the figure to match her skinny jeans, opened the car door and a small dog leapt up and began licking her face. Her partner caressed the dog's head and beamed. As they drove away Sally knew she couldn't do it. Whatever Paul had meant to her she couldn't face meeting Katie; to try and piece together a friendship would leave them more likely to permanently avoid each other, not less. But she could at least absolve herself of guilt and offer an apology for not speaking to him properly at the conference. She began to text:

I wanted to say that I'm sorry that I didn't have time to speak to you … but that was a lie and the least he deserved was honesty.

It was good to see you … also a lie.

I hope you enjoyed the conference. There were some good talks … missing the point rather.

It was interesting to see your stall at the conference. Things have been quite challenging with us as you probably guessed but it's turning out OK. Sally … She didn't want to rely on the sympathy vote, but she didn't have a better idea.

The text was still unsent when Darren came out.

"What's up?"

"Nothing – I was just trying to call my friend."

"She's not answering?"

"Actually I spoke to his wife."

Sally pressed send without another look at the text then followed Darren back into the pub.

* * * * *

Mel was away again the next weekend, so Sally agreed to spend an afternoon at a 'poetry surgery' in London with Liz. Liz had conveniently omitted to explain that it was a specific anti-capitalist group. Each poet, ranging from a teenage Goth to a man who could have been her grandfather, stood to read their poem. Then, after a pretentious explanation, they opened themselves to criticism from the floor. At this point Liz would nod vigorously in agreement with whatever was said. Sally understood most of the words from each poem, and lots of the phrases, but somehow nothing once it was all put together. She rarely got any of the references to capitalism.

When everyone but Sally had shared a poem, someone ordered a round of drinks and the poetry discussion continued more informally. Sally still didn't grasp what was going on, but she was happily storing up anecdotes and caricatures she could entertain Mel or Darren with. As the second round of drinks was ordered, the conversation broke up and Sally found herself chatting with Liz and one of her friends. She was about their age and had read one of the more overtly anti-capitalist poems.

"So what do you do?" She asked Sally.

"I'm a scientist."

"That's cool, what do you work on?"

Sally glanced over at Liz; she felt the need to be on best behaviour and not let Liz's image down by revealing she'd brought a GM scientist along to an anti-capitalist meeting. "Agriculture – crop improvement."

"I see, genetic modification."

"Actually, not all crop improvement is artificial genetic modification."

"But that is what Sally works on." Liz sounded amused to drop Sally into it.

"How can you justify the risks of genetic modification when we have enough food already?" The girl put her drink down and looked at Sally with genuine confusion.

"We don't have enough food. A billion people are already going hungry, and the problem gets bigger the more the population grows."

"We have distribution problems, not shortages."

Sally felt momentary relief that to be faced with a claim she was comfortable dismissing. "That's an age old argument which doesn't stack up. Shipping food round the world is unsustainable and traps people in poverty because you saturate local food markets."

"Is your work directed at areas where there are local farmers with food shortages?"

"Well, no, not exactly, but it's early days, and there are reasons that GM crops will be beneficial in developed countries too…"

"There are more reasons why they won't be. When the problem is basically excessive consumerism and global inequality, you're developing a solution which will increase both those things."

Sally watched as Liz sipped her drink in silence. This was Liz's day and these were Liz's friends; Sally didn't want to say anything which would make her look bad. But this wasn't about Liz, it wasn't even about the poet who was quizzing her. It was about Sally facing the issues which she feared the most. She wasn't going to back down now. "We want everyone to benefit from our technology, so we can lift people out of poverty."

"With particular benefit going to the patent owners and big businesses? You're throwing science after a social problem. Here," she said smugly, "we're trying to address the social problem."

With poetry? Sally wanted to say, but not in a room full of poets. "Science has shaped our society, you can't distinguish the two."

The girl smiled sweetly. "And poetry has been shaping civilisation for longer."

It really was time to stop; that wouldn't be an argument she could win. Quickly, Sally drained her glass. "Who's for another drink?"

Both Liz and her friend looked disappointed that the conversation was over, but handed over their glasses and requested refills.

"What did you think of the poetry?" Liz asked as they headed for the station.

"Well, I liked yours the best, it was the only one I understood."

"It makes more sense once you're used to it."

They stopped at a pedestrian crossing, and Sally wondered whether any amount of time and study would allow her to understand Liz's poetry. She had enjoyed her afternoon and nobody had held any grudges as soon as the GM debate was over. Now she was out in the fresh air, Sally was relieved to feel that the arguments put forward by Liz's friend weren't hers to answer; she had to tackle the moral dilemma which was. Liz had been brave enough to invite Sally to an event Sally may have scorned, and now Sally felt she could repay her by asking for advice.

"Liz, if you thought a law was wrong would you break it?"

"You mean letting you put my copy of The Grease Megamix on your MP3 player, or murdering someone I thought should be in jail?"

"Kind of somewhere in between."

"Why do you ask?"

"I read the program while you were off talking. I might not have understood any of the poems, but apparently they were anti lots of things, and it got me thinking." Her view into Liz's world had made Sally interested to turn to her for advice, but it hadn't brought her close to explaining why the advice was needed.

"Poets aren't all anarchists you know," Liz said.

"I did just go to an anti-capitalist poetry surgery, something I had no idea existed until this morning. Anyway, I'm asking what you think, you don't need to answer for poets as a species."

"OK, I may think our whole political system is wrong but undermining it in petty ways won't help."

"Ever?" Sally searched for an analogy she could safely try Liz with, but failed.

"My uncle was caught driving over the alcohol limit and got fined and banned. He claimed it hadn't affected his driving, and I'm sure he was right. But he deserved what he got – if everyone made their own judgements about what was safe, then some people would make the wrong ones and more people would die."

Sally wondered what Liz's poetry friends would think of her law-abiding attitude.

"But if the motivation was to do something good, not just because they were too stingy to pay for a taxi."

"I know what you're getting at, and I totally see your point, but still no. Why do you suddenly want to know about this anyway?"

"I went to poetry surgery to discover what it was like to be a poet, and now I'm even more confused than ever. I thought artists didn't like rules." Sally laughed, pleased with the fluency of her cover-up.

"No wonder we have a bad name if you hold onto views like that. Being anti-capitalist isn't being anti-rules, and the only rules a poet needs to break are the confines of the written and spoken word…"

"Bad grammar?"

"You will never, never understand."

Now the two of them were laughing, and the closeness Sally felt to Liz lasted all the way home.

Chapter 15

The next day Sally's phone rang with an unknown number. Anticipating a sales call she almost didn't answer it. She picked it up on the fourth ring, unsure of whether it had already cut to answerphone.

"Hello?"

"Hi Sally, it's Paul."

"Hi." Her voice came out unnaturally high-pitched. She stood up and began walking in cramped circles around her room, trying to concentrate on sounding normal.

"Sorry I missed your call," Paul said.

"That's OK, sorry I didn't call, well obviously I did, but you know what I mean…" Sally cringed; she didn't even know what she meant. She hadn't called a second time because she didn't want him to answer. "How did you know it was me?"

"You texted me after you called and I added your number, and then the last call came up as you."

He'd added her to his phonebook: her last text hadn't been taken as a civil goodbye. She began talking about the first thing that entered her head.

"Did you see us in the paper?"

"Yes, I'm sorry, are you OK?"

"We're fine, I kind of feel guilty about how lightly we got off, given that the farmer lost his house."

"Why is it that the person least to blame feels the most guilty?" Paul said gently. "That goes for everything."

"Probably the same reason that the people who aren't responsible suffer the most."

She told him the story of the day after the fire: the weird phone calls, the blackened fields, the fire crews. He laughed when she described her noble attempt at speaking to all the journalists.

"I didn't know you did a line in inspirational speaking. You should write something for us. Everything's so bureaucratic; every pro-GM sentence has so many additions to it that it's half a page long. We could do with something a little punchier."

"I think I need the pressure for it to work though. If only writing my thesis had come as naturally as justifying my existence to journalists."

"Well, I'm glad you're standing up for what you believe in."

She realised she'd spent too long looking at the photos taken outside the scorched farmhouse. They had been carefully composed to make her appear sinister, and she had started to believe them. Talking to Paul, she returned herself to the status of hero. She stopped pacing and sat on her bed.

"Look," Paul said, "would you like to come over for dinner some time?"

Sally tensed again, her fear of Katie rapidly resurfacing. She paused for long enough for it to be noticed, but knew she was too weak to turn him down. "Yes please."

"Are you free next Saturday?"

"Yes." Meeting Katie would at least provide hours of analysis with Mel. Excitement was already beginning to catch up with Sally's fear.

"7.30 OK?"

"Sure."

"Great. I'll text you my address and see you then."

"See you Saturday!" Her phone beeped as they both hung up.

She lay back on her bed, smiled and started to plan her outfit.

* * * * *

When Saturday night came Sally was ready with an hour to spare. She sat on the sofa clock-watching and wondering exactly how many minutes late she should be. Her calculations were interrupted when the front door opened and Mel loudly announced her return.

"So, tonight's the night! What are you going to wear?"

"Um, this." Sally brushed imaginary fluff off her jeans and sat up straighter to show her floral top to its full potential.

Mel eyed her critically. "Sure I can't persuade you to wear a skirt?"

"Sure."

"OK, we'd best make the most of what we have then. Go and fetch your makeup."

"It's not really…"

Mel broke her off with the wave of her hand. "No excuses, and make it quick, I'm starving."

Sally returned with her meagre make-up collection and tipped it out on the coffee table. The sweet smell of hairdressing salons escaped from the bag.

Mel crouched down next to it. "OK, sit down so I can see you in the light."

"I'm only going round to his house."

"You're meeting his wife – you have to outdo her." Mel laid Sally's eye shadows out in front of her and began opening them one by one.

"Mel, stop. I'm not up for playing games."

"Quit the pretence."

"I'm over him."

"You're lying."

Sally wondered how transparent she was to everyone else. She slumped backwards in her chair, leaning further away from Mel and the make-up. "You know, I'm not sure this is a good idea. If I don't want to play games maybe I shouldn't meet her. Perhaps I should just arrange to meet him for coffee one day." She reached for her phone. "I hope they aren't already cooking…"

"Meeting him for coffee without her there isn't playing games? Come on, I've got a better lipstick than this in my handbag, why don't you go and fetch that."

Reluctantly Sally went into the kitchen to retrieve Mel's handbag. Amongst the receipts and painkillers Sally found a battered collection of lipsticks, all far darker than she ever dared to wear. She returned to where Mel was sitting.

"I know you wear them to work, but I think they're a bit much for tonight…"

"Just try it." Mel twisted up a plum-coloured lipstick and handed it to Sally. "You'll get used to it."

As she stepped outside into streaming sunlight, Sally looked at her watch; she was already late. She squinted as she hurried through the centre of town, barely noticing the churches, colleges and shops. As Victorian terraces replaced the grand college lawns she began to imagine what she would say when Paul opened the door. Nothing seemed natural.

When she rounded the corner and saw a red door with the number 5 on it, the butterflies dancing in her stomach instantly solidified into concrete. She slowed her steps and gave serious thought to turning around. Ideas for excuses she could give both Paul and Mel distracted her sufficiently from the fact that she was still walking, and she arrived on his doorstep before she'd had the chance to decide against it. She paused before she lifted her hand to the tarnished knocker, but just as she touched it the door swung open.

"I saw you coming." Paul stood aside and held the door open so there could be no awkwardness about how they should greet each other. Sally smiled and walked past him into the hallway, still unsure about what to say.

"Sorry about the mess," Paul said. "And that goes for the whole house."

Sally blinked as her eyes got used to the dim light. The hall was lined with cardboard boxes, giving the same feeling of lives in limbo that she had experienced on her last visit to his house. A house that was just a few streets away, but in a situation so different that Sally felt she might as well be looking at someone else's memories.

"Are you moving in or out?" she asked.

"In, thankfully. But things aren't quite straightened out yet, so you'll have to imagine what it'll look like in the end."

In front of her, a staircase bare other than carpet grippers led to a lonely pot-plant on the landing. Paul closed the front door. "Bear with me a moment while I stir the supper, and then you can have the grand tour."

As Sally followed him into the pokey kitchen she was hit by a delicious smell of roasting vegetables. The work surfaces were full of clutter and it looked like he'd used every kitchen implement he possessed. Three saucepans bubbled on the hob.

Paul kept on chatting, but Sally couldn't concentrate on what he was saying. She knew she was making him work hard, filling up silences so she didn't have to. But all she could focus on was the moment Katie would come in. Upstairs she heard a floorboard creak, and she listened for footsteps on the stairs.

Paul sipped the gravy. "What do you think?" He handed Sally the spoon and she leant closer so she could dip it into the pan. Heat radiated off the oven, but she felt as if it was coming from Paul.

Suddenly the door kitchen door swung open behind them. Sally leapt sideways as if her thoughts alone meant she'd been caught in the act.

Paul laughed as he scooped a large tabby cat into his arms. "It's only Bernard. My sister helped me move in and as payment I have to look after him while she's away."

"He made me jump." Sally gave a relieved giggle as she reached out to scratch the cat's silky head.

"Come on, there's time to see the front room before this is done."

She followed him into the front room. The walls had been stripped down to the grubby plaster, but the ceiling was painted white, and a plaster rose surrounded the light fitting. The bay window still had some original panes in it, making patches of the street outside appear in low resolution.

"Do you like it?" A grin spread across his face. "It's mine, as of last Sunday."

Mine, he'd said, not ours. The bare walls meant she was given no clues about his life, and no preparation for when Katie would come down the stairs to meet her, if indeed she would. His grin began to fade, and Sally realised she was meant to be showing her enthusiasm. "It's beautiful."

Still in Paul's arms, Bernard began to purr.

* * * * *

Sally's cheeks were flushed with warmth and excitement when she returned to her waiting housemates. At some point while Paul laid only two placemats on his makeshift table she had relaxed. The food had been delicious, but she had been so wrapped up in listening to Paul that she had almost forgotten to notice.

"You look happy," Liz said, "what's up?"

"Sally's been on a date with a married man."

Liz couldn't have looked more shocked if Mel had just told her Sally worked in a brothel.

"I wasn't on a date."

"Oh, sorry, just dinner was it." If there was one thing Mel enjoyed more than teasing Sally, it was winding up Liz.

"I don't even know if he's married."

Liz's expression didn't change. "If he's keeping that quiet about that, he's effectively cheating on her before he's even started. Lying by omission."

Mel ignored her. "How can you not know? I thought scientists were meant to notice things, work stuff out. You need to be nosier."

"He had just moved in – there was nothing on the walls or anything."

"Does he wear a wedding ring?" Mel asked.

"Well presumably not if he's pretending he doesn't have a wife." It was clear that all the evidence was going to point in one direction for Liz.

Sally waited for them to finish, then shook her head. "He didn't. But that doesn't mean anything. Some men just don't wear one."

"I think you're being somewhat naive." Liz sounded just like her mother, and Sally thought the accusation a bit rich coming from someone who had never had a proper boyfriend or even a proper job, but it worried her all the same. Had she been naive?

"So what did you talk about?" Mel asked.

With a disapproving frown Liz got up and left. Sally and Mel giggled like schoolgirls.

"Everything – his work, my work, his new house, his sister's cat, my annoying housemates…" Without Liz's scepticism to keep her down to earth, Sally gave up trying to hide her smile.

"Sounds suspiciously like there's no wife…"

"I'm honestly beginning to wonder."

Mel was quiet for a moment. "Whatever Liz thinks of me, you know that really I believe you're worth far more than being someone's mistress."

Mel's words, meant to reassure her, made Sally shudder. Whatever the situation, she never wanted to be someone's mistress. She was relieved when Mel changed the subject.

"That guy you brought to my party, Darren was it? He seemed alright."

"Yeah, he is. We argue sometimes in the lab, I guess, but I like him."

"Invite him over for supper and I'll stop pestering you about Paul."

"It's a deal."

Chapter 16

Late on Monday morning an email from Vangelis arrived in Sally's inbox, with the draft paper attached. It was accompanied by an enthusiastic note about the importance of submitting their work to *Nature* as soon as possible. She glanced around the office before she opened the paper, as if merely reading it was a criminal offence.

Mel had once got hold of a paper Sally was trying to read and entertained herself by calculating the percentage of words in the title she understood. She was pretty much limited to 'the', 'and' and 'in'. When she'd gone on to compare the language with the small print of an insurance certificate, Sally had become indignant, but mainly because she knew Mel had a point. The pompous, wordy sentences which had found their way into Sally's thesis and papers made her wonder at what stage in her life she had become so dull. So the attachment to Vangelis's email surprised her. It was punchy, lively and persuasive. Pages of minute details had been condensed into an accurate overview of what they'd done. But above all, it was convincing. Maybe the optimism she had felt with Paul the night before had infected the rest of her brain, but as she read how her work would be presented to the world, she felt proud.

These were not the thoughts she needed to confront Vangelis. By going along with things now, she reassured herself she wasn't backing down, just choosing her moments. So she began the process of combing through the document for inaccuracies, inconsistencies and improvements, and frugally added her comments. Eight different people had their names on the paper, and no doubt they would all want to stamp their mark. She didn't want to join in a contest of who could write the most. The chances were that even the order of the authors' names wouldn't pass without a fight. In academia publications are everything, and where your name appears on the list of authors flaunts your importance.

On the computer next to Sally, Amy was on her favourite website – findacareer.com. She would open the details of endless jobs she'd be hideously unsuitable for, regularly latching on to obscure options. In the last week these had ranged from manager in a garden centre (she'd typed in that she worked with plants) to database designer (she worked with numbers for her thesis…). When Sally looked over to see her browsing the fitness instructor section she decided it was time to intervene.

"Your inability to get a job in science will be a self-fulfilling prophecy if you spend your life researching how to be a bin man. Have you taken a look at this draft of the paper?"

Amy brightened at this prospect. The paper was one thing that could bring her closer to a career.

If gazelles assert their dominance using their horns, scientists do so with Track Changes and blunt comments down the margin. Words get needlessly replaced with favourite phrases, and sentences get torn to shreds. Over the next two weeks the paper went through six versions, during which Sally was mostly a passive bystander, adding only her agreement. If there was online silence for more than three hours Vangelis would send out an email which pompously explained the urgency.

On a sunny afternoon, just three weeks after the paper did its first circulation, Darren found Sally alone in the office.

"We're done," he announced. "I'm just collecting everyone's signatures then we're submitting tomorrow."

"And you want mine now?"

He handed her a pink coversheet. Seven authors had signed their consent for the paper to be submitted; the only gap was next to Sally's name. She smoothed the paper out in front of her and reached for a pen. It was her last chance to say no.

For Sally, school English lessons had been constant re-reading of books, plays and poems about characters she felt no affinity with. Her copy of the *Crucible*, grey round the edges by the time she carried it into her GCSE exam, contained the ultimate example of someone whose motivations were alien to her: John Proctor was hung for witchcraft rather than signing his name to a confession. But now his words resonated: *Because it is my name! Because I cannot have another in my life! Because I lie and sign myself to lies!*

If he was willing to sacrifice his life for the integrity of his name, she seemed to be selling herself short by forfeiting her honesty for the sake of a research paper. Realising that once her signature was on this form there was no turning back without revealing their fraudulence, Sally wavered. She'd been swept along by the familiar process of finalising a paper; now she wanted to make a decision not just agree by default.

"I think I need to talk to Vangelis about this."

"What do you have left to talk about?"

"Possibilities, implications."

"But, everything's sorted. Sign your name here and you don't need to worry about any of this again."

"I can't sign just to stop feeling guilty."

He took a step closer to her. "You can sign because it's the only reasonable thing to do."

Sally shook her head. "See you tomorrow Darren." She gave him a look which said 'don't argue', and went in search of Vangelis.

It was gone 5.30pm and the corridors were quiet; a sunny evening had called everyone to the pub, the park or the sports pitches. She was relieved to see Vangelis in his office still engrossed in a report. Her knuckles jarred as she knocked loudly on his door, still not sure what she planned to say. Vangelis looked over his glasses and smiled when she entered. "Ah, Sally, you've managed to complete the forms? Thank you very much."

In silence Sally removed the pile of books from his spare chair so she could sit down and face him. She placed the pink form down in front of them and explained simply why she had come. "What we're doing is wrong."

Vangelis nodded slowly as if to show he'd already considered and dismissed the problem. "As with many things, that's a matter of definition."

"I think illegal and dishonest come under most definitions of wrong." She concentrated hard on keeping her voice steady. If he wanted to make this a fight of clever words, she was ready to take him on.

"So, tell me Sally, do you think that our slight modifications have in any way affected the outcome?"

"No, but…"

"So our conclusions are honest and, more importantly, true."

"Not all the authors even know."

"It's better that way, nobody who was directly involved with that aspect of the work needs to be burdened with the details."

"But I know, and I'm not sure I can go through with it." She had wanted to base this argument on science and not her conscience.

"If you want to commit professional suicide and remove your name from this paper then that is your decision not mine, but I will not let you jeopardise the future of our colleagues and our lab." Vangelis's tone was calm and rational but his look was piercing.

Sally held his gaze. "There's more at stake than my career."

She pushed the form closer towards him, but he resisted, picking it up and holding them out to her.

"Take the forms away with you tonight, and I want them on my desk by 9am tomorrow, with or without your name on them. But before you make any decisions, I'd like you to give serious thought to what its absence will do for your future prospects."

Sally took the papers in silence and stood up to leave.

"Sally."

She turned round to face him.

"If what we're about is advancing scientific knowledge then surely, surely, you recognise the value of submitting this paper."

With only a nod for a goodbye, she walked out of his office.

The sun was still warm when Sally left the department, and the pavements were full of women whose bare shoulders were turning gently pink. The evening was too good to waste and her body needed movement, so she strolled towards the river, hoping that watching the ducks and the flow of the water would help clear her head.

She had been walking for nearly half an hour when she saw a familiar shape on a bench: a round belly, hunched shoulders and a collection of carrier bags. It was the same seat Sally had met her on last time. Sally sat down on the bench next to her and was hit by the smell of dirty laundry basket.

"Problems again, my dear?"

"I guess you could say that."

"Then tell me."

Sally took a deep breath, wondering how to start. "Have you ever lied?"

"I don't know a soul who hasn't."

"I don't just mean 'dinner was really tasty' when actually it was disgusting, I mean for real."

"You know m'love, it's all the same, it's still lies."

"But complimenting the food just makes someone feel good. Lies can end marriages, start wars, cause people to refuse life-saving vaccines…"

"There's only two kind of eggs – a good egg and a rotten one. And's the same with lies – some are told for good, some for bad."

"Well tomorrow there's a chance I will sign my name to a lie. It's been sold to me as a modification of the truth, but that's just for the benefit of my conscience. It's a lie. And I don't know whether it's a good one or a bad one."

"It's one or t'other."

"It's wrong because it's for personal glory, and for my colleagues I guess, but still selfish. But it's right because it was an experiment, and it's giving the right answers."

"Are you doin' it for yourself m'love? Cos there aint a man in the world who's worth lying for."

"I feel like I'm living a lie – that I'm lying to friends who don't even have anything to do with my work. They all believe

I'm honest, committed to my work, doing it not because I want to make a name for myself but because I want to make a difference."

"You ever been to the rail station? Watched all those people in their suits? Their whole lives are a big act, they're lying to everyone they meet. Until you say what you want and don't just follow like a bleating sheep then you're lying to your friends. Even to yourself. I should know dear, 'cos I tried it as long as anyone else."

Sally turned to the lady with interest. "What were you before?"

The lady was silent and Sally feared that she had overstepped the mark, and broken the understanding between two strangers – the ability to speak honestly to someone whose life is entirely tangential to yours. But the lady was concentrating intently on rearranging her shawl so its fine crochet sat neatly over her shoulders. When she was eventually satisfied she spoke.

"I was a lotta things, but I can tell you what I wasn't, and that's happy."

Sally nodded as if she understood, trying to imagine lives the lady could have lived, and what could make the one she'd chosen be more attractive. She stayed on the bench enjoying the warmth of the sun on her arms and face. The peace was shattered when her phone rang. Sally nodded an apology to the lady as she answered it.

"Sally, I've got some fantastic news from your brother."

"Hi Mum, what is it?"

"He's been made a partner!"

Knowing this would be a long one, Sally wearily stood up and began her walk home. She waved goodbye to the bag lady, but her eyes appeared milky and unseeing as she stared out over the river.

"Great! What does that mean?"

"Um, it means that he's done well… it's a big promotion you know."

Although she had no idea what this meant in business terms, Sally knew exactly what it meant to her mother. It meant he was important and he was rich. It meant his status was recognised in a career that her friends respected.

"Well he's certainly worked hard for it," Sally said. "And I hope they pay him well to sleep with his BlackBerry under his pillow."

"Oh they do. He only heard today but he's already talking about buying somewhere bigger than his flat, you know, somewhere more appropriate for a family."

"That's good." Her brother didn't even have a girlfriend.

As her mother continued to give the reaction of each of her friends to the news, Sally let her mind wander to her surroundings – the barges moored on the river banks, the children playing in the fading sunshine. Her mother's proud chatter was reassuring, even if her words would be irritating if Sally listened too closely.

Her attention was jolted back to the conversation when her mother asked her a question, "So Sally, is there any news in your career?"

"Yes in fact there is. Tomorrow we're going to submit a paper to Nature. It's one of science's top journals, as in, one of the places where your research gets most people actually reading it. If you have a *Nature* paper on your CV it shows that your work isn't just good, it's important."

"Well done, dear. If it makes you happy, that's what matters most."

Normally this kind of comment wouldn't be worth replying to, but if Sally couldn't fight for her mother's approval when she was published in *Nature* there was no hope of ever getting through. "Many people wait most of their careers for this. Even outside academia it looks good, really good."

"Well you do work hard so I'm glad someone's noticed."

That would have to do.

On the way home she stopped at the fish and chip shop. It amused her to think of her brother ordering champagne while she was feeling guilty about spending £3.50 on a bag of chips.

When Sally arrived home Mel was eating a salad at the kitchen table. Sitting down opposite her, Sally opened the greasy parcel of chips, releasing a warm smell of vinegar and deep-fat fryers.

"I hope I can tempt you to counteract some of that lettuce?"

Mel nodded eagerly and Sally shovelled a lump of chips onto her plate.

"What's the occasion?"

"It's a celebration – my brother has been made partner."

"He's done well. How old is he?"

"I can't remember. 35? Anyway, he's reached new levels in my mother's estimation."

"You know if you got yourself a boyfriend I bet you could rise to meet him."

"I tried to impress Mum with our success in the lab, but she didn't really get it."

"These biotech companies make a fortune, I'm sure you can match your brother if you put your mind to it."

"I don't want to work for them. They make money not food."

Mel didn't look like this was a debate she had any interest in starting. Instead she went to the fridge and pulled out a half-empty bottle of wine. She handed Sally a glass.

"Here's to your brother, who's earned the ticket to abuse his workers in the name of making money."

"You're such a sceptic. Does everyone in charge really have to trample on those below them?"

"If you can get to the top in science without cheating anyone then make the most of it."

Sally opened her mouth. The words *tomorrow I have to make a trade-off between getting to the top and keeping a clear conscience* rose in her throat. But they didn't come out.

Chapter 17

As she lay in bed that night, the effort of not thinking kept Sally on the cusp of sleep. But when her mind finally let go of consciousness, her sleep was deep and dreamless.

She awoke the next morning with a clear head. The alarm clock read 7.30, just an hour and a half until she needed to face Vangelis with her decision. She allowed herself to think through the arguments she had blocked out the night before. As her radio alarm reached its second song, the answer came to her, so simple it shocked her that she hadn't thought of it before. If she told one of the other authors, they would make their own decision and she would be released from guilt and from the pressure to decide.

She mentally ran through the list of names, very quickly deciding on Andrew, the scarily intelligent statistician who had designed the trials and analysed the data. The scheme was perfect; the decision was out of her hands – if he believed it was wrong then she could fade into the background as he retracted his signature and blocked the paper from publication. If he was in favour of going ahead then she would respect his judgement and the guilt would be transferred from her shoulders onto his.

When she arrived at the department Sally didn't visit Andrew immediately. Instead she came into the office to turn on her computer and take off her jumper, perhaps only as a form of procrastination. Günter, Amy and Darren were all working in there and Sally quickly got sucked into conversation. Their talk darted erratically from problems with one of the PCR machines to how they would celebrate when Amy submitted her thesis. At last they returned their attention to their computers and Sally realised the time had come. But still she lingered. She looked at the back of her friends' heads and at the science on their screens.

It was almost unheard of for anyone under the age of 30 to get a permanent job, and they were all on fixed-term contracts. She had over two years left, but Darren was now counting his time there in months not years. Thoughts of their future occupied her as she dragged her feet on the way to Andrew's office. Günter at least had two countries to look for jobs in, and anyway computers were cheaper than labs, so people needing only a PC to do their work were more in demand. But if a career in academia was denied to her, would Amy choose Monsanto or the garden centre?

When she knocked on his door Andrew look surprised to see her.

"What's up Sally?"

"Hi, how are you?"

"OK, thank you."

There was silence and Sally's eyes darted round the room. His officemate Ben was covering pieces of scrap paper with a spidery sprawl of numbers and symbols. He sniffed loudly and Sally wondered whether acting as awkward as she felt would encourage him to leave. But Ben was known for bluntness and lack of subtlety; he wasn't going to take the hint.

Andrew, however, was used to dealing with him. "Hey Ben, it's 9.26 and you haven't visited the coffee machine yet. My brain is caffeine starved, and I think Sally could do with something too."

Ben smiled and left, presumably oblivious to the fact that he'd been sent away for Sally's benefit. He didn't share any of Andrew's charm, but the two of them were close friends.

Andrew closed the door behind him. "What can I do for you?"

Sally sat down in Ben's chair and listened to the blood pumping in her ears. "Sorry, Andrew, I didn't mean to bother you. I just wanted your advice."

"Go on."

"You've worked with Vangelis a long time."

"Five years and counting."

"Do you always trust his judgment?"

"He's a great scientist and has done some impressive work, I have a lot of respect for that. We've had our differences. As a statistician I'm used to that – I design the perfect experiment and then someone says they don't have the resources to do it."

"And you compromise?"

"Experiments wouldn't get done if we always insisted on our way, and they wouldn't be worth doing if we didn't say what data is needed to make the results meaningful."

"That's true."

There was a silence while Sally tried to collect her thoughts into a coherent explanation.

"Have you had a disagreement?" Andrew asked.

"Yes, I guess we have."

He didn't push her to say what the disagreement was.

"Look, if I have one piece of advice, it's that you live in England in the 21st Century. Gone are the days of strong hierarchies – if you have an issue with something, then say so.

Vangelis may be a professor, but your views are as valuable as his are."

Sally nodded. "That's good advice."

At that moment Ben returned with two plastic cups of coffee. He stopped when he saw Sally sitting in his chair. "Oh, Sally, sorry, I forgot."

"Back you go, Ben." Andrew pointed to the door.

Sally watched him place the two cups on the desk, wincing as hot coffee spilled onto his fingers. It was cowardly to pass the decision on. If she had any ambition of making it in science she had to take responsibility for her results and for her actions. Granted, publishing fabricated data could be the end of the whole lab if they were discovered, but the chances were slim. Vangelis and Darren had already decided it was a risk worth taking.

She had to make the choice herself. "No don't worry, I'd better do some work. Thanks for talking to me Andrew."

"Any time, you know where I am."

She walked down the corridor to Vangelis's office, stopping only to rest the form on her leg and add her scribbled signature. When Sally handed the completed coversheet to Vangelis he greeted her cheerfully, and she was annoyed that he showed no sign of having feared her decision.

"Thank you very much for this. I'll submit right now." He took the form from her and placed it on his keyboard, the only clear space. "How's everything going?"

They talked about the experiments she was working on, the first experiments in this lab which were entirely hers. He bombarded her with so many tips and ideas that her brain quickly reached capacity. She began making excuses to do with timings in the lab and slowly backed towards the doorway.

Only when she said goodbye and reached for the door handle did he lower his voice.

"Sally," he said. "You're doing the right thing."

As she left Vangelis's office Sally felt liberated. She could continue with her experiments, a new project not tainted by the failures of the old one. Science could once again be about creating results, about discovery, not about guilt and dishonesty and tactical career moves. The sense of power was so strong she even contemplated calling Paul. The moment passed – he was at work and she didn't actually have anything to say – but she did have the courage to invite Darren round as Mel had requested. If it was unexpected, Darren didn't show it and readily accepted.

* * * * *

Mel was adding the final touches to her seafood paella when Darren rang the doorbell. Pleased to be freed from kitchen duties, Sally let him in and led him into the kitchen. He'd brought a bottle of wine, which he handed straight to Mel.

When they sat down at the table Darren didn't waste time in getting on to personal questions. "So Mel, Sally told me you don't like your job."

"Oh did she? And don't tell me she said I should quit?"

"As a matter of fact she did – your boss isn't worth it and you work too hard."

"Well I'm glad she's stopped boring me with this crap and started annoying someone else with it."

Mel reached for the salad servers in a way that suggested this conversation was over. Sally thought back to all she'd told Mel about Darren, and wondered whether Mel would bring it all up as punishment for telling Darren too much.

"Actually," Darren said, "I agree with her."

There was a silence. This wasn't how it was meant to be. When you introduce two friends there's meant to be small talk and pleasantries, not a betrayal of confidences. Mel looked up from the salad to Darren, and Sally wished she could disappear.

"Well she's probably failed to tell you that without my salary we can't pay the rent, that this is how life is in a law firm, that if I didn't work these hours by boss would make my life miserable, that it's the way I'm trained to work. And anyway, it's fine for you to be motivated by your values, but I'm not."

"So, basically, you work all hours to pay Sally's rent?"

"Sally can pay her own rent, I work to pay the rest of it."

"Liz's poetry is still pre-profit," Sally explained.

"That figures. So, what do you like about your job?"

"Well, I guess…" Mel faltered. Sally had never seen her without a quick answer before, but it was a long time before she continued. "I like being quick thinking, outwitting people. I'm good at it, and I'm proud of that. It's not as if I'm good at many things."

"That's not what Sally tells me."

Sally had told both of them far too much – the kind of things you pretend you don't know when you actually meet the person. She hadn't realised that Darren would break this social nicety.

Mel raised her eyebrows at Sally and said to Darren, "Tell all."

"For a start, she says you're smart. And that means there are lots of things you'd be good at, if only you tried them."

Sally was nervous about joining the conversation but couldn't help it. She'd had so many abortive attempts at persuading Mel to quit that she wasn't going to let her off now. "It's true, you should try them. Why not?"

176

"What's stopping you?" Darren echoed.

Again Mel dwelt on this, and Sally looked down at her paella.

"There're two reasons, I guess. You're both genuinely keen on what you do, but there just isn't anything I'm into that much. And…" Mel paused. "What if I'm not good at it?"

Sally shifted uneasily; she wasn't ready for Mel to show cracks in her perfect exterior.

Darren too seemed nervous about this admission, and his questioning became more tentative. But he continued. "What are you into?"

"Not much."

"That's not true. And it doesn't have to be something you're into already," Sally said, "just something you believe in. I never really understood how GM crops can help people until I was doing my PhD. So what's motivating me now I used not to know about."

Mel turned to Darren, who was picking out the prawns to eat first. Sally hoped he'd put things into words better than she had.

"Why do you spend your life working on molecules you'll never even see?"

"I like the challenge. It's amazing, when you think about the four letters that control life on Earth. Everything from bacteria to the human brain, all made possible because of the letters A, T, C and G."

"Four letters that rule the world? I didn't realise being into something meant obscure philosophy." Now the attention had turned to Darren and Sally, Mel had recovered.

"They're not letters," Sally said. "They are nucleotide bases, the four building blocks of DNA. We give them letters for our own convenience."

"Letters are just human definitions was that? I thought you guys were scientists not existentialists."

Darren continued as if the discussion was still serious. "The DNA bases, A, T, C and G, are the code of life – each of these DNA building blocks has a slightly different structure and they make a code. Everything on your computer screen is created by a string of zeros and ones, but every protein in your body is created by a string of A,T,C,G… It's amazing."

"Have some more wine."

Sally held out her glass and accepted some lukewarm wine. "But it's not just that it's amazing – it's for some good. We're actually doing something that makes a difference."

"Darren?" Mel asked.

"I guess that's true." He sounded reluctant. "But it's more than that it's just interesting."

"But… if all that interests you is how fascinating it is, isn't there a danger you forget the bigger picture about what it's all for?" Sally could feel herself being too intense for a dinner party.

Darren shrugged. "You just need to understand the science. Anyway, deciding whether it's good for people is someone else's job, not mine."

"OK, Sally," Mel said. "If you had the choice of a boring desk job that you believed would help feed people and a job as a scientist studying something that was interesting but entirely pointless, what would you do?"

"I don't know. I am glad I don't have to make that choice."

"Sally, you're crazy," Darren said.

"I'll drink to that."

Mel and Darren clinked glasses.

They moved on to the kind of subjects Sally had assumed they would talk about: cyclists without lights in Cambridge, a video of a man being attacked by a bear on YouTube, jibes at politicians which were fuelled more by drink and fun than by any kind of understanding. She happily went along with it, but her mood never properly lightened.

It could be considered rude to leave your own dinner party early, but Mel seemed more than happy to play the hostess, so when the plates had been cleared after their pudding Sally said her goodnights and went to bed.

Just occasionally, the times when your friends speak the most openly with you are the times you feel you know them the least. She had never considered the possibility that Mel actually liked parts of her job, or that she would be scared to leave. It had taken a stranger to get these things out of her. And worse, she had assumed that Darren was similar to her in so many ways. But to not really care about the ultimate point of their research, that was as far away from her philosophy as Mel's was. But what filled her with fear most was the idea that Vangelis might be the same. He justified submitting their research despite 'modifications' because of its value to the cause of food security, but was that just because he knew how to win her over?

She found herself wondering what Paul would have made of Mel and Darren's revelations. But for the first time things had changed: she wasn't imagining the opinions of the Paul who existed in her head, she was thinking about the real Paul she had seen last week. Before she could change her mind she texted him, simply *Hope you're well, would you like to meet up sometime soon?*

She had hoped that sleep would come quickly, but she was wrong. She lay with eyes open watching her silent phone and listening to Darren and Mel in the kitchen. She'd never thought that falling asleep to the sound of your friends laughing could feel lonely.

* * * * *

When Sally came downstairs the next morning Mel still wasn't up. The kitchen was in a state; dirty plates were piled around the sink and empty bottles had collected on the table. Clearly Mel and Darren had carried on drinking long after she had left. Slowly and methodically Sally separated out recycling from washing up and eventually the kitchen table was clear. Darren's jumper was hanging on the back of a chair, so she put it in her bag ready to return the next day at work.

Even when the washing up was done Mel hadn't emerged. Sally hung around, hoping to see her. She wanted to do something light-hearted with her, to forget the uncomfortable conversations of the night before. They often went to the cinema at the weekend, or shopping or for a pub lunch. But when there was still no sign of Mel, Sally began to wonder whether she'd gone out already. In the end she went to the cinema on her own.

She kept her phone close, still hoping for Paul's call. Even though it never made a noise, she couldn't help lighting up the screen at regular intervals, just to check that a message hadn't arrived. But when it maintained its silence, she began leaving it where she wouldn't be able to hear it. She missed a trip to the pub because she didn't hear Amy's call. Her mother left a couple of worried answerphone messages, and Sally imagined her pleasure at the idea of rescuing her daughter from a minor drama. She went to bed still without a response.

Chapter 18

The next day the lab was busy. A research group working on seed germination had hired some summer workers. They were all immersed in their experiments, wandering round the lab with headphones in. Judith had been 'tidying up', and Sally entertained herself by returning everything to its original position.

Her work was going well; she had already inserted the new gene. Next to her Darren wasn't having so much luck. Their new project hadn't encountered any major setbacks, but nobody was immune from regular minor ones. He entertained her with good-natured cursing as his results proved only that he was using defunct enzymes. Although she hadn't yet seen Mel, Sally was reassured by the fact that everything was normal with Darren. But their conversation over dinner had left her dissatisfied. As they stood next to each other, pipetting, mixing, failing, discovering, working towards the same goal, she wanted to know what that goal really was to him.

She started tentatively. "What you said to Mel about how amazing biology is, that it's crazy how DNA shapes all life forms from amoebas to us, I think you had it just right."

"Of course, that's because you understand."

"We're lucky to work in a lab, learning about DNA and changing it."

Darren looked at his failed experiment. "Speak for yourself!"

One of the summer workers was pouring molten agar into Petri dishes, and Sally watched as the viscous liquid solidified into a smooth gel. She felt awkward about continuing their conversation in front of him, even though she knew he wasn't listening.

"But we're doing this for the value of the results, not for fun."

"Well I can assure you it's not fun today."

"But don't you see what I'm saying?"

"What the heck does it matter anyway?"

It mattered because they had lied. The bag lady had divided lies into two separate categories – the good and the bad. She'd intended hers to be good, but had the same lie from Darren come with the wrong intentions?

The uneasy feeling she carried round with her for the next few days was broken only by a text from Paul. He'd been away for the weekend and wanted to cook her supper.

* * * * *

As soon as Paul opened the door Sally could see his house had gone through a transformation. The boxes lining the hall had been replaced by cans of paint, and there was a lingering smell of white spirit. He led her into the living room, now painted an olive green, and went to the kitchen to make tea.

The walls were covered in pictures, giving it the permanent feel that her rented house with magnolia walls and greyish carpet would always lack. Unsure of whether to sit down, Sally concentrated on the feel of the varnished floorboards under her bare feet.

Above the fireplace was a photo of a red sandy track leading to a jagged rock structure. When Paul returned with two steaming mugs he saw her looking at it. "New Mexico, I went for a road trip there when my contract ended, just before I moved back to the UK. It was stunning."

Sally focussed on the contrast between the orange rocks and the blue sky. "What was it like in America?"

"Beautiful ... Unhealthy ... Tough ..."

"Tough?"

Paul looked at her in confusion. "I went to America to get married and I came back single."

Sally's heart gave an unhealthy thump. "I'm sorry." She was sorry to have been tactless, but she couldn't bring herself to be sorry about what he'd just said. This was the confirmation she had been waiting for. She pushed her hands into her pockets in an effort to keep herself immobilised.

Thankfully, Paul seemed oblivious to her excitement. "Sorry, I like to think everyone knows, that way I don't have to tell them."

Sally didn't point out that there was nobody to tell her; their only shared friend was a cat. She kept her eyes on the photo so they didn't betray her. "I hope it's easier now you're back," she said. "And Cambridge is healthy as well as beautiful."

"It's true, I can't describe how much better it is to be here."

"But you stayed in America?"

"Yes, well, it's a long story." They looked at each other, Sally wondering whether it was a story she was going to hear. Eventually Paul gestured towards the sofa. "We might as well sit down."

They sat at opposite ends, but the sofa wasn't large enough to allow the space between them that Sally felt the situation deserved. Paul turned to face her, bringing one leg up on the sofa so his knee splayed out sideways.

"I went to America and it was amazing. Everyone was friendly, the weather was perfect. And it was only when I saw Katie that I realised how much I'd missed her."

Sally looked away and hoped Paul couldn't see colour rising in her cheeks.

"But all that didn't last long. As soon as I started work, I realised that America's national parks may be stunning, but I would never find time to visit them. Even worse, it was practically impossible to make friends. Everyone was so conservative, and deeply religious, and most people in my lab had children – they led completely different lives to me. I lived in constant fear of offending someone, and I realised I often didn't say things because I couldn't be bothered to explain them. Everyone was kind to me, and they were nice people. We just didn't understand each other."

"Did Katie have friends?" It felt odd to say Katie's name out loud.

"Maybe she had a magic touch that I just didn't. Everyone loved her. She would invite people over and be the centre of attention. But I just found her friends annoying. I think that was the first sign something was wrong. And my job was getting me down, I had got my PhD, yet here I was the most junior technician. It felt like such a backwards step, and I didn't take kindly to doing other people's work."

"Nor would I."

"It wasn't long before she started staying late at work or spending the evening with friends. The less I saw of her, the more time I had to wonder whether doing a rubbish job and having no friends was worth it to be out there with her. I'm pretty sure I wasn't even making her happy; I think she saw me as a burden, holding her back."

Sally was struck by the matter-of-fact calmness Paul was telling his story with. It was the same accepting tone she often marvelled at on the radio. People called in to tell stories of missing spouses or terminal illness which made Sally want to cry, but they were told with total pragmatism.

"I don't believe you were a burden."

Paul shrugged. "She sometimes made me feel that way, and sometimes I believed it. We didn't decide to put off the wedding, and we certainly never talked about whether getting married was still the right thing to do. I don't really think that had crossed my mind properly. We just never spoke of it at all. But then I saw a job in California, where I could do my own research and showed the advert to Katie. She couldn't believe I was even thinking about it, and just wasn't willing to talk about compromises that would affect her career."

"That's so unfair." Sally felt genuine outrage for him.

"I applied anyway and I was offered it three weeks later. I went, and she didn't try to stop me." Paul picked at the bottom of his jeans, frayed where his heels had been treading on them. Sally wanted to reach out and take his hand, to hold it still. But she hardly dared move in case it put him off telling his story. "Pride wouldn't let me come back to the UK less than a year after I'd left, and for my career it was an opportunity I wouldn't have got back here. But it took me three years in California to get my self-respect back. And, well, here I am in Cambridge."

"I'm glad you came back."

"Thank you." He smiled and reached for his cup of tea, as if to signal that the story was over.

But for Sally he had left it incomplete. For her, it began before he left the country, in his house in Shelton Road with boxes lining the hall to mark the end of his student days. This was the only point she had touched Paul and Katie's story, but had the memory of that night affected the outcome? If it wasn't for her, might they have worked things out? That was a burden of guilt she didn't want to shoulder. His pain which, even years later, clearly had been dulled but not extinguished, could perhaps have been avoided. But what might be even worse was knowing that she was irrelevant to the story. One of the things that had reassured her when she thought he was gone from her life was that he had been hers, even if only for a night. She at least held some claim to him.

On the other end of the sofa Sally brought her knees up to her chin and steeled herself for the question she needed the answer to, the part of the story she would never hear if she didn't bring it up herself. She felt her heart grow louder, then asked, "Was it me?"

"Sally, it's completely not your fault." The calm detachment he'd spoken with was lost. "You can't possibly take any blame. I'm so sorry if you ever felt guilty."

She was silent, waiting for him to answer her question.

Eventually he took a deep breath, his shoulders rising. "That's something I've spend too long asking myself, mainly during sleepless nights. But every time I come out with the same answer: it wasn't at all. In fact, I think it gave us more of a chance – I was so determined not to have ruined things that I tried harder. What happened didn't seem to be a valid reason for our relationship to end, so I didn't let it become one."

The door swung open and Bernard walked in, his tail twitching in agitation. He jumped onto the sofa and settle in

186

Sally's lap. She hugged him too tightly, making him squeeze free and jump over to Paul.

"Has your sister abandoned him?" Sally had heard enough; it was time to return their conversation to the cat.

"She said he could keep me company for a while."

"I like him."

They spent the rest of the evening cooking and eating. Sally stirred the soup and let Paul's talking drift over her. Her head felt swollen with thoughts of what she'd just learned. She'd spent years picturing his life as Katie's new husband. The Paul who was standing there explaining his creative plans for decorating was leading a very different existence to the fictitious Paul who had inhabited her head.

Supper was delicious but strained. In the entire time she'd known Paul, Katie was a topic of conversation Sally had avoided. But tonight she mentally checked everything she was about to say for links to her. Now the topic seemed taboo, Katie was all Sally wanted to talk about. She left straight after they'd eaten, hoping he hadn't been offended by her mental absence.

It was still light by the time Sally returned home. The walk had cleared her head, and she was already wishing she could return to Paul's and start the evening over again. Mel and Liz were sitting in the kitchen, a pile of chocolate wrappers on the table between them. Sally greeted them, trying to work out if the chocolates were hers.

"How was your date, Sally?"

"It wasn't a date," Liz said.

"Katie wasn't there – she's gone."

"This calls for celebration. Who's got more chocolate?"

Sally opened her cupboard where two bars of chocolate were hiding at the back. She pulled out the largest and broke it in to pieces, the last of the frustration she'd felt when she left Paul's rapidly disappearing.

"So, Paul's single." Mel pulled the pile of chocolate towards her. She didn't deserve to stay thin.

"But is he really?" Liz looked at Sally with concern.

"Yes, I've been to his house, you can't hide a wife!"

"What else?" Mel said.

"Surely that's good enough gossip for you?"

"You've basically known that for weeks. What about you and Paul?"

"There's nothing to tell. He's pretty cut up about Katie, and I just don't think he's looking for anyone else. But that's fine, it's still easier for me that Katie's gone."

"Problems, problems, Sally – it's always problems!"

"You're right to take it slow; problems are usually real." Liz was doted on by her father, and no other men seemed good enough for her or her friends. "If he's been married, you never know what went wrong, or whether he's just making the most of things before he goes back to her. You don't know that he's even properly divorced."

"He never was married. He told me everything. It's for real."

Sally began smoothing out the wrappers, channelling all annoyance at Liz into creating beautiful metallic squares. Liz was wrong. By doubting Paul's character, she'd only made Sally realise how much she trusted him.

"Tell all, Sally," Mel said.

Omitting only the part where she was involved, Sally told them everything.

Thoughts of Paul kept Sally awake most nights. When, five years earlier, she left his bed unnoticed she'd had no expectation or intention of seeing him again. It had been a natural conclusion to their relationship that never was. She'd gradually come to define herself as a lost cause, absurdly loving a man she would never see again. She'd given up her fight of trying to forget him, instead living with the knowledge that Paul's memory left little room for future lovers. A quitting smoker can control whether their fingers reach for a cigarette, but no amount of will power will stop them craving it.

Now Paul was back, pointless longing could be replaced by hope. There was an overwhelming temptation to say this was fate: she'd kept loving him because she knew they would meet again. Her scientific mind knew she was simply infatuated.

She thought of what she'd told Mel, of reasons Paul had no interest in her. But gradually she realised the problems in her head were no different to the ones Liz had created for her. They were dreamt up based on nothing but supposition; they weren't things Paul had told her. She wanted them to be wrong. She wanted to disprove them.

Sally endured a weekend with her parents. Being smothered with attention and treated like a teenager was much easier to stomach in small doses. She could at least count herself lucky that any pressure to be a better daughter, visit them more often and get a boyfriend was delivered not by subtle emotional blackmail but by well-intentioned demands from her mother. It was vaguely comforting to hear her mother's fussing over whether she had enough money and did she separate out whites and colours for washing. And, like a preoccupation with Paul, it was a welcome distraction from the eroding guilt she still felt about 'modified' data, guilt that was numbed by her choice to submit the paper, but not extinguished.

Her father played his normal role, maintaining the peace. When he was alone with Sally he asked her about her work. He listened diligently to the progress of her experiments and Sally knew he was proud.

The house was quiet when she arrived home on the Sunday night, but there was a note waiting for her on the table.

Here's my CV, 1st draft, look OK to you? Be nice, Mel.

Sally read with fascination the summaries of contentious cases Mel had worked on, each of them carefully avoiding the confidential, and hence most interesting, details. The ephemeral nature of science jobs meant Sally was an expert in commenting on CVs. But the ones she normally saw were carelessly modest, with dull details standing in the way of the salient points. Mel's was perfectly crafted to sound exciting and impressive, ironic given that Mel claimed she found her job deathly boring. Somehow Sally felt proud reading the CV, despite the fact she'd had no input into Mel's academic success. It was satisfying to think Mel might actually use her skills for something that made her happy.

That week Sally saw so little of Mel she almost wondered if she was avoiding her. Mel always worked late, but she was taking it to extremes. Sometimes when she was in bed Sally would hear the rustles and bangs of Mel returning and making herself something that passed for supper. Sometimes she'd be fast asleep.

On Saturday morning Sally found Mel in the kitchen, placing large scoops of coffee into the cafetiere. Mel was wearing skinny jeans; Sally was in her pyjamas. They exchanged moans from the week – Mel about the amount of work she had,

Sally about Paul not getting in touch and about old samples ruined by a catastrophic failure of the -80°C freezer.

When that ritual was over Sally began the talk of jobs. "Your CV was pretty impressive. What's it for?"

"Keeping on file."

"Very funny."

Mel continued fighting the cafetiere without answering.

"You were being serious weren't you?" Sally said.

"Having a CV doesn't mean much."

"Come off it, even your draft was printed on posh paper; that definitely means it's going to be followed by the real thing. You didn't just do it to boost your ego by writing down how good you are."

"Just because you're too stingy to use posh paper for anything at all, doesn't mean you can be a detective about my motives. And don't underestimate my ego."

Sally gave a pointed sigh and wondered whether Mel found her just as perverse when she was making excuses about Paul. "OK, hypothetically speaking, where would you want to work?"

"Somewhere my boss wasn't a jerk."

"Good start, but they don't normally put that on the job description."

"Somewhere that the right answer to every task I'm set isn't so clear."

Sally tied her dressing gown tighter around her. "If the answer was clear they wouldn't need to pay someone as expensive as you to find it."

"All I do at the moment is apply laws someone else has written. Yes, I try and find loopholes, but basically it's clear cut. There are right answers. I want somewhere the territory is new, where laws are changing, and new cases challenge the law."

Mel had clearly given this a lot of thought.

"Have you seen anything?" Sally said.

"Honestly, I've no idea where to look and I haven't had a chance to try."

"I can look for you. My colleague Amy, she could do a PhD on researching jobs. I could at least find where you could start."

"Do you guys ever do any work?" Mel was comfortable giving help, not accepting it.

"I'll do it while my experiments are running."

Having beaten the cafetiere's dying plunger, Mel stirred milk into two coffees. "Thanks, Sally, I'd actually be really interested to see what you come up with, just for ideas. Who knows, you've got to start somewhere."

Chapter 19

Sally waited for the dust to settle before contacting Paul. She texted to thank him for supper but hadn't suggested meeting. She justified it to herself that the ball was in his court now he had told her about Katie. Maybe it changed everything, maybe nothing, but that was his decision.

By the time Paul got in touch Sally was almost giving up hope. Even Mel had got bored of listening to her fret about how she'd offended him, how he'd misinterpreted her silence after she'd heard about Katie. But his email contained an invitation for Sunday lunch.

For the next few days Sally lived with the kind of excitement her childhood birthday parties used to induce. When she arrived at his house she chatted happily, the awkwardness she had felt after hearing Katie's story entirely forgotten. Paul had put a lot of effort into the food. He showed her the chocolate mousses setting in the fridge ready for dessert and directed her to a ready laid table. "Now I've got a smart house, the cooking has to live up to it."

Paul divided the mashed potato into even portions, and Sally tried to imagine what Bernard would think of them, if only cat courtship was as complex as it was for humans and he could understand a word of what they were saying. She and

Paul were talking and laughing like friends. There were no fluttering eyelids, no lingering looks, no hands subtly brushed against each other. But they were sharing a three-course lunch; two people who normally ate sandwiches from plastic lunchboxes were now drinking wine from the correct glasses. All that was missing was the candlelight.

After lunch they had coffee to counteract the wine, and Paul suggested exercise to counteract the food. "I've got bookshelves to fit together in the spare room, and I need some artistic advice on positioning."

Sally stroked the smooth spines of the books as she arranged them on the shelves, sorted by genre. "Are you just very careful with your books or have none of them been read?"

"They've spent three years in boxes, so I can barely remember which I've read. Makes you wonder what's the point of reading them. It's so satisfying to see them on the shelves though."

Sally looked at the half-filled shelves. Most of the book collection she'd been amassing since she was a teenager lived under her parents' spare bed. "I know what you mean."

It was late afternoon by the time Sally got up to leave. Paul opened the front door for her, and they stood awkwardly on the threshold. The light-hearted mood had vanished and Sally wondered whether he was about to say: *when can you come again* or *I don't think we should keep seeing each other.* Bernard ran between them and jumped out onto the pavement. Sally watched as he disappeared behind the neighbour's hedge.

Eventually Paul spoke. "I do really appreciate you coming."

"I like it, and your food is delicious." She had no idea how serious he was being.

Paul fiddled nervously with the lock. "Thank you, but I mean I know your boyfriend doesn't like it, so I wanted to say I'm glad you come."

"Sorry?" Sally felt her face adjust into an *'are you mad?'* expression.

"He makes it pretty clear I'm not wanted."

"I don't understand."

"It's OK, I completely see where he's coming from; I'd probably do the same if I was in his position. I don't think badly of him."

"Paul, stop!" Sally reached out to shut the door. He let it swing closed, blocking out the sunlight. "I have no idea what you're talking about. I don't have a boyfriend."

There was silence as their eyes adjusted to the gloom.

"But…"

"Who do you mean?"

"Darren – he acts like he owns you."

"He's just my friend, we work together."

"But every time I see him he tries to get in the way. I even came to your lab and he just told me you were busy."

Sally thought through the occasions when Darren had met Paul. She remembered their first meeting in the pub – the relief she'd felt when Darren came to rescue her. Ever since then Darren had tried hard never to leave her alone with Paul. It all made sense. "I'm sorry."

"No, I'm sorry. I guess I just always saw you together." Paul didn't look convinced.

"Did he really tell you I was busy?"

"He said he'd let you know I'd been there, but when you never got back to me I guessed he hadn't."

"That's so rude, I had no idea."

They stood in silence, not looking at each other. Outside a blackbird was singing.

Paul reached out again to the door handle. "I'd best let you go, sorry I got things wrong."

"I'm sorry about Darren."

"It's no problem."

Sally stepped out onto the pavement and wondered what on Earth this all meant.

When Sally got home, Mel was sitting at the kitchen table surrounded by documents. She tilted down the screen of her laptop and looked at Sally.

"Sally, what news? This stuff is dire, I need entertainment."

"I've just been to Paul's."

"I knew that much. And?"

"Paul thought Darren was my boyfriend."

Mel pulled a face. "I thought Paul was meant to be smart."

"Actually, I can see why. Every time he's met Paul, Darren's acted like an idiot. It's almost, I don't know, as if he's possessive."

"One word from Paul and you'll convince yourself of anything."

"No, listen. Paul came to the lab to see me, and Darren told him I was busy and never told me he'd been. All that time I spent worrying I hadn't heard from Paul, it was Darren's fault."

"He probably saw you drooling over Paul and thought it best to save you from yourself."

Sally tried to ignore the sneer in Mel's voice. "I don't drool, and why would Darren feel the need to save me?"

"Because you act like you need saving."

Sitting down at the opposite end of the table, Sally began to fiddle with Mel's biro. "Mel," she said, "you don't think Paul could be right, that Darren does actually like me?"

Mel returned her attention to the laptop. "Don't flatter yourself."

Sally felt the sting of Mel's words. She searched for anything she could have said wrong. "Sorry, I meant to ask about your job hunt. I did find you some websites, they looked really interesting. There was a biotech one."

"Drop me an email sometime. I'm snowed under with this, but I might get round to looking at them." She didn't look up.

* * * * *

Sally wasn't going to let the matter drop with Darren; there was no way that not telling her Paul had come to visit her had been an oversight. They were both in the lab on Monday morning, surrounded by the normal whirrs and beeps of equipment. She avoided eye contact and spoke to him in monosyllables. Her pointed sulking gave the same kind of satisfaction as playground squabbles.

Whenever anyone else spoke to her she made a show of being nice to them, to prove that she wasn't just being grumpy. She even asked Judith how her weekend had been, although somehow her answer gave no information about what she had done but still contained a complaint about purchase requests being handed in without project numbers.

The more Sally avoided talking to Darren, the more he talked to her. Filling her silences with inane chatter, he gradually became more controversial to try and elicit a response. Sally's irritation built steadily along with her anger at the way he'd treated Paul. By the time Sally left her bench and headed to the prep room she was ready to slap him.

As she had hoped Darren followed her and joined her in the stuffy prep room. He put down the box of clean pipette tips he'd been carrying and came to stand in front of her. He squeezed her arm. "Are you OK, has something happened?"

A look of worry had replaced the fake smile he'd been wearing all morning. Sally faltered. She'd never noticed how brown his eyes were.

"No nothing's happened."

Still he didn't let go of her arm.

"You can tell me," he coaxed. One of the freezers began to hum.

What if Paul was right, and she had been blind all along? What if Darren loved her?

"Don't worry, nothing's wrong." She spoke gently. "But actually there was something I wanted to talk about. Why did you tell Paul I was busy?"

"Who's Paul?"

"My friend who came and asked for me." There was no way he couldn't remember who Paul was.

"You were busy." His expression seemed to harden; the tender look that had disarmed her earlier had vanished.

"I'm always busy doing things, that doesn't mean I can't be disturbed. I'm not Vangelis when he's writing a paper. And why didn't you tell me afterwards?"

"I forgot."

"Really?"

"What does it matter? You found out, didn't you."

"And why…" The question was meant to end *why does every encounter you have with Paul become a battle of wills.* But if he loved her, confrontation wouldn't make him admit it. "Why don't you like him?" She hoped if she said this gently enough it wouldn't sound like a challenge.

"I don't even know him!"

"But still, you don't seem to…"

It sounded wrong, as if she was asking his advice about Paul's character.

"Sally, I don't know where this is leading."

Nor did she. She wanted to hear answers to questions she didn't know she needed to ask, or at least questions she didn't want to. What was going on in his head was a mystery to her, but she wanted to hear it. She didn't know what she would say to him, now or for the rest of the time they worked together, but something would come to her.

There was a clatter in the corridor and Amy walked in – she'd been clearing samples out of the freezers ready for her departure. She didn't greet Sally and Darren but looked at them as if trying to gauge whether she'd interrupted anything.

Darren made for the door. "We're done in here. Make sure you have everything out of the -80°C as well."

* * * * *

For the next few weeks speculations about Darren's motives for warding off Paul filled Sally's head whenever she spoke to him, but he behaved normally. His actions gave nothing away.

True to her word, Sally emailed Mel with details of job websites. She received a grateful reply, but had no idea whether Mel had actually looked at them. Whenever she tentatively raised the subject, Mel suddenly became very busy, so Sally quickly gave up. But one afternoon Sally arrived home from work to find Mel with the entire contents of the kitchen cupboards out on the worktops.

"You're home early – day off?" Sally said.

"Yep, first of many, and we haven't cleaned the kitchen properly since we moved in."

"I hope you're doing something more exciting with your holiday than cleaning."

"It's not holiday, it's gardening leave. I handed in my notice today and was promptly ordered to clear my desk."

Sally went to hug her. "You never told me!"

"I only found out about my new job yesterday."

"New job? You applied, had an interview and had an offer without actually telling me?"

"It all happened a bit fast. I thought I was just testing the water and, well, here I am."

"So, what is it?"

"Relatively small London firm, only established in the 90's, with an office of eight people in Cambridge, total turnover of £9.8 million…"

"I don't care about that, what will you actually do?"

"Oh I'm not too sure, they obviously don't tell you much because it's confidential, particularly as lots of the applicants will be working for competitors."

"Surely you must know something."

"All I can tell you is that I'll be working on fewer, bigger cases, maybe even some high profile ones, and I found the advert on one of the websites you sent me."

"A biotech one?"

"Maybe."

"You owe me one."

"I'll take you out for supper tonight, and Liz if she's around. Is that a good start?"

"It certainly is. I'm so happy for you."

Sally came to hug Mel again. She brushed her off, laughing.

"Go and get changed, while I try to remember which cupboard I got all this junk out of."

Chapter 20

For the next few weeks Sally led the kind of life she had assumed Vangelis's lab would provide: business as usual with more progress than setbacks and nothing to keep her awake at night. They broke a centrifuge machine and managed to persuade Vangelis to buy them two new ones. They coaxed Amy through the third results chapter in her thesis. They watched as the trees showed the first signs of autumn.

Mel started her new job and was soon into the same routine of long evenings in the office. Her complaining, at least, had diminished, though she was even more cryptic than normal about what she was working on. Sally hoped that pride wasn't all that was keeping her from grumbling about this job too.

Sally's meetings with Paul became more regular. They walked across Midsummer Common together, the same route they had taken when Sally was an undergraduate. As they dodged families with pushchairs and students with bikes, Sally had to suppress a smile at her change of fortunes since then. She was now a Dr, a scientist in her own right, and Paul was her equal, not her teacher. He cooked for her again, and in return she helped him restore law and order to his postage-stamp garden. Nothing was said about Darren, and Sally worried that Paul assumed there was more going on. She felt she should say that she'd spoken to him, pass on an apology and explain that she'd cleared things up. But there was no apology and nothing had been cleared up, so she remained silent. Mel's assessment of the situation was *The human race would be extinct if everyone courted at the same rate that Sally does*. Liz was smug. But Sally's panic whenever Paul didn't reply to a message had diminished; she was confident a reply would come.

On a slow afternoon in the office Darren came to get Sally for a meeting with Vangelis. He told her nothing as they walked to a meeting room. Sally looked through the glass in the door and saw all the co-authors of the paper in there. She stopped and turned to Darren.

"What's happened?"

Darren pushed the door open and went in. Six faces focussed on them.

"Sorry we're late." Darren lifted two chairs from a tatty stack.

"No problem, I think we're all here now." Vangelis was standing addressing the room. "I wanted to bring you all together to tell you the good news: *Nature* has accepted our paper. This is just recognition for years of hard work – congratulations."

Somebody cheered. Congratulations were exchanged, hands shaken. Vangelis went round the room to thank everyone individually, offering generous praise. From the row in front of her Amy turned round and grinned at Sally, who leant forwards to put an arm round her. "I told you things would turn out right."

Darren gave Sally a satisfied nod.

"You knew, didn't you?" she said.

"Maybe. I didn't want to spoil your surprise."

But soon the chatter died down and everyone began to bombard Vangelis with questions. He returned to the front of the room.

"I have reports from the three reviewers, all of whom recommended publication with only minor alterations." He waved a crumpled wad of paper. "They all chose to keep their reviews anonymous, but one did suggest the insertion of three references from the same research group in Dublin, so no prizes for guessing where he comes from." Where 'He' comes from: sexism wasn't dead, but Sally was too excited to let Vangelis's assumption bother her.

Günter reached for the reports, and people either side of him crowded to look.

Vangelis continued, "I'll forward the email to you all so you can read them for yourselves, but they all commented on the importance of the work…"

Sally took this information in. It was important; they'd produced valuable results. Publishing it benefited science and farmers.

"… And every one of them mentioned its thoroughness."

Sally reached out to take an annotated copy of the paper from Günter. The reviewer was right: their research was thorough, the conclusions had been drawn from lots of data, everything had been taken into account. The experiment that had been destroyed was in itself an extra check, and the volume of data they had originally planned to collect showed how seriously they had thought everything through.

Vangelis addressed the whole group again. "This afternoon I'll be submitting the grant proposal with Amy as the named post-doc, and with the positive response to our work we've just seen, along with a forthcoming *Nature* reference, I rate our chances of success as very high."

Amy was beaming, perhaps for the first time since she started writing her thesis.

"And," Vangelis said, "the results in here from Darren's experiments showed exciting potential for expanding this to different crops, so Darren you will be doing a funding application too."

There were nods of approval. Sally tried to catch Darren's eye, but his attention hadn't left Vangelis. Neither of them revealed any more, and Vangelis sent everyone back to work.

Nobody managed to achieve very much for the rest of the morning as word of their success rapidly spread across the department, and it was quickly decided that a pub lunch was called for. Ten of them gathered outside in the quad to head to The Eagle. As they walked down the sunny streets, Sally tried to get Darren to drop back with her. He seemed reluctant, always talking to someone else, but eventually he fell into step beside her.

"I never knew you were applying for funding."

"I've been thinking about it for a while, but I only decided I would when Vangelis suggested it this morning."

"What money are you going to apply for?"

"A fellowship probably." He kept his gaze on the paving stones in front of him, seemingly embarrassed. "I know it's a long shot but it seems like the next step, to have a bit of autonomy, and I'd like to stay here. It feels like we have something good going."

Sally had expected Darren to need an ego-check not encouragement. "You're in a perfect position to apply," she said. "You've got as good a chance as anyone, in fact probably better."

Sally and Darren were being propelled along in the centre of the group. Nobody could hear what they were saying above the hum of traffic, but Sally lowered her voice anyway. "I am glad we've been accepted. I think we did the right thing, submitting it I mean."

Darren looked alarmed. "You shouldn't be worrying any more, everything's sorted."

"I can't forget about it."

A delicious smell of chips and beer welcomed them as they entered the pub and offers of drinks put an end to their conversation.

* * * * *

They returned the corrected paper to the journal in under a week, and when they had the email confirming its final acceptance Vangelis invited them all to an evening celebration. When they received the invitation, Darren embarked upon a long story about the last time he'd been invited to Vangelis's house, but Günter was unimpressed.

"He just wants to show off his big home."

"Remind me not to invite Günter to a party," Darren said.

"Darren, you live in a glorified bedsit," Amy said. "Nobody can accuse you of showing off if you hold a party there."

"Fair point."

"Free alcohol, don't ask questions." Sally didn't want even friendly bickering to spoil her fragile good mood.

Günter scrolled down to the bottom of the email. "It says bring guests. Maybe Amy will bring her new boyfriend and we will get at last to meet him."

"Only if you remember that just because he *might* be my boyfriend it doesn't mean you have to act as if he's from a freak show," Amy said.

"What about you?" Darren turned to Sally. His look was challenging.

"I don't need to bring anyone."

If Darren was going to make this into a confrontation, there was no way Sally was going to invite Paul to endure an evening of it.

"Oh," Darren said. "I thought you might bring Mel."

"She's not exactly my date."

"Guests don't have to be dates."

Günter shrugged. "You have a flatmate that is closer than Darren has come to having a girlfriend for more than two years."

"Look who's talking." Darren threw a ball of paper at Günter.

"OK," Sally said, "I'll ask her."

When Sally asked Mel that night she said, without a pause, "No".

"Why not?"

"I'm not acting as your pseudo-date because you're too shy to ask Paul."

"That's not why I'm asking you."

"Why don't you ask him then?

"Actually it was Darren who suggested I invited you." As soon as she said this Sally was struck by how this must sound to Mel: Darren again trying to control her, helping to keep Paul away.

To Sally's surprise, Mel didn't seem to notice. She said, "Then I can be Darren's guest."

Being able to say that Mel was coming made it feel vastly more normal to be inviting Paul. He accepted readily and Sally arranged for him to meet her, Mel and Amy at her house so they could walk to the party together.

When she arrived Amy eyed Paul with interest. They stayed chatting in the kitchen while Sally fussed around them. If any of them were nervous, they didn't show it. The air was cool when they stepped outside. Sally was wearing open-toed sandals and she could feel goose pimples reaching up her legs.

Vangelis lived on the outskirts of Cambridge, in a residential area with detached houses set back behind hedges. Paul directed them with a map printed from Google, while Sally wondered whether this was a world she would ever inhabit. When they finally reached Vangelis's doorstep, Amy reached up to the heavy brass knocker. It was Darren who opened the door and he greeted them as if it was his party. "Come on in. You can leave your coats in here." He opened the door to a large study. "And go through to the room on the left for the punch."

He kissed Amy, Mel and Sally on the cheek. Then Paul stepped inside and Darren's smooth act was broken. They stood looking at each other. Sally waited, watching them. The sounds of the party reached them, and she realised how many people she would have to explain Paul's presence to.

"Good to see you again," Paul said. He was a bad liar.

Darren didn't attempt to sound welcoming. "There are lots of people here, I'm sure Sally will introduce you."

Without a smile, Darren went to guide Mel and Amy towards the drinks, leaving Sally and Paul alone. Paul looked as if he wondered why he'd come. Thankfully ahead of them the door to the kitchen was open, and Sally saw a way to delay facing the entire party. The scene in the kitchen was one of domestic bliss. Vangelis's wife and three children were preparing cupcakes on large trays. The two older children were carefully tessellating rows of cakes. They were attractively dressed from yummy mummy catalogues. The youngest, a boy, was standing on a stool in order to dust the cakes, and himself, with icing sugar.

"Pleased to meet you, I'm Christiana." Vangelis's wife held out her hand. Sally was surprised at how attractive she was.

"I'm Sally."

"Ah, Sally, I've heard a lot about you."

Sally felt she'd been caught on the back foot; if it wasn't for the ring on Vangelis's finger she wouldn't even have known he was married. She was saved from embarrassment as Christiana began to introduce her children. They obediently shook hands with Paul and Sally in turn.

When the children returned to their work, Christiana asked Sally a flow of questions about the lab. She was genuinely interested and seemed to treat Sally with slight reverence. She'd done a science degree herself and had thought of becoming a scientist before she had the children. The *Nature* paper was clearly important to her, as if she was achieving her success through Vangelis. Her accent didn't sound English, but Sally couldn't work out what it was. Sally kept glancing at Paul who gradually looked less out of his comfort zone.

When four trays of cup cakes were neatly ordered and sugared, Christiana and the children carried them out of the kitchen. Sally and Paul followed, Paul poised to catch a plate held at an alarming tilt by one of the children. Christiana had made them feel welcome; Sally felt more ready to face the party and was grateful for that.

Vangelis did a clichéd speech about how they'd all come together to do great science, and Sally was caught between wanting to vomit at his pomposity, and lapping up his compliments.

The invitation list was larger than Sally had expected, and lots of high-profile figures from the university were there. The party was clearly a tactical move on Vangelis's part, reminding everyone of his success. There were people Paul had known during his PhD, and he was pleased to be re-united with them. Occasionally Sally would find herself watching him, happy to see him so relaxed, imagining bringing him to these parties as her boyfriend.

When she saw him laughing with Darren and Mel, Sally felt as if she had 'I love him' tattooed on her forehead. She decided it was time to speak to someone else. The room was getting stuffy and Vangelis was no longer there, so she assumed the party had expanded into other rooms. Her first point of call was the kitchen. Quietly spoken Christiana seemed like someone Sally might even be tempted to share her story with. The scene of domestic bliss in the kitchen, however, had deteriorated; the youngest child was crying and pieces of a broken plate were scattered around his feet. Sally paused unnoticed in the door then slipped away in search of the rest of the party.

Alone in the hall she realised how grand it was. The ceiling was high and botanical drawings hung from the picture rail. Light from the hallway shone through the study door, illuminating a pile of coats hanging over the back of a chair. Sally was about to walk past when she saw Vangelis's arm reach towards a coat. Next to him in the gloom Judith was preparing to leave. Gently, Vangelis eased Judith's coat over her shoulders. Judith smiled and for the first time Sally saw kindness in Judith's face. She felt as if she had pried on an intimate moment.

A second crash came from the kitchen, the sound of china meeting a tiled floor. Vangelis turned. For a moment before Sally retreated their eyes met.

Sally slipped immediately into the bathroom and locked the door. She listened to their footsteps on the wooden floor and then the opening of the front door. There was a moment's pause (a stolen kiss?) followed by the click from the closing door and the sound of Vangelis's retreating footsteps. When she felt safe to emerge from the bathroom Sally didn't rejoin the party but instead stepped outside.

The front curtains were open and, although the darkness kept Sally invisible, it gave her a full view of the party. She could see Paul playing with Vangelis's children, their tears forgotten. But she couldn't go and join them; knowing about their father's affair left her unable to look them in the eye. She could see impending doom for their family harmony.

She stood outside in the dark, knowing that her strapless dress wouldn't allow her to stay there for long. It was the kind of time she wanted Darren to come out and find her. He knew how much Vangelis and Judith bothered her and always managed to justify that it wasn't her problem. But he was inside standing over the punch bowl with Mel. And infidelity certainly wasn't an issue she was keen to discuss with Paul.

When a cold gust of wind made her shiver she returned to the party, where older members of the party seemed keen to impart their wisdom on the young. A bearded professor entertained her with stories of life in the lab when it took weeks to produce enough DNA for an experiment. She began to enjoy herself again, thinking wryly about the skill she had developed at ignoring uncomfortable facts so she could have fun. It was almost a relief to concentrate on forgetting someone else's problem rather than her own.

The party began to disperse at 11.00, and Mel invited everyone back for an after-party. At one in the morning there were still a dozen people in Sally's living room, gradually cleaning them out of alcohol. Eventually Darren, Mel and Paul were the only people left.

Darren was the first to admit defeat. "I'd better be heading off."

"I'll show you out." Mel stood up to follow him and there were calls of good night as they left.

Alone with Paul, Sally's confidence died away. In the morning, she fully intended to give Mel a hard time for so obviously ensuring she was left alone with him, not that it would make the slightest bit of difference.

Paul, however, was smiling. "They're sweet."

Sally was relieved he didn't seem to feel the pressure. "They are, I'm lucky to have them as friends."

"They're sweet together I mean."

Sally frowned at him.

"Sally, you do know that he's not really leaving?"

Sally stared at Paul as the pieces fell into place. She felt her eyes widen in panic, and she jumped up towards the door.

Paul caught hold of her wrist and pulled her back down onto the sofa next to him. "Leave them be." He was laughing.

Realising how absurd it would be to try and stop them, Sally relented and fell back into the sofa. She couldn't fight the feeling that she really didn't want this to be happening, but her head was too fuzzy to identify why. Jealousy? Fear that if they had each other they would no longer need her? Her thoughts were still racing when Paul released her wrist and handed her a full glass of wine.

She took a sip and listened hopefully for the sound of the front door.

With Mel and Darren gone the party atmosphere disappeared. Sally and Paul stayed talking, but the laughter had died. When their eyelids began to droop Sally decided it was time for bed. It was 3am.

"Do you want to stay over?" she said.

Paul remained motionless and Sally suddenly realised how her offer could have been interpreted. She rushed to explain herself.

"I just thought you might not want to walk home in the cold, but it's up to you. The sofas are comfy, we have lots of blankets, or we might have an air bed in the cupboard…"

"Yes please."

The shelf in the airing cupboard was stuffed with blankets and pillows, and Sally stood on a chair to reach them. It was a desk chair on wheels, saved when Mel's office had a clear out, and the seat swivelled precariously every time Sally turned to hand Paul another item of bedding. When she pulled out a second pillow she finally lost her balance and jumped to the floor. Paul held out a hand to steady her, and they both burst out laughing.

Back in the sitting room Sally piled blankets on the sofa then turned to leave. In the doorway she turned and lingered.

"Goodnight," Paul said. "Thank you for inviting me. I had fun."

Sally allowed herself to wonder whether the sofa really was where he wanted to stay, and whether she should let him know the sofa wasn't what she'd hoped for. Was it clear to him that his friendship wasn't all she was interested in? The question burned on her tongue, but all that came was "goodnight".

When Sally came downstairs the next morning she found Mel tidying up. A pile of bottles stood ready to go out for the recycling. She stopped when she saw Sally, a bin liner still open in her hand.

"So, what's Paul doing sleeping on our sofa?"

"What's Darren doing sleeping in your room?" Sally couldn't match Mel's friendly tone.

Mel raised an eyebrow. "I'm really hoping your question is rhetorical, but mine wasn't."

"Why shouldn't Paul sleep on our sofa?"

"Because, Sally, he should have been in your bed."

"Quit it Mel, he didn't want to."

"Did you ask him?"

"Of course not, it's not the kind of thing you just come out with."

"So how do you know the sofa was where he wanted to be?"

"I do, OK?"

"Sally, you're an idiot."

At that moment the kitchen door swung open. Paul paused in the doorway and looked from Mel to Sally. Sally could only hope that if he'd heard what they were talking about he wouldn't have come in, and his reluctance now was only because he'd heard Mel's final comment.

"What do you want for breakfast?" Mel said brightly.

Paul seemed to relax and he came into the kitchen. "What's on offer?"

Sally smiled weakly at Paul and went to her room to get her water glass. Her mouth was dry, and she was teetering on the edge of a headache. She jumped when Darren came out of the bathroom in front of her. His hair was wet, and he was wearing only a towel. He smiled when he saw her. "Morning, Sally."

Caught off guard she didn't know what to say, so she stood facing him in the hall. When she eventually forced a greeting her voice came out croaky. "Good morning." She stood aside to allow him access to Mel's bedroom, hoping he'd interpreted her silence as hangover not shock.

Safely in her room, she sat on her bed and rubbed her eyes. This immediately let her headache loose. Her sheets were still warm, and the duvet inviting. She didn't want to return to the kitchen to face Mel and Darren; the sooner she could forget that Darren was still here the better. But she couldn't just leave Paul with them. She picked up her glass and drained the stale water.

The smell of cooking greeted Sally as she returned to the kitchen. Mel carefully laid a rasher of bacon into a sizzling pan. "Sally, I can offer you bacon or aspirin."

"Or both," Darren said.

The last thing Sally wanted was a stodgy breakfast with Mel and Darren cheerily acting as if everything was normal. "Or neither?"

Mel shrugged. "You know where the cereal is."

Sally didn't want a bad mood to show in front of Paul, but disagreements with Mel always upset her. She already regretted being confrontational about Darren, but she wasn't yet ready to apologise. She sat down with them at the kitchen table and forced a smile while the others chatted around her. Paul looked at her with concern and she was grateful. It gave her the energy she needed to get through breakfast, and even to show amusement at Darren's jokes. As soon as Paul and Darren left she returned to bed.

Sally saw little of Mel over the following week; it seemed she had taken working hard to a new level. Whenever their paths crossed it was fleeting and cool. On Friday Sally came home to find Mel sitting with her laptop at the kitchen table. She glanced up when Sally came in, but her fingers didn't stop typing.

Sally sat down directly in front of her, maximising the chance of making eye contact, and tried to make the peace.

"How are you?"

"Busy."

"Look, I was thinking about the cinema tomorrow. Are you in?"

"Sorry, too much to get through."

"But it's the weekend." Sally tried to gauge whether she was being brushed off.

Mel shook her head. "This case doesn't take weekends."

There was a silence in which Sally flipped aimlessly through a pile of unwanted post. "What are you working on?"

"I could tell you, but I'd have to kill you…"

"Is that true?"

Mel pulled a face. "Lawyers aren't that evil."

"I didn't mean literally." Sally couldn't help the edge of frustration in her voice.

"Of course it's true that I'd be in serious trouble if I leaked any of this."

Again there was silence. Sally had always relied on Mel to say exactly what she thought. Now she had no idea if Mel was angry with her, and she had no idea what was happening with Darren. Mel wouldn't even say what she was working on.

The next day Sally went to the cinema with Liz. She told herself Mel was spending the weekend in the office, but she couldn't suppress the feeling that Mel had fobbed her off with the age-old excuse of *I'm working late.*

Chapter 21

"*Protesters today have gathered outside the UK office of Tewx Technologies on the Cambridge Science Park...*" The BBC voice sounded crackly and formal through laptop speakers. Darren, Amy, Günter and Sally were crowded round the screen, which displayed jerky images of the crowd and their banners. "*A protest is taking place as court proceedings get underway in the state of Karnataka, India where Tewx Technologies is suing three farmers for replanting genetically modified seed from the previous year's harvest.*" The presenter turned to the crowd, and banners were pushed higher to accompany some tentative booing. He turned back to the camera. "*Joining me today from Cambridge University we have Professor Vangelis Papadakis, an expert in genetic modification.*"

The camera shifted to Vangelis, wearing a striped shirt and floral tie.

"What's he wearing?!"

"It's hideous!"

"Why is he doing this anyway?"

"*Professor Papadakis, can you explain more about what is going on?*"

"*Certainly. When a company sells genetically modified seed they have the option of putting in a molecular mechanism to ensure* the crop produces sterile seed, in the same way that hybrid seeds from conventional crops are often sterile. This means the GM crop can't be planted the following year unless the farmer purchases more seed from the supplier. However, these farmers produced fertile seed from their GM crop last year and have replanted this seed."

The presenter nodded. *"And this particular crop was meant to produce sterile seed, but for some reason the farmers have ended up with seed they are able to plant year after year?"*

"Yes, that's right."

The presenter turned to his right where a smartly dressed woman was waiting. *"Here we have Vanessa Frances-Smith who has organised today's protest. Vanessa, why have you started this campaign?"*

"What we have here is a multi-national company with an annual turnover of billions suing three Indian subsistence farmers. These are not large farms of the type we are used to; they are men who are growing food for their families and for surrounding villages. We do know they were unable to afford these seeds for a second year running and so couldn't have grown this year's harvest if they hadn't reused seed, so Tewx here are not losing business, even if we considered it ethical to ensure crops don't produce fertile seed.

We believe that once a farmer has bought seed it should be his to reuse; he shouldn't be forced to buy new seed each year from huge corporations like Tewx. If I buy vegetable seeds for my garden, I expect to be able to use what I produce the following year. And this goes for farmers too; it's how they have always worked."

"What would you say to that Professor Papadakis?" The presenter pointed the microphone to Vangelis.

"Actually the law quite clearly states that farmers are not necessarily able to replant seeds from their harvest; companies are completely within their rights to sell seeds for a single use only."

His cold tone made Sally shudder. "I can't believe he's sticking up for them."

"He's only saying what's true," Darren said. "That is the law."

"But he made the protester look foolish."

Darren shrugged. "That's because she's foolish."

"It's not all about the law, it's about the people."

"Whatever. I don't think that stacks up in court: 'I was breaking the law, but it was OK because of the people'…"

The microphone was held out to a middle-aged lady whose T-shirt had a 'stop GM' logo stretched over her bulging stomach. She looked at the microphone rather than the camera and said with a fenland accent, *"I think it's disgusting really. The whole world has gone wrong, you know; everyone is just looking for more profit, all the time. It's all about the money, that's what it is."*

"Thank you. This is Mark Cartwright reporting for BBC Look East. Back to the studio."

Darren paused the programme, and they returned to their desks.

"At least now they have something more important to protest about than our field trials," Günter said.

"Maybe we should join the protests." Amy didn't sound as if she was entirely joking.

"Why? None of them have a clue what they're talking about." It was clear Darren was doing more than just sticking up for Vangelis.

"Exactly, that's why we should join them," Günter said. "We can't moan that imbeciles have the argument if we don't do anything."

"They're not all imbeciles," Amy replied. "They just can't think how to make things work, how to actually ensure people benefit from what we do."

Darren raised his eyebrows. "Are you going to tell them how things should work?"

The issue was too murky in Sally's head to want an argument, but she resolved to speak to Amy about it when they were alone. It seemed arrogant to think that because they had skills in amplifying DNA they were qualified to pass judgement on transforming the socio-economics of the agricultural industry, but if she didn't like the status quo, perhaps she should do something to try and change it.

She followed Darren into the lab; it was a relief to focus on the minutiae of experiments rather than the ambiguities of court cases.

* * * * *

At the weekend she visited the Chilterns with Paul and some friends. His friends were welcoming, and Sally was pleased by how they reacted to her: their inquisitive looks at Paul made it clear what they were thinking.

She returned tired and happy to find Darren sitting in the kitchen eating supper with Mel. They seemed genuinely pleased to see her, and Mel, for once, seemed relaxed and carefree. Sally, however, was annoyed that they were seeing each other without getting her to arrange the meeting. Of course it was a crazy idea that they should still need to communicate through her, but she couldn't help feeling superfluous. She banged around the kitchen looking for something to eat while Mel and Darren quizzed her on what she'd been doing. She answered evasively, not wanting Darren to know she'd spent the day with Paul, and not sure why it would matter.

They never ate meals in their rooms, and to do so would be more of a statement than she was willing to make. Instead she stood around awkwardly and ate a bowl of cereal.

Mel and Darren were discussing space travel, something neither of them knew anything about. Whenever they couldn't agree on a fact they deferred to Sally who offered vague answers. The harder it was to extract information from her, the harder they tried. Leaving her cereal bowl in the sink, Sally put her phone down next to Mel – "you can Google it…" – knowing full well that they weren't questioning her simply to find out about space.

* * * * *

The protest outside Tewx Technologies gained momentum. Within a week they had pitched a camp and made the national news. New information appeared in the form of bland statements of confidentiality from Tewx and rumours from unknown sources.

An eloquent human rights lawyer was interviewed on Radio 4, explaining that the seed was designed to protect against a particular species of insect which that year hadn't caused problems: *"The farmers spent their entire savings on seeds which then provided them with no benefit whatsoever because there was no pest outbreak."*

Darren nodded in appreciation when the presenter played devil's advocate: *"Last year it was too cold for me to use my BBQ but that doesn't mean I'm going to ask for my money back".* Sally kept quiet.

A spinout protest even set up outside the university. The protesters had heard Vangelis on TV and had developed a conspiracy theory about his involvement with multinational companies, Tewx included. In the university a flurry of emails passed between the communications team and the head of department to agree their stance, leaving the office with an air of nervous excitement. But then Sally and Darren went out at lunchtime and found that the 'protest' was really three people standing around with cups of coffee.

When Darren was back in the lab Sally found herself reading endless comments under online newspaper articles. There seemed to be an equal number of expressions of horror that a large company would pit itself against village farmers and accusations of hippy protesters failing to understand how the world works. It looked as if she and Amy were the only people with sympathies on both sides.

When they were alone in the office Amy summed up Sally's concerns in a way that she hadn't yet put into words: "It's almost like Tewx owns the farmers, not just the seed."

That night Sally got home to find Mel and Liz in front of the TV watching the news. The presenter picked his way through the Tewx Technology protest, pointing out camping stoves and tents laid out ready for erection. Sally sat down next to Mel on the sofa, leaning her head against the cushions. It was a relief to see Mel doing something other than work.

"How was your day?" Mel asked.

"Other than a half-hearted protest at the department, pretty good."

"How do you cope? Tiananmen Square all over again," Mel said dryly.

They sat in silence as a spokesperson from Tewx came on.

"Companies are there to make a profit," Sally said. "I can live with that. But to take on peasant farmers like this…"

"They're not peasants." Mel's attention was still on the TV, where the man from Tewx was making bland corporate statements.

Sally kept going. "It's not even in Tewx's best interest – this is pretty bad PR, not just for them but for GM full stop."

Protesters entered the camera's field of view and jeered, but the spokesperson didn't flinch. "*This is not an isolated event and it is not limited to single farmers. There is evidence of patented seed being distributed through local village networks.*"

Liz scowled. "Can't they see that patenting plants is an idiotic idea?"

"Liz what century do you live in?" Mel sounded irritated. "Patents protect the people who do the work."

As the news turned to politics they watched in silence. Sally wasn't sure whether Mel was genuinely annoyed, and she wasn't sure she wanted to find out. The three of them shared a pizza for supper, but no conversation would come.

* * * * *

The following day Sally left for a conference in Vienna. She caught the train to the airport before Mel was up, and by lunchtime she was settled in a tired hotel next door to the university. Vangelis, Darren, Günter and Amy were all there and excited to be away from the lab. Amy was there thanks to a travel grant, and more than anyone she needed to get away from the tedium of her thesis.

For two days they went to presentations on everything from bioenergy grasses to plant compounds in medicines. Sally enjoyed the talks. They were relevant enough to be useful but not so relevant that she had to take notes. In between talks tables of limitless food were brought out, and at the end of the day the food was replaced with wine.

The session on GM took place on the penultimate morning. The room was small and stuffy, with cramped rows of plastic chairs. Sally balanced her notebook awkwardly on her knee and attempted to take notes. The talks made her brain ache. Signal pathways, gene expression, nutrient flows – all presented in chaotic style. She was relieved when they broke for refreshments. They all loitered next to the coffee and let Vangelis do the talking. He was moaning about tiny inaccuracies in the talks, knowing full well that only he had noticed.

When the session reconvened Vangelis was the first speaker. They had moved to the main lecture theatre with tiers of seats designed for two hundred undergraduates. There must have been over 50 people in the audience but in the large lecture theatre they seemed lost.

The session chair introduced Vangelis and left him alone on the stage. He told the story neatly: the genes they had modified, the protection from pests, the healthy growth of the crop, the favourable comparisons with existing crop varieties. From her seat in the front row, Sally looked anxiously behind her. In her own presentations she had learnt to ignore the blank faces, understanding their expressions said nothing of what they were thinking. But for some reason, today their approval really mattered to her. If this work wasn't well received – results that were good enough to lie for – then nothing she produced would be.

When the session was over a stream of admirers came to talk to Vangelis. Relieved, Sally joined the group and discussed implications and future plans with anyone who had given up hope of getting to speak with Vangelis himself. At the same time as needing their appreciation, their praise made her shrink. Their support would evaporate if they knew the full story.

Nerves had left her exhausted, so when Darren suggested skipping the afternoon session she readily agreed. Amy stayed behind, trying to impress a professor who might have a job going.

"I feel so guilty, but I don't even know whether my grant application to stay with the lab will be funded," she told Sally.

"There's nothing wrong with keeping your options open."

"I don't exactly have many."

"Go and talk to him; you don't need lots of options, just one which works out." Reassuring Amy always made Sally feel better, and it was hard to remember that less than two years ago she had been in the same position: driven mad by writing up her PhD and in a blind panic about how to get a job.

On the tram into town Darren read aloud from the guide book. As they planned a route to take in monuments and churches he supplied her with history. Dates meant little to her, and she'd already taken in too much information for one day, but she appreciated his enthusiasm.

In their third church, Sally reached out her hand to feel the cold, rough stone of a carved pillar. The stone carving of a bishop peered down at her. Next to her a spiral of steps led to a pulpit, with dips worn into each of them by nearly 900 years of preachers' feet. It was intricately carved, and its elegant roof was adorned in gold. The silence of the church was broken by a group of severe Austrian ladies preparing for their choir practice. Chairs were scraped and a general murmur filled the nave, followed by a chord from the organ and the powerful voice of a soprano. The contrast to the morning's lecture theatres made her smile. Amy was still in a bland room and, while these ladies lost themselves in song, tried to find herself by searching out potential employers. The choir probably had no idea that the human genome had been sequenced, and Amy couldn't read music. Perhaps she should have brought Amy with her; if there was ever a time to get trapped into unhealthy feeling that your whole identity was based on being a plant scientist, it was conferences.

There was nothing like stepping into a different world to make you feel unimportant. Posters announced a concert that night. The church would be packed with people listening to the choir. The bishop who had been immortalised in stone must have delivered sermons to thousands of people. Would anybody ever listen to her? Getting 50 plant scientists to sit through a talk was a start, but it wasn't exactly going to change the face of modern agriculture.

Travel often gave Sally these feelings of helplessness. It revealed quite how many people there were in the world, all needing food and all going their own way about getting it. But the thought-provoking atmosphere hadn't rubbed off on Darren. "It stinks of incense in here; it's time to get back for some food."

That night the conference dinner began with a drinks reception. Vangelis seemed proud of them all, and he boasted loudly about how good his 'students' were. Darren lapped it up, but Sally didn't feel like being Vangelis's fashion accessory. She managed to slip away from her colleagues and found herself talking to a young professor. They discussed some of the morning's talks, and Sally began to enjoy herself. But, inevitably, he asked who she worked with. When she told him it was Vangelis he spouted stories about Vangelis's great ideas and how he was reliable, trustworthy. Sally didn't know how much he was doing it to flatter her and how much he really believed it. Whatever, she was accepting his compliments on false pretences.

It was nearly midnight by the time they returned to the hotel bar for a final drink. Sally reluctantly sipped the whisky that was placed in front of her but hastily said her good nights when a second round was suggested. As soon as she was out of the bar, she slipped off her shoes and walked barefoot on the carpet. She felt herself swaying as she stood waiting for the lift, more as her legs recovered from heels than from alcohol. As the lift arrived she realised Darren was standing next to her.

"Hi," she said without looking at him. They stepped into the lift, and she pressed the button for the third floor. "Which floor are you on?" she asked.

The doors closed with a ding and they were alone.

"What's up?" Darren kept his gaze on the metal doors.

"Nothing."

The lift began to move with a jerk.

"I know that's not true."

Sally remembered all the times she had escaped from social situations and been followed by Darren. Whatever her excuses, Darren always saw through her. There was no point in avoiding his question.

She took a deep breath. "Don't you get this constant feeling that…"

With another loud ding the lift stopped and the doors opened to reveal a waiting couple.

"This is my floor." Darren stepped out of the lift.

"OK, good night."

"Come on out for a moment," Darren said.

"Don't worry, we can talk in the morning."

The other couple, now in the lift, watched them impatiently, but still Darren waited for her. She stepped out and the doors closed behind her.

"Come to my room for a moment."

Sally shrugged then followed him, still carrying her shoes.

Darren was sharing a room with Günter, and when they walked in he hastily gathered up the clothes that were strewn on the floor. Sally perched on the end of a neatly made bed, and the mattress tipped sideways when Darren sat down next to her.

"Tell me what's up."

"I just can't forget what we did. It's like a heaviness I can't shake."

"The paper?" It sounded as if he genuinely wasn't sure what she was talking about.

"The data which came from your imagination."

"Stop torturing yourself like this Sally. It's done with."

"It feels like I'm lying to everyone I meet. And not just here, even my Mum; she's hoping I'll grow out of my scientist phase but at least thinks I'm honest." Sally had a Pashmina around her shoulders, and she began to play with the tassels. "The only person who understands the truth is you."

"And Vangelis."

Sally shook her head. "Sometimes I think he understands the least. He's so good at lying to himself he doesn't even see what we've done as wrong."

"You're focussing on one tiny bad thing. All these results we've got, they're important. Then you let one little detail get in the way."

"My career is based on a lie."

Darren reached out and put an arm round her shoulders. "Your career is based on your skill and your dedication."

228

They could see themselves in the large mirror which covered much of the wall, and Darren smiled at her reflection. She smiled back and for the first time was reassured by his presence, almost glad to be telling him exactly the things she'd wanted to hide.

When she continued there was less determination in her voice. "Amy doesn't even know that the foundations of her career are based on fiction."

"Burdening her would achieve nothing. And anyway, without this paper she wouldn't even have a career."

"It is actually possible to have a career without a *Nature* paper you know."

"OK, you know what I mean."

Sally was quiet for a moment. She felt the pressure of needing to publish as much as Darren did. The whole system of academia was draining her, with its way of judging people based on journal publications, not their talents.

"Maybe I need a new career…"

"Don't be ridiculous."

This came as a relief – the words had come out without her thinking; the idea had only just struck her, but it had instantly made sense. She didn't want to continue this line of thought, but neither did she want to leave. Instead she deflected conversation away from herself.

"Mel was brave enough to take on a new career."

"New job – not quite the same thing."

"She never tells me anything about what she does."

"She can't."

"I know, but…" Sally wanted to ask whether Mel told him about her work, but she knew she might not like the answer. Instead, she said, "You really like her, don't you?"

"I do." He was smiling.

This left Sally deflated. She had first tried to secure Paul's affection more than five years ago, and still she'd got nowhere. Without even trying, Mel had gained the attention (or maybe even love?) of someone caring, confident and, ultimately, attractive. "Then I hope she knows how lucky she is."

Darren looked baffled, and Sally realised it was time to leave.

"Thank you. Knowing secrets can make you feel, well, alone. I'm glad I can share them with you." She was genuine, and she hoped Darren realised this.

"Good night, Sally. Stop worrying."

Back in their room Amy was sitting on her bed still in her dress. She grinned when Sally walked in.

"And where have you been?"

Sally sighed and threw herself on her bed. "Nowhere."

"Oh really?" It was clear from Amy's eyes what she was thinking.

"Amy, shut up."

Amy looked offended, and Sally snapped out of self-pity. She rolled over onto her side so she could look at Amy.

"Have you had a good day?"

"I have, thank you," Amy said. "We were having fun down there without you."

"I'm glad. And how was your flattery in the name of chasing jobs?"

"A waste of time. I thought it was going perfectly – he was all interested and keen. Then I met his research group at the dinner. They were all pretty girls, and the only one I spoke to was really irritating. He was buying them all drinks and looking smug."

"Vangelis bought us drinks," Sally reasoned.

"Not like this he didn't."

"At least that means he thinks you're pretty."

"Great. If all else fails I can always seduce a grey-haired professor with a liking for young girls."

"It's an option."

They both paused while they considered the image then simultaneously began to laugh. The laughter did something to shift the heaviness in her chest, and just for a moment the pressure seemed to ease. Later, listening to Amy's rhythmical breathing, it wasn't hard to get to sleep.

Chapter 22

Back in her own bed, Sally got up late on Saturday morning to find Mel in a good mood. Still in her pyjamas, Mel made them both coffee and omelette while Sally sat at the kitchen table. At the same time as filling the kitchen with the smell of singed egg, she quizzed Sally about the conference: how was Vienna, was the food good, what did everyone at the conference think of Tewx Technologies? Sally flicked through photos of the city on her camera screen and assured Mel that most people had been too absorbed in their own research to talk about events on the news.

When they had eaten their omelettes and drained a second cup of coffee there was a lull in the conversation. Sally was relieved to have her friend back – the Mel she could speak openly to. She felt happy speaking openly about Darren.

"When we were there I spoke to Darren."

"What, you spent five days in Vienna with him and you two spoke? Amazing." Already Mel's jovial mood seemed lost.

"You know what I mean, spoke to him properly."

"No, I don't know what you mean."

Sally cut to the chase. "Mel, he really likes you."

"Thank you." Mel displayed no interest, and Sally thought bitterly of all the times she had told Mel everything she felt about Paul. Mel clearly wasn't going to reciprocate with the same openness.

Sally realised she hadn't planned the next part of the conversation but kept on going. "Just don't, I mean…"

In the years Sally had known Mel she had never seen the flash of anger in her eyes that those few words caused.

"What? Don't hurt him, don't lead him on? Is that what you think of me – oblivious to how I might upset someone? Totally uncaring?"

"That's not what I meant at all!"

"It's exactly what you meant. You complained he was possessive of you, and here you are protecting him, warding off his girlfriends. Just because you were too weak to tell Paul how you felt, don't get jealous of anyone who's capable of a functional relationship."

Sally panicked, said everything that came into her head. "I'm sorry, I know he wouldn't want me to say anything, it really wasn't for me to get involved…"

Mel stood up and looked Sally squarely in the eye. "Sally, did you stop for one moment and think maybe I like him?"

Sally did stop, and realised what a total misjudgement she'd made. "I'm sorry, I'm sorry." She stood up, hoping to hug Mel, try and give an apology, but she was already walking away.

Mel cleared up the kitchen, noisily and angrily, then put the frying pan in the sink to soak. Sally looked on helplessly; there was no way to unsay what she'd just said. Mel left the kitchen without another word.

Sally sat at the table, waiting for an answer to come to her. For nearly an hour she searched for ways to diffuse the situation, then realised she had to get away. She couldn't face Mel again.

She closed the front door and started walking, briskly but in no particular direction. She had nowhere to go. The wind was surprisingly cold, and she pulled her sleeves over her hands to keep them warm. When walking couldn't keep her from thinking she called her mother and explained the whole stupid story. Her mother cooed soothing words, which Sally appreciated, even though she didn't believe them.

"You were only trying to look after your friends, love."

"Not very well though."

"You weren't to know. Anyway, you did her a favour. Too many men don't tell girls how they feel, and now she knows."

And it's not just men who keep quiet, Sally thought. "Yes, at least she knows."

"I hope when you get a boyfriend your friends will be looking out for you, too." Her mother would never lose confidence that a boyfriend was coming soon.

It was midday by the time it dawned on Sally that she was very thirsty and at some point had to return home. Even now, avoiding the situation was the only way she could think of dealing with it. She contemplated going into the lab but hadn't brought her entry card for the department. She had no money for a cafe, and anyway to sit there alone as a refugee from her own house was the one thought more depressing than seeing Mel. So she turned for home, hoping she would be able to pass the few metres from the front door to her room without being noticed. Then, as Saturday shoppers bustled around her at a pedestrian crossing, she realised there was an alternative. She could go and see Paul.

By the time she knocked on his door her stomach was rumbling and she was thirsty enough not to worry about whether he'd be surprised to see her.

"Sally?" Paul leant on the doorframe and smiled.

"I was just walking this way and thought I'd call in, if that's OK?" Surely she could have thought up a better excuse than walking.

"Of course, come in, do you want something to drink?"

"Oh yes, please."

Sally downed two glasses of water while Paul made them tea.

"You weren't busy, were you?" she said. "Sorry just to turn up – just tell me to go away if you had plans."

"None at all. My sister's been here, helping me with more decorating – unfortunately you just missed her. I'll show you what we've been doing."

Sally smiled. "I hope you're looking after Bernard very well in repayment for all this DIY help." She looked around, surprised Bernard hadn't come to greet her yet.

"Well, actually, that's another reason she came, to take Bernard away with her." Paul looked disappointed, and Sally too realised she would miss him.

Handing her a mug of tea, Paul changed the subject. "Did you have a good time at the conference?"

"Yes, thank you." Sally hoped she sounded convincing. When she had agreed to 'exaggerate' the truth about her data she had no idea of the smaller lies that would be needed to keep the real lie afloat. They sipped their tea in silence, Sally glancing constantly at Paul to try and gauge what he thought of her unexpected visit.

"Sally, is there something wrong?"

At that moment, everything felt wrong.

She nodded, relieved to tell him. "It's Mel, I was so stupid, I said something I really, really shouldn't have said."

Paul listened to the whole story, a look of concern in his eyes. When she had finished he said, "She's your friend, she'll forgive you."

"I've never really fallen out with her before – there's this whole side of her I don't even know."

"I know you would forgive her if it was the other way round," Paul said gently. "So I'm sure when she's calmed down she'll do the same."

If it had been the other way round, if she'd admitted to Darren how much she liked Paul and he was the one to pass it on, then he really would have been doing her a favour. But still she was too scared to say it herself.

Paul reached out a hand and squeezed her arm. "Do you want to call her? Or is it best to give her some time?"

"I think time is called for."

"In that case, let's have some lunch."

"Thank you, I'm starving."

When lunch was over and Paul showed no signs of sending her back home, Sally offered to help with the decorating. The house was almost finished, and they had moved on to the landing. Sally had never felt the desire to own a house before, but as she saw the care with which he painted his skirting boards, she suddenly saw the appeal. She wondered at what stage she'd come to feel more attached to Paul's house than to her own. As the afternoon turned to evening, they watched a film, sitting next to each other on the sofa. Paul rested his feet on the coffee table while Sally huddled into the corner of the sofa, more aware of his physical presence than of the storyline. It was dark by the time they finished.

"Do you want to stay over?" Paul asked.

"Don't worry – it might be time to face Mel."

"It really wouldn't be a problem. I bought a house with a spare room so my friends could come to stay, and so far my sister is the only person who's used it."

"Thank you, but I'd better go home."

"OK, do you want me to walk back with you?"

Sally shook her head. "But thank you, and thank you for letting me stay this afternoon."

"Any time, you know that."

Despite what waited for her back home, Paul's care filled her with momentary happiness.

When Sally got back there was no sign of life. She hoped Mel had gone to Darren's and not to work, but was just relieved that she was somewhere other than here. The relief only grew when she managed to avoid them on Sunday too, and on Monday morning she sneaked out of the house unnoticed.

* * * * *

Sally returned home on Monday night, again consumed by fear of meeting Mel. However, when she got in it was Liz not Mel who was waiting for her, sitting at the kitchen table looking grim.

"What's up?" Sally asked.

"I take it you have been following the story of Tewx Technology?"

Sally's heart sunk at the idea of Liz harassing her about GM. The Tewx trial was nearing its final stages, delayed by complications and demands for changes to the law. It looked increasingly likely that Tewx would come off well, in legal terms if not in popularity. The images of scientists and businesses had fared badly in the media, so it was no surprise that Sally, by proxy, could be assumed guilty.

"I have," Sally said cautiously. "I think there's a lot wrong with what's happening."

"So do I."

Liz picked up a wad of paper and passed it across the table to Sally.

Sally looked at the front page. It was a report about Tewx Technologies. "What's this? Did you get it from the protesters' website or theirs?" Sally didn't have the emotional energy to fight someone else's battle and dreaded Liz trying to drag her in.

Liz shook her head. "It's not from the internet, look at the name."

Sally looked. "Melissa Richardson."

"Mel left her notes out and I happened to see it. It's her. She's one of the lawyers for Tewx Technology."

Sally stared stupidly at the report. It all made sense: Mel's secrecy, her long hours at work, her defensiveness when they talked about Tewx. She looked up at Liz. "How could she?"

"We can't let her."

"Does she know you have this?"

"Not yet."

"Alright, may I have it? I'll talk to Mel when she comes home." Sally didn't trust Liz to approach this calmly or rationally. Whatever argument followed, it would be worse if Liz started it. Unlike Sally, she wouldn't be willing to hear Mel's side of the story.

Liz looked sceptical. "We can both wait here until she comes home."

"She might be late, I can do it tomorrow when I've read this through. I'll let you know everything she says then we'll all talk about it together."

The room was gloomy, making the report hard to see. Sally flicked through the pages without reading them, waiting for Liz to answer. She tried to imagine the confrontation between Liz and Mel, and what it would be like to live with them afterwards. Where could she live if she didn't live here? The point was irrelevant; they were tied into a contract.

"OK," Liz said eventually. "I'm in tomorrow evening. I'll see you then."

"Thank you. I'll talk to her and find out everything I can. I'm sure there's more to the story than this."

Sally slept fitfully, and her dreams were haunted by arguments with Mel. Two days ago there was nothing she wanted more than to win Mel's trust again, now she was trapped into confronting her. She spent most of the next day in the glasshouses; there was no one she wanted to speak to. When Paul texted her to see how things had gone she imagined running to him, letting Liz and Mel fight without dragging her in. Hopefully they would be so worried that she'd disappeared for days everything else would be forgotten when she returned home. But it would be an empty friendship when they accepted her back, if she'd just ignored their arguments, and if Mel was genuinely suing a farmer for feeding his family.

When she came home she sat at the kitchen table reading and waiting for Mel. The report was safe in her room, unread; it was best if Mel thought Liz had only looked at the report and not taken it.

She didn't have to wait long. Mel came into the kitchen and, without a word to Sally, made herself a sandwich.

"Mel, can we talk?"

"What 'talk properly' you mean?" Her harsh tone suggested she hadn't mellowed since their last meeting.

"Yes."

Mel sat down in front of Sally. As always, she looked pristine. Her nails were done in the same dark blue as her silk blouse. Sally felt so detached from the businesswomen sitting in front of her it seemed impossible their lives had ever met on equal pegging.

"I'm sorry," Sally said. "I realise how totally I'd got things wrong."

"Good."

Sally searched for ways to show how genuinely she had changed her mind. "I think Darren knows how lucky he is."

"Stop telling me what Darren thinks."

"I'm sorry." Sally looked down at the cold mug if tea in her hands. "I guess it was a way of telling you what I think."

Mel acknowledged this with a slight nod.

Realising her apology has taken her as far as it could, and that it was going to be overshadowed by what came next anyway, Sally moved on to what she really had to say.

"Mel, are you working for Tewx?"

The look on Mel's face wasn't the anger Sally had been expecting, but blankness. For a moment Sally hoped she had got things totally wrong, then she explained, "Liz saw your report."

"God, has Liz no idea of privacy?"

"I think you'd left it in the living room."

"So? That makes no difference," Mel said.

"She shouldn't have done it, but that's not the point."

"Liz snoops around, starts discussing confidential information, and that's not the point?"

"We know Tewx Technologies is your client."

"And?"

"A multi-national company taking on Indian farmers, you have to agree that's totally wrong." There was a hint of mockery in Sally's voice, as she felt a surge of righteousness. Now it was Mel who was in the wrong.

"I don't actually. And I know your boss has spoken out to defend them."

"I'm not Vangelis."

"Now you and Liz can stop talking about things you don't understand."

Sally worried there was some truth in this accusation; maybe she should have read the report. It seemed wise to shift blame onto Liz. "Liz was mad when she told me, but I persuaded her to let me speak with you. I know things are never so simple, so I wanted to give you the chance to explain what's going on. Anything I don't understand is because you never tell me the tiniest detail about what's going on."

"What's this – innocent until proven guilty? Who are you guys? This is my work, I'm entitled to do what I want and tell you as little as I want. I can assure you, there's very little I want to tell you."

"I'm sorry, I know you're not answerable to us, it's just that you're supporting…"

"Telling me that you're sorry doesn't entitle you to keep going."

"Your colleagues are explaining this in a court of law, the least you could do is let me know how you justify what Tewx is doing."

"OK. Tewx is upholding laws that are essential the viability of their business. Farmers aren't forced to buy GM seeds, but without this kind of regulation they wouldn't have the choice."

"Why not?"

"Without this kind of protection against people stealing your technologies, it's not economically viable to do it."

"An interesting definition of stealing."

"Sally, you tell me these great things about how GM can tackle hunger, and I often agree with you, but you have no idea about the practicalities."

"My research is different." Sally felt her self-righteousness sounding naive. "We're not a company out to make a profit, we have Government funding because they believe what we're doing will help global food security."

"Great, good on you. But businesses don't have the luxury of Government funding."

"You only get funding when you're acting for the public good."

"And businesses never act for the public good? Look at it this way: you'd never get public funding to develop a wonderbra, but that doesn't mean society hasn't benefited."

"It's a whole different mindset when you're not motivated by profit."

Mel rolled her eyes. "That hasn't even worked for golden rice. It sounds like a perfect situation: some guy adds vitamin A to rice with the sole intention of improving nutrition, no profit required. But look, even that's failing."

"It hasn't worked yet, but that's to do with laws that will probably change. Anyway, that's a perfect example. I'm not anti-patenting, I'm not Liz, but for golden rice patents have been waived so that the poorest farmers can benefit from the technology. Business isn't all about enforcing patents."

"Why do you see GM foods as so different to the pharmaceutical industry? Patenting drugs so people can't get them cheaply? I don't see you complaining every time you get a prescription. And I can assure you that without patents there would be no prescriptions to get."

Sally wasn't going to get sidetracked by bashing the pharmaceutical industry. "Can't we work out a way to balance profit and public benefit a bit more?"

"Be my guest, but don't be so naive as to think this case is special because it's GM. It's no different to the rest of agri-tech." Mel said. "Are you going to stop people buying fertiliser because big businesses make it?"

"But suing farmers, it's evil!" Out of arguments but still convinced she was right, Sally began the move towards exchanging insults.

"Until you have any intention of trying to understand I suggest you save your rants for Liz."

When lovers quarrel they can say 'I love you' and made up; there's no option of simply avoiding each other. When housemates quarrel there was nothing to stop them walking away. Mel went to bed with their arguments unresolved, and Sally lay sleeplessly in her bed, wondering whether just a few metres away Mel was doing the same.

Chapter 23

Sally waited for a time when Mel was out so she could talk to Liz without fear of being overheard. They perched on the edge of different sofas, Liz looking expectant, even excited.

When Sally spoke it was with an air of defeat. "I talked to Mel, and she believes what she's doing is right. She's upholding the law and that's her job."

"I knew you'd get nowhere with it. Our only choice is to go public."

"And do what?" Sally pulled a face, confident that Liz was all talk.

"Oh, I don't know." Liz shrugged and raised her palms as if to show that such practicalities were for someone else's problem. "Look for something in the report, tell the protesters what we know, tell the local papers."

"That's ridiculous. We'd achieve nothing. I don't for one moment believe there's anything illegal in the report – all we'd do is embarrass ourselves."

"With the lawyers for things like this there's always something, maybe not in the report, but in an email, in another document. It won't be hard to get into her emails – she leaves her BlackBerry lying around."

With a twinge of dismay, Sally realised that Liz was serious. "She's our friend!"

Liz eyed her coldly. "Some things are more important than protecting our friends."

Sally paused at this. She prided herself on sticking up for her principles, but how much was she looking for an easy life, making sure her friends liked her?

Liz misinterpreted her silence. "She's talked you round – is that it? That didn't take much."

"It's not that. It's because I think it's all a crazy idea, and because taking the law into your own hands generally ends in disaster. There are probably lots of laws in relation to biotechnology I disagree with, but I do believe these things are better fought in court rather than by housemates stealing their friends' BlackBerrys."

"But what if there's something for us to discover? Something courts don't know."

"Oh, and why don't we hack some phones while we're at it?" Sally didn't want there to be anything to discover, but most of all she didn't want anything to do with underhand tactics. "Look, Liz, you found the report – it's yours. I'll get it for you in a minute and you can do what you like, but I really think the best place for it is the shredder."

"That's fine," Liz said. "I thought you'd care enough to do something."

As Sally watched Liz walk out it was exhaustion she felt, not fear. She knew that Liz wouldn't act on her own. Thankfully, Liz's grudges were short-lived and Sally had no concerns about letting her down.

* * * * *

At work Sally often saw Darren at his computer reading about Tewx, and she begrudged it. She felt certain Mel had told him freely what she was working on, and she was also sure Darren would agree with everything Mel said. She kept quiet about what she knew, and he showed no sign that Mel has told him. But still Sally pictured the conversation they could have had about her. Complete isolation between her lives at work and home had meant she always had an escape route from problems in one of those situations. No one is always on your side, but that way there was always somebody to agree with you.

On Saturday Sally woke up early and tried fruitlessly to relax again. She felt as if her resting heart rate had become 20 beats higher than it used to be. This wasn't a sustainable way to live.

She arranged a weekend's escape to Paul's. It hadn't taken long to build up the courage to ask if she could stay over. She told herself she'd been brave enough to ask because they were becoming closer, more relaxed, but she couldn't pretend that desperation to get away didn't have something to do with it.

She walked along the riverbank, killing time until it was reasonable to turn up at his house. It was deserted except for rowing coaches on their bikes, shouting encouragement and criticism at their crews in equal measure. The sun was beginning to shine through the clouds when Sally saw the shape she'd been hoping for: the bag lady. She sat down next to her, the dew on the bench seeping through her jeans.

"How are you?" Sally handed the lady a chocolate bar from her pocket.

The lady fingered the wrapping lovingly. "Very well, thank you m'dear. Where do you get this kind o' thing from?" Ripping off the wrapper she took a bite of chocolate. "Well I d'know if it's legal but it ain't half delicious!" She cackled in delight.

"It's just a chocolate bar."

The lady stopped and looked at her. "Wait, don' we know each other?"

"Yes, we've talked a few times. You showed me the ducklings, remember?"

The lady's eyes lit up in understanding. "You were on the ship – I knew it!"

"The ship?" Sally glanced around them at the meadow, as if that might provide some answers.

"You don't remember?" The lady sounded disappointed. "Well, a lot o' folk don't seem to remember things nowadays."

Sally wondered how many people stuck around long enough to discover what a crazy bag lady thought they should be remembering. "Well, if we went on a voyage together, then maybe you can give me some advice."

"Anything for you m'dear."

"I'm just trying to decide if it's always right to stick by your friends whatever they do. I know that nobody can look after the whole world, you have to start with the people you know, but sometimes is sticking up for what's right more important than protecting your friends?"

"Do yer friends do this boat nonsense?"

Sally listened to the rhythmical sound of eight blades hitting the water simultaneously. A boat came round the corner, jerking slightly with each stroke. "Not anymore, but they did when I was still a student."

"I thought you was too young to be a student."

Sally pictured the lady's brain, which must have come to resemble her holey grey scarf even more than it had on their last meeting. When she spoke about her loyalties she hoped that it was the holes she was speaking to.

"My colleagues asked me to lie for them, and I did. Part of the way I justified it was that it was helping them; they needed the paper we were publishing. Now I wonder whether my motivations were right at all."

"Havin' colleagues is more trouble than it's worth! I've worked on three ships and two trains – every one of the crew were liars or crooks." The lady turned her milky eyes to Sally. "Other 'n you that is."

"It's too late to do anything, but maybe I can at least learn from this." Sally took a deep breath, steeling herself to move on.

"And your man, are you happy together?" The lady said, in what seemed to be a moment of lucidity.

"Yes thank you, I'm going to visit him now."

"Thanks for comin' to see me, pet, and watch out for the ducks."

"See you soon!" Sally stood up and waved. She resolved to visit with food offerings more often. Her troubles seemed slightly dulled if she could associate them with a delusional old lady thrilled to receive a chocolate bar.

She walked slowly towards Paul's house, imagining an alternative life spent on a ship with a crew of liars and crooks. The idea held some romantic appeal.

Her day with Paul was grounded with reassuring normality. They went shopping for DIY, and Paul let her choose fabric to replace the moth-eaten curtains he'd inherited with the house. She helped him prepare a roast chicken, and they ate it with large glasses of wine. When the evening turned cold he lent her one of his jumpers, with shoulders that seemed to almost reach her elbow. He laughed when she rolled back the sleeves like a school child given clothes they would grow into. "*I should be so happy,*" she thought. "*But instead I feel I'm spinning a lie just by keeping quiet.*"

She was alarmed by how dependent she'd become on him. She'd been clinging onto sanity, and without him it might slip through her fingers. She feared losing him, and to tell him she loved him would risk pushing him away. But it also nagged that this kind of unequal friendship never worked in the long run. At the moment she could act as if she was happy to just have him as a friend, but how long could she keep that up? The question of whether to tell him how she felt was entirely hypothetical because she would be too scared, but she thought it was at least best to decide whether telling him would be the right thing to do.

In the evening as they went to bed, Paul poured them a glass of water each. They paused before they climbed the stairs, and Sally thought maybe this was the moment where they admitted that she wasn't really there so she could stay in the spare room. But the moment passed and they went their separate ways.

Sally's bed was cold, and she arranged the duvet so it covered her ears. She contemplated putting Paul's jumper back on but that would involve getting out of bed, and sleeping in his jumper felt like a greater intimacy than he'd intended by lending it to her. She watched the red digits on the alarm clock slowly advance and thought about her situation. It seemed that her fortunes had changed not when she found her field trial destroyed but when she saw Vangelis's lab book and its make-believe data. Her thoughts wandered between what had possessed her to go along with it and the statistical implications of simply stating a larger sample size. The only way she could see to free herself from the burden of her guilt was to leave the lab entirely, get a new job somewhere else. But that was only freeing herself from her conscience; she would still be guilty.

She must have dozed off because she was woken at just gone one o'clock by footsteps. Paul was walking downstairs. She waited for a few minutes then pushed back the duvet and stood up. The air was cold round her neck, and she had no choice but to pull Paul's jumper on over her pyjamas.

She found Paul in the kitchen making a mug of something hot. He hadn't turned the light on; instead he was using the light that spilled in from the hallway.

"Hey Sally, what are you doing up?"

She moved into the kitchen so she wasn't blocking his light. "Sorry, I heard you were awake."

"That's OK, do you want a drink?"

Sally shook her head and wrapped her arms around herself.

"Are you cold? Would you like a blanket?"

Again Sally shook her head, and then immediately realised she would like a blanket, though that wasn't what she'd come down to say.

"What's up?" he asked.

"Paul, I know the middle of the night isn't the time to be saying this, and I am sorry to burden with you with it, but I don't have anyone else I can tell…"

Paul stopped making his drink and came to stand directly in front of her. "Tell me, and whatever it is we can work it out."

"I didn't want to, right from the start I knew what a bad idea it was, and now I can't take it back." She was garbling, trying to defend herself even before she'd said anything incriminating. "I know I let Vangelis bully me into it, and I knew it was good for my career, so I went along with

250

everything. There's no going back; I'm stuck with the consequences and I don't know how I'm going to deal with it."

Paul reached out to take hold of both of her hands in front of him. "I'll look after you. Sally, we'll work this out, I promise you." His intensity startled her, but then she realised: he thought she was pregnant. She pulled her hands away. "No, it's not like that at all, I wouldn't do that." For the first time in the conversation she raised her eyes to look at him, trying to register what he'd meant, what he'd been offering to do. Then she said more calmly, "You know we were published in *Nature*?"

Paul seemed to have recovered, but somehow he didn't look relieved. "Of course," he said cautiously. "I went to the party. It's brilliant, you shouldn't be shy about letting everyone know."

"But that's the problem. It's not brilliant. It's a load of rubbish."

"How do you mean?"

"It contains fabricated results – for data we couldn't collect when the field trial was destroyed."

It was Paul's turn to take a step backwards. He stood for a moment without saying anything, his mouth hanging slightly open. "How bad? Genuine rubbish?"

"No, not that bad. We had some samples collected already, so we took the results from those and just pretended we had a large enough sample size. And it was just one experiment. The irony is, I think our conclusions are right. All the papers out there have genuine data but draw the wrong conclusions, and ours is the one that constitutes fraud."

Sally watched as Paul processed this, and when he didn't speak she grew increasingly nervous. Eventually she asked, "What are you going to do?"

"I'm going to go to bed and in the morning we're going to talk about what *we* are going to do."

"Thank you. I'm sorry, I hadn't planned to tell you all this, I just felt so trapped."

"Time for bed." He placed his hand in the small of her back then pushed her gently towards the stairs.

Back in bed Sally slept almost immediately. There seemed to be no more choices to make, she had passed that on to Paul, and so she was able to clear her mind. As soon as she heard Paul get up the next morning she followed him downstairs.

"Morning," he said cheerfully. "Did you sleep well?"

"The bed's very comfy thank you."

"What would you like for breakfast?" Paul opened a cupboard of cereals and let Sally make her choice. They carried breakfast into the dining room and sat down opposite each other. As she poured them both some orange juice her fingers trembled not from cold but from fear. It seemed surreal to finally find out what Paul ate for breakfast so many years after they first spent the night together. She was relieved when Paul spoke.

"So, what are we going to do?"

"I honestly have no idea," Sally said.

"What options are you considering?"

"Tell someone I guess." Sally played with her cornflakes, pressing them with her spoon until they compacted.

"So you've decided to do something?"

Sally looked at him, uncomprehending. "Now that I've told you, I didn't think doing nothing was an option anymore?"

"You told me as a friend, nothing to do with my work, and I trust you. If you're genuinely happy to let this pass then I'll support that."

252

The burden of his trust suddenly seemed crushing. She'd thought the decision was at last out of her hands. "If you were me," she said, "what would you do?"

"I would tell someone, without a doubt."

Hearing this, Sally knew there was no turning back. Her resolve strengthened. "I can't believe I got myself into this position – scientific misconduct, fabrication – how?"

"You're getting yourself out. That's the important thing."

Sally nodded but didn't speak, but examined the table instead. It was an old one his parents had given him and it was covered in indentations from where he and his sister had pressed too hard when doing their homework. It was almost impossible to make out the words, but if she dragged a finger over them she could feel the tiny dents in the wood.

"If I'm the whistleblower," she said, "what's going to happen to me, to Darren, to Vangelis?"

"I don't know."

"I know it's selfish, but I worry about them hating me more than I worry about what will happen to them."

"Look, I had this idea." Paul's voice was suddenly uncertain. "I'm not totally sure it would work, but I think I could arrange it so there was an inspection. We might be able to make sure it was discovered without anyone knowing a tip-off came from you."

"OK," Sally said slowly, processing what this meant.

"It depends totally on whether you'd rather be a whistleblower or be accused of fraud."

The bluntness of his words made Sally give a short laugh, forced and unnatural. They weren't words she had ever thought she'd hear. "One of the ways Vangelis sold this to me was so that it helped my career. Now it's driven me to risk my job and my reputation."

"It may not be as bad as you think; Vangelis will get most of the blame."

"I'm under no illusions. If I'm going to do this I have to be ready to be shown the door."

"Let's cross these hurdles when we come to them. Think about it and if you want to work out an accidental discovery then just say the word."

"Thank you." Different scenarios were rushing through her head, all dramatic and disastrous; she couldn't begin to approach the decision.

Paul reached out to take her empty cereal bowl and piled it on top of his. "I'll do the washing up later, we've got some painting to do first."

As they layered olive green emulsion onto the landing walls Paul seemed distant in a way he hadn't done the day before. Although he'd been sincere with his offers of help, it had a business-like feel about it. The way a teacher has to help out a pupil regardless of whether or not they deserve it. They stood next to each other and dipped their rollers into the same tray, breathing in the fumes. Sally constantly stole glances at him, trying to understand what he was thinking. But then she would realise how long she'd lapsed into silence for and wonder if his remoteness was her doing.

* * * * *

Over the coming weeks house relations were strained. Mel was still speaking to Sally, but it was always functional, non-committal. They made no attempts to see each other more than they had to. Whenever Mel had Darren round, her manner towards Sally would soften, but Sally knew this was all in the name of appearances, eliminating any danger that Darren would feel the need to stick up for Sally. Liz appeared to sulk, disappointed by Sally's refusal to expose Mel and her report. But then the Tewx Technologies case was closed, and Liz seemed to forget it as quickly as the papers did. When Tewx's victory was reported with finality on the national news it seemed strange they had ever believed they could make a difference. Once she was back on friendly terms with Liz, Sally found her house easier to bear.

At work what had been bad became good and what had been good seemed bad. When she was forced to do jobs she hated she felt a sense of relief she would soon be free of them – she sat at the fume hood crouched over chemicals, neck aching, and took deep breaths of the acrid smell to remind herself exactly what she would be missing. When results in the lab were coming fast and easily, which they often were, she tried to push them from her mind. The successes she'd hoped for, the results she'd believed in – they seemed tantalisingly close if she didn't work hard to block them out. When her experiments fell foul to contamination or unprovoked failure, she felt liberated; results were going to be no good to her anyway. When she shared a joke with Darren and Amy, or when she listened to Vangelis give an inspiring seminar to the department, her heart sank lower.

It hadn't taken Sally long to decide to take up Paul's offer of an inspection to discover the fraud 'just by chance'.

"Some people would think it mad to do things like this," he said. "To risk your career for the sake of your colleagues' good opinions, but I'd do the same. My friends are more important than my job."

"You don't think it's dishonest, do you?" Sally asked him.

"Dishonest to expose a lie? No, you're doing the right thing."

She hoped he could see how grateful she was, but feared no look on her face could display the physical relief she felt as he said this. Whenever he gave her updates of how documents were travelling between departments to ensure her inspection, she knew he wasn't just doing this because he'd promised to help her.

There were plenty of times when, if she could have told Paul to call off the whole plan, she would have done. But there was no going back, so Sally focussed on her next meal, her favourite TV shows, phone calls to her mother and, most of all, time spent with Paul.

Chapter 24

The day the inspection began, the first of the autumn swallows collected on the phone cables. It was bright as Sally walked to work, but the air was cold and the sun cast long shadows. She arrived before the inspectors and worked silently in the lab, showing none of the restlessness that had gripped her colleagues. The inspectors came before lunch, three men dressed in suits, conspicuous in a building full of jeans and lab coats. The youngest of the three was Paul. He nodded when he saw Sally, but they displayed no signs of recognition. She obediently surrendered her lab books then escaped to the basement where decades worth of samples were stored and where liquid nitrogen was dispensed from giant cylinders. It was half way through the afternoon when Darren found her. She had her head in a -80°C freezer, sorting through old samples. Many of them were labelled with the names of people who had left years before, so she was being ruthless with her clear-out. She ignored Darren and continued with her task.

"You know it will be OK, don't you?" Darren said from behind her.

"No, I don't know."

"Vangelis didn't leave any of this to chance."

The freezer started an angry beeping as the thermometer reached -76°C, and Sally straightened up and closed the door. "We'll wait and see."

"Running off down here, it looks like you're guilty." He was grinning, and Sally saw he genuinely meant it as a joke. When she didn't laugh his expression turned to reassurance. "And anyway, one of the inspectors is your friend Paul. I admit we didn't completely hit it off, but I'm sure he wouldn't land you in anything…"

Sally still had her hand on the freezer door and opened it very slightly to let more cold escape. Sure enough the alarm started again and Darren was cut short.

She went to the department computer room to work. It was something she never did; being surrounded by undergraduates reminded her too much of her student days in the computer room, a permanent feeling of knowing too little and panic about the next assignment. But she had a productive afternoon writing up her results, fuelled in turns by the desire to leave everything in order for whoever took up the work once she was gone and a freedom that came with knowing that anything she wrote badly was no concern of hers. The project didn't have to die along with its current leaders, and it felt good to work magnanimously for a success which wouldn't be hers.

At the end of the day Sally returned to the office to pick up her coat and left as quickly as possible. Half way down the corridor she heard footsteps and Paul came to walk alongside her, still in his suit and tie. He had clearly been waiting for her.

"How are you?" he asked.

"OK."

"Really?" Paul stood still, and Sally was forced to turn and face him.

"I hid pretty effectively."

"I noticed."

A post-doc from the lab next door walked past them, with a look of unashamed curiosity. Sally turned away from Paul, and as soon as they were alone again she said, "let's go."

"Would you like to get a drink somewhere?"

They walked in silence through the busy streets until they found a pub. Their feet stuck to the wooden floor as they walked thanks to a permanent coating of spilled beer. They found a table surrounded by enough people that their conversation would be drowned out.

"You survived your day?" Paul loosened his tie; he looked tired.

"Actually I was very productive: ruthless sorting in the morning and speed writing in the afternoon. When I'm alone in the department and not thinking about my labmates I feel almost released."

"We had a productive day too."

Any sense of freedom Sally had felt was immediately extinguished. "Did you find anything?"

"We just did what we needed to do. You don't have to wait much longer, and we can put this behind us."

He said us, as if there would still be a 'we' when this was over.

Sally lowered her voice so she could barely be heard above the noise of the pub. "Thank you for doing all this; I'm so sorry it all happened and I had to drag you in."

"No, I'm glad you told me. Thank you."

They made feeble small talk while they finished their drinks, Sally all the time imagining what it would be like to have his arms around her.

* * * * *

Sally spent the next morning tidying cupboards in the lab, slightly wobbly after a sleepless night. After lunch Paul came into the office to say his colleagues would soon be there to speak to them. As he left, Sally felt her heart pound as if it were a blue whale's. She thought of all the waits she'd endured. Standing outside the school gymnasium in an alphabetical line waiting for her A level exams, scanning for her name on the list of degree results, reading the notice boards outside her examiner's office while he debated whether or not to give her a PhD. Uniquely, this time she knew what fate awaited her, and unlike her previous waits, this one was not going to end well. She reached for her water glass the way you reach for your wine at an awkward party and realised her hand was shaking. Behind her Amy was teasing Günter about having something to hide, and Sally couldn't begin to tell her what poor taste her joke was in. Darren hid his fear in silence.

When the inspectors returned Sally met them with a level gaze. '*You've made your bed, now lie in it,*' she repeated the words in her head until they obscured what the first inspector was saying. When his colleague, stout and balding, began to speak her thoughts were brought rapidly back into the room.

"I'm afraid I have some bad news." His tone was flat, with none of the accusation she'd expected. She imagined Amy assuming he was about to lecture them on the format they used in their lab books or writing in the wrong coloured ink. He cleared his throat and continued. "It appears from your published results that when your field trial was unfortunately cut short you had already collected enough samples. However, this was not the case."

The words were painfully simple to be sealing her fate. She glanced around at her colleagues. There were no gasps of shock from Günter and Amy, just looks of total incomprehension.

The inspector continued. "This does, of course, constitute scientific fraud – the publication of fabricated data."

The words prompted Amy into action. "What are you talking about? There's no fraud."

The taller inspector spoke calmly. "I'm very sorry, but Professor Papadakis has admitted it. I know this comes as a shock; it was all carefully planned to ensure none of you were aware."

It was Sally's turn for disbelief. She stared, her eyes darting from one inspector to the other, searching for confirmation of what had just been said. For the first time Paul looked up, warning her to not to react.

Thankfully the balding inspector spoke. "We won't keep you for long, but we do need to ask you all some questions individually." He nodded to Sally. "Miss Jones, can I ask you to wait here until we're ready for you?"

The three inspectors led away Darren, Amy and Günter. Sally was glad that Paul went with Amy; she knew he would be gentle with her. She didn't point out to the inspectors that she was Dr Jones not Miss. It seemed irrelevant now anyway. She wasn't going to be a scientist for much longer.

There was nothing to make her stay; none of these people had any power over her. It seemed a good enough reason to leave a job without giving notice; she could walk away right now and never need to look back. She turned off her computer, then collected her mug from the kitchen and wrapped it in a tea towel to keep it safe in her bag. She collected the few books she owned and added them to her backpack. She had a friend teaching English in Thailand. If all you wanted to do was earn your keep it wasn't hard to get work, and her friend could probably arrange visas, work, accommodation or weekend trips to beaches, jungles and cities. Flights to Bangkok were easy to come by, and she could wait a few days to get one cheap enough. She could sub-let her room if she wanted to come back to it. That seemed unlikely; she could leave her housemates to sort it out. These practicalities weren't important; all that mattered was that she knew they could all be overcome. She was free to go. She had waited five years for Paul, and if he wanted her it was his turn to wait. If she wasn't worth the wait, then clearly nor was he.

She swung her heavy backpack onto her shoulders and, with a final glance through the window into her deserted lab, she left. She picked her way through the streets, wondering why there were so many people not at work. Her phone rang in her pocket, and she ignored it. Almost as soon as it cut to answerphone it rang again, and again. She pulled it out of her pocket, deciding only Paul would be worth answering. But it was Darren's photo that came up on the screen. There was a slight pause before it rang for a fourth time. This time she answered; she wasn't scared he would persuade her to come back.

"Hi."

"Sally, where are you?"

"Not waiting around to put my energy into a lost cause."

"But Vangelis…" Darren faltered.

"He got what was coming, and there's nothing we can do to make things any better." Saying this she felt virtuous, even powerful.

"You were right all along, and I messed it up, and I'm sorry, sorry." His voice was pleading, and it scared her.

"Are you OK?" She said more gently.

"What do you think?" His tone wasn't unkind, more deflated.

She tried to think of anything she could say to reassure him. "It's all done. If anybody blamed you they would have turned you in." The calm provided by an escape plan to Thailand was still there in her voice.

"Are you coming back?"

"I don't know, I don't see any reason I should wait around to have inspectors tell me what I already know."

"Please, Sally, come back just for a moment. I'm not going to make you talk to the inspectors. I just want to... to talk."

Sally stopped and the lady behind her banged a pushchair into her legs.

She had done this to him; if she'd had the guts to refuse to be part of the fabrication then she could have stopped it without anybody else needing to know. The least she could do was help pick up the pieces. She took a deep breath. "OK, where are you?"

"Outside the department."

"I'll be five minutes."

She walked briskly back, the straps of her bag digging into her shoulders. She had no idea what she would say. She'd had months to make decisions, come to terms with what they'd done and the emotions that came with it. She'd forgotten that for Darren, this feeling of helplessness was totally new. He'd been too cocky to envisage himself in this position.

She found him perched on a wall in the car park and came to sit beside him. He looked calmer but his face was pale.

"You cleared your desk then?" He pointed at her bulging backpack.

She shrugged. "Thought I might as well get it over with."

Darren sighed. "I have no idea what I am going to do."

"Nor do I, but we don't need to decide now. We've got lots of choices."

"What about Vangelis? He's left with nothing, absolutely nothing."

"He'll sort something out. You're just as good a scientist as Vangelis is, he's just had more time to prove it. And plenty of people have had science careers denied to them for far lesser reasons than this."

"But what can he do?"

"Why are you so worried about Vangelis?"

"Because we shouldn't be out here, we should be answering questions about what we knew. We should be learning the penalties for misconduct, not walking away from them."

It was true; they should have all have gone down. That was what she had prepared herself for. "How did this happen?" she said eventually.

"He was clever. Looking back, I think he'd thought it all through." Darren shook his head. "He never let me write fabricated results in my lab book, it was always in his. I thought it was because it would look as if I'd processed more samples than was humanly possible. But why would a professor spend so much time doing dull sampling? That must have looked odd in an inspection."

Sally sighed, reassessing her view of Vangelis over the last few months. "So, he was only risking himself." She watched as a small crowd of undergraduates filed past them, clearly just out of a lecture.

"I knew as well as he did what we were risking, and now I've taken none of the blame."

"Vangelis wouldn't protect you if you didn't deserve it. If he didn't think your reputation was worth saving then he wouldn't lie for you."

"We were right, Sally, that's the worst thing, I'm sure every conclusion in that paper is right."

"I know."

They sat in silence as the last of the undergraduates dispersed.

Suddenly Darren spoke. "God, not now."

Sally looked up to see Paul walking towards them, his expression determined. She felt trapped momentarily between Darren and Paul. She'd walked away when the inspectors were waiting for her, leaving Paul to keep the investigation together without her. But she didn't want to force Darren to speak to him. Paul was just metres away from them, close enough to make eye contact. He met her gaze, and then she looked away. Immediately, Paul changed his course awkwardly and walked past them towards the department. Sally could almost feel his humiliation.

"Thank you." Darren had clearly noticed. Sally felt, after months of worrying about the right thing to do, that she had finally done something selfless.

Darren's phone rang. He looked at the screen but didn't answer it.

"Mel?" Sally asked.

Darren nodded. Sally thought about how badly the loss of Mel's friendship had affected her, and the reason she had lost it. If she was genuinely disappearing to Thailand, now was a moment to think what was best for her friends.

She took a deep breath. "I know Mel seems so *together* all of the time, but she understands. You don't always have to pretend you're fine – I can assure you I don't."

Darren stared at the tarmac of the car park, not acknowledging whether or not Sally had understood the problem. The phone rang again.

"Are you coming to work tomorrow?" he asked.

"Probably not, are you?"

"I've no idea."

Just as the call threatened to cut to answerphone Darren accepted the call and waved goodbye.

Sally watched his back until he disappeared, then she texted Amy: *'Remember, they don't have to make you do anything, you're free and you'll be fine. Call me tomorrow if you want to talk.'*

She knew now she couldn't just run without calling Paul.

He answered without even a Hello. "What's going on?"

"I'm sorry, it just all seemed too much, so I left. I'm sorry if I made your life harder."

"But I just saw you in the car park."

"I came back to see Darren."

"To see Darren?"

Sally thought of the strength it had taken to look away as Paul approached them, willing him not to stop and so choosing Darren above him. She shouldn't have said it was Darren she came back for.

"He just had no idea what to do, and I was worried about him. He's gone off to see Mel now."

Paul considered this in silence.

"Is everything OK, would you like me to come back in?" Sally's fear of speaking to the inspectors was rapidly replaced by a fear of upsetting Paul. She would submit to a whole night of interrogation if it would make Paul forgive her.

"It's a bit late for that," he said.

"I'm really sorry."

"It's alright, I covered for you."

"Thank you, I'm sorry…"

"Stop saying sorry!" This sounded like irritation not forgiveness.

"OK." Sorry was the only thing she wanted to say. "Would you like to" She was too scared to finish her sentence asking him to do something together.

"Would I like to what?"

"Meet up?" She had the feeling that she was asking a favour, and that she'd used up a lifetime's worth of favours by asking him to solve her professional problems.

Paul, however, suddenly seemed to lose his anger. "Are you still in the car park? I'm not done for the day, but I'll come down for a bit."

"Thank you."

"See you in a mo." He hung up.

Out in the car park Paul picked his way between reversing cars to reach her. He had lost his jacket and tie, and with them his look of confidence. He looked a little bit like an overgrown school child, and Sally ached to hug him.

"I feel guilty that I put you through this whole thing," she said.

"It's my job. At other times I enjoy it."

"You do good things through it."

Paul smiled wearily. "Thank you. I like to think I did today."

"You did." Sally was relieved to remember this wasn't just about her; it was about everybody's integrity. She chewed at her fingernails. "Why did Vangelis lie for us?"

"I guess he realised he'd achieve nothing by handing you in. It wasn't your fault, and it's not like you'd make the same mistake again."

Darren's words about where they should be rang truer than she had admitted to him. "I wish he hadn't."

"You won't be saying that in a few weeks' time."

Sally was reassured by Paul's tone, but still didn't believe him. "I thought we'd be given the same treatment as Vangelis, and that science would be over for me and Darren. I have options I didn't think I'd have."

"Sally, you made probably the toughest decision of your life getting me to do this. You took your future in your hands. You don't need every decision from now on to be made for you."

They were still leaning on the wall, and Sally looked at his hand resting on his thigh. She could reach out and hold it. Even if he pulled it away it would be better than waiting, not knowing.

"They'll be wondering where I've got to." He stood up. "Look after yourself."

"Thank you for everything."

"You're welcome, now go home."

He faced her for a moment then turned to leave. She watched him disappear back inside, a wasted chance to tell him how she felt. Thailand seemed less appealing while she still hadn't found the courage to discover what Paul wanted from her, but a solo trip to a new continent seemed to require less bravery than to ask Paul the question she needed an answer to.

Chapter 25

It was partly morbid curiosity that took Sally to the department the next morning. There was no sign of Darren at home; Sally couldn't even work out whether he or Mel had been in the house overnight. She hoped she would find him at work.

She got inquisitive looks from everyone who passed her in the corridor, but nobody seemed brave enough to speak to her. It was a lonely walk through the department to her empty office. She settled down in front of her computer, wishing she hadn't entirely emptied her shelves. The Head of Department had already emailed asking her to come to see him. Pleased to have something worth doing, Sally went immediately. She averted her eyes as she walked past Vangelis's door, not wanting to know how soon his office would be cleared or whether he'd be allowed back to do it himself.

The Head of Department, Professor Downes, was grey-haired and smiling. He wore shirts that seemed to press into his neck, and managed to greet every student jovially but with the wrong name. He'd always been supportive of Vangelis's work, and his expression turned to concern when he saw Sally at his door. "Come in," he said. "Take a seat. How are you?"

"I'm OK, thank you." She wasn't ready to give a more accurate answer.

Professor Downes tugged at his tie. "I know yesterday must have been very hard on you, so I wanted to say that you have the full support of the department, and that we do recognise the important contribution you've made in the time you've been here."

"Thank you."

He continued a stream of compliments and reassurances. They were kindly meant, but Sally hadn't come looking for sympathy. The more he explained why things were going to be fine, the more she thought about the reasons they might not be. She felt quite battered by the time someone knocked at the door. Professor Downes stood up to go and speak to them, and Sally was left trying not to eavesdrop.

She looked around the office, its tidiness a painful contrast to Vangelis's mess. The only papers were in neat trays, labelled by his secretary. Sally read the one closest to her. It was Judith's resignation.

Darren arrived late and subdued. Sally tried to draw him in to conversation about what they were going to do but he resisted, answering only in monosyllables.

"Judith's gone," Sally said in an attempt to prompt a reaction.

"Gone?"

"Resigned."

Darren shrugged. "No great loss. I can order my own reagents without her getting in the way."

He went to work in the lab and Sally followed. She kept glancing over to where he was lethargically pipetting out samples. He might be continuing his experiments, but Sally guessed it was just because he didn't know what else to do with himself. It didn't mean the lab was going to pull through.

* * * * *

Over the next few days Sally regularly picked up her phone to text Paul but each time put it back down again. With Mel still frosty and distant, Sally turned to Liz for help. Liz had been sympathetic about the inspection, but still Sally had been light on the details. She found Liz in the kitchen stirring a wok full of vegetables and leant on the worktop next to her.

"You know my friend Paul?" Sally said cautiously.

"The no-longer-married one you pretend not to fancy."

Sally nodded. This was going to be easier than she'd thought. "Yes, and I swear he likes me." Liz continued stirring her vegetables, but Sally could feel herself blush. "He's done so much for me. I just don't think we can go on like this for much longer. We nearly argued last week, after the inspection. I don't even know what about, I think we're just too scared to say what we really mean."

Liz laughed. "You need to get drunk and build up some Dutch courage."

"You sound just like Mel."

"Well, just occasionally, Mel's right."

"It's not quite what I had in mind."

"You are actually planning to do something though I hope."

"Yes, I am. Whatever happens, it's best to know."

"Totally. To put you in the right mood bring Paul along to my friend's party. He's celebrating his first anthology in print next week, and he'll kid himself that anyone who comes is one of his fans."

Sally had no better ideas, and Liz's party seemed less of a contrived situation than any she could think up. She texted him and he replied with a yes. It was a relief to have Liz on her side, and Sally wondered why she had always chosen to confide in Mel. Every time they met over the next few days Liz quizzed Sally about Paul. It was good to have the attention, and the more Liz talked about it the more excited Sally was about the possibilities the party held.

* * * * *

Sally began a dissatisfying regime of turning up in the lab when she felt like it, doing experiments until she was bored and intentionally ignoring the results. Darren and Günter still came in, and at times it was possible to imagine nothing had changed. None of them mentioned Vangelis or the future; they just generated results because it was the easiest thing to do. They never saw Amy; she had submitted her PhD and no longer had any reason to be there.

One day Sally found herself alone with Darren in the lab. She had separated out DNA fragments of different lengths just like school children separate the colours of ink in a felt tip pen in chromatography experiments. But there were fragments of different lengths that shouldn't be there. She was about to throw the contaminated experiment in the bin when Darren said, "Do you want to come to the prep room for a minute, just to talk."

"There's nobody else here, it's OK to talk."

Darren shook his head. "Come to the prep room."

Sally followed, confused and reluctant.

In the prep room Darren switched on the lights and closed the door. The room was hot and stuffy and brought back memories of the tedious hours they'd spent processing samples. Hours, it now seemed, they'd wasted. Darren cleared a place on the workbench so he could sit down, pushing aside the detritus of someone else's experiment. Sally sat down next to him.

"You know Vangelis isn't coming back?" he said.

"Of course."

"Well, they've suggested that I might be in a position to apply for group leader."

"That's brilliant!" Sally leant towards him, unsure of whether or not to give him a hug.

Her words were heartfelt, but Darren showed no signs of excitement. "I just wanted to know what you thought?"

Sally looked at him in confusion. "What do you mean? That's the kind of position you've spent your whole career working towards."

Darren raised his hand to silence her. "It just feels wrong."

"I know, I guess everything feels wrong at the moment. But we have projects that deserve to be finished, and you're the best person to keep them going."

"Thank you. Are you going to stay?"

"I honestly don't know. I'm still thinking about everything." Whenever things got too much for her, dreams of Thailand kept Sally sane – the temples she'd visit, the train rides she'd go on, the people she'd help. But she hadn't told her friend in Thailand that she was thinking of joining her; she hadn't even looked at prices. While Darren waited for her to explain, she thought through all the things that could keep her in England, in her job: a dysfunctional friendship with some housemates, some great colleagues who were now struggling to keep things together, a paper that was meant to be a high point in her career but would now have to be retracted, a mother who was waiting for her to grow up…

"You'd be fine without me," she said. "My contract's got two years left on it – and Amy would be very happy if you employ her for the rest of it."

"You know I'd love to have Amy back, but, to be honest," he said quietly, "things would be much harder without you."

It felt as if it had cost him a lot to admit this, and Sally accepted the compliment gracefully. She knew he was right. "I do think things would be good with you in charge, and I think all our plans are worth doing."

"But?"

"There are lots of things to think about."

If anything made her life in Cambridge worth preserving was Paul. If she was to rebuild her life somewhere else, the one thing she seemed unlikely to find was someone like him. If he didn't love her there seemed little hope of their friendship continuing. Without Paul, picking up the pieces of her old life seemed a depressing prospect. Starting again seemed the only option, whether it was teaching in Thailand or staying with her parents and applying for jobs so she didn't jeopardise her career.

"If we stay in the lab we'll make it work, I know we will," Darren said.

"I'll decide soon," she said. "And I promise I'll be as useful as I can even if I go – I won't just board the plane tomorrow. Maybe you can Skype me in Thailand to tell me about any lab disasters then listen to stories of sunny beaches and Thai curries." They both smiled, unconvincingly, and began to chat about more immediate issues – what they were doing in the lab and where they were getting lunch.

* * * * *

When Paul arrived for Liz's party, Sally had just finished trying on every skirt she owned, only to be told by Liz they were too severe, too plain or just too wrong. She brought Paul into the kitchen and offered him a drink. It felt wrong not to mention the inspection, to ask him how the aftermath had been or at least thank him one more time. But Liz was waiting to leave so there was no time to be alone. Sally wasn't brave enough to suggest they stayed behind.

The party was in the back room of a pub. A few copies of the book were carefully placed on the tables, and Sally was glad they'd come along to boost the guest list. Someone made a painful speech, but otherwise it passed like a normal party. Liz had told them what the book was about, and Sally and Paul amused themselves by telling other guests what they thought of each poem, getting bolder with their claims each time. Thankfully, when they got it totally wrong they were just seen as wacky, and the person they'd been speaking to would soon make excuses to move on.

When last orders were called rumours started about an after-party, but Sally wasn't sure how much she believed them. Liz drummed up support for a few people to come back to theirs for a last drink. They were still in Sally's living room at 1 am, surrounded by Liz's friends discussing politics. Sally let the conversation drift over her; neither she nor Paul had anything to contribute. Sleepiness was catching up with her, and the wine was having a greater affect than she'd meant it to. But she wasn't going to forget what the evening was really about. Whatever happens, Sally thought, there's always Thailand.

She rested her head on Paul's shoulder. He didn't flinch. Almost immediately, Liz caught Sally's eye and began to usher her friends out, saying she was ready for bed. Paul said goodbye to the others but made no attempt to leave. The CD had finished, and Sally got up to put some more music on, fumbling in the dim light.

She returned to her position on the sofa, her head again on Paul's shoulder. They didn't talk, just listened to the muffled sounds of Liz making her way to bed. Cautiously, Paul reached out an arm and placed it lightly round Sally's shoulders. She smiled, certain that she already had her answer, though suddenly and inexplicably nervous about what would come next. The room had grown cold and Sally was glad of the warmth Paul's body provided. But Paul shifted and she sat up, too abruptly. They sat awkwardly, not touching, and Sally worried he was about to leave. Panicking, she ran through ideas of what she would say to keep him there. But he didn't leave.

"Sally?"

She turned to look at him, their faces close. He leaned forward, and they kissed.

Sally woke up hot and early, unused to being pushed against the wall. The happiness she felt overshadowed the trials of the last few weeks so completely that it seemed absurd they had ever worried her. She turned over, ready to reach her arm round Paul's sleeping figure. But all she felt was empty bed. She brought her arms outside the covers in an attempt to cool down, happy that this meant he was awake. She listened for sounds, the flow of the bathroom tap or footsteps on the stairs, but the house was quiet. Paul's side of the bed was still warm; he couldn't be far away. She pulled some clothes on, still in the dark, then cursed as she tripped over Paul's shoes. But they weren't Paul's shoes, they were hers. His were gone. She ran down the stairs, not caring who she woke, and opened the front door. The streetlights had been dimmed, but she could still see to both ends of her road. There was nobody there. She didn't shout, but stood disbelieving on the doorstep, a fine drizzle coating her hair.

She went to get her phone and called him. There was no answer, and she didn't leave a message. She called again, and again, then sent a text, but there was no reply. She sat in the dark at the kitchen table, holding her silent phone. Bitterly, she hoped this was how Paul had felt when she'd left silently while he slept. A warm trickle of tears fell down her cheek and dropped onto the table. She didn't think even Thailand could cut it.

Eventually, as the blackbirds announced the arrival of dawn, she went back to bed.

Her head thumped as she woke up and reached for her phone. Nothing. She got up and dressed carefully, still checking her phone between each item of clothing. Tears falling again, she went to the bathroom. She splashed cold water on her face then put the plug in and filled up the sink. She dropped her phone with a splash. Air bubbles rose out of it and she watched with satisfaction as the screen flickered then died. Now she wouldn't be waiting hopelessly for his call.

She couldn't stomach any breakfast but went to make herself a cup of tea. She took scalding sips as she tried to calm herself down.

"Why is your phone in the sink?" Mel appeared at the kitchen door.

Sally couldn't speak. She hadn't sunk so low that she didn't care what Mel thought. She felt that every part of her life had successfully fallen apart, yet she was too proud to admit any of it to Mel.

But Mel could see her red eyes.

"Darren told me everything about the inspection, and I'm sorry, but it looks like you've found your feet again."

Sally wondered whether 'everything' included the fact they had been in on it too.

"It's not that."

"Paul?"

Sally nodded.

"Oh, Sally, there are other men. It needn't be this hard you know." Mel put an arm around Sally, and Sally rested her head on Mel's shoulder, just as she had to Paul the night before.

"I know."

"Try and sound a little more convincing."

"I know there are other men, but will they be free, will I want them?"

"OK, let's not worry about this now. I have to go out, just for a bit. I'll see you later."

Mel gave Sally's shoulder a squeeze then left. Unable to find the energy to move, Sally stayed sitting on the kitchen table, her feet resting on a chair. She stayed motionless, trying to convince herself that Mel was right, there were other men, it was finally time to realise this.

By the time Darren came in Sally had forgotten he was even there.

"What's up?"

"I'm OK."

He frowned and said gently, "I know that's not true, tell me."

His tone was intimate, the voice he saved for when one of them was vulnerable, and who knows, maybe a voice he saved for her. She knew that whenever she saw his bravado stripped away she was always going to reciprocate with honesty. "It's OK, it's just, I know you always thought there was something between me and Paul. But there never was. I thought it for a while, but now I know there was nothing."

Darren looked at his feet, bare on the kitchen floor, and was silent.

"Sally." He looked up at last. "You're beautiful, you're kind, you care about your work and the good it's doing. Don't waste your time on someone who doesn't see that."

"Thank you. But I can't blame him."

"You should blame him." Darren stepped closer, so his legs were touching hers. "You know I'm not just saying that to be kind."

Sally was aware of her red bloodshot eyes when his were clear and caring. But all she could think of was Paul. Even as Darren stroked her hair and she fought back tears determined not to cry in front of him, her mind was running through the times she'd spent with Paul, reassessing them in the light of his sudden departure. "I know you're not, and thank you. You're as good as Mel."

Darren dropped his hand.

"When's Mel coming back?" Sally asked. "Can we do something, I don't know a pub lunch, or punting or something? I can't sit here on my own."

"Of course." With a final squeeze of her hand he turned away. "What would you like for breakfast?" He opened the fridge and started removing everything which could be part of a fry up, regardless of whether it was in date.

"Thank you, but I'm not sure I can eat anything."

"Wait 'til you see what I'm cooking for you."

Sally watched him in a daze. The smell of frying sausage assured her she was hungry after all. When he placed an ad-hoc breakfast in front of her they ate in silence, occasionally exchanging tentative smiles. Her breakfast was settling in her stomach as nausea by the time the doorbell rang.

She looked pleadingly at Darren. "Can you?"

He shook his head. She searched for signs that she had offended him, that his kindness was now costing him more.

"It's your house," he said.

Sally's body ached as she went to open the door. Her tired fingers fumbled with the lock.

"Hi." It was Paul.

Sally gazed at him, too tired or too scared to be angry.

"Can I come in?" He asked eventually.

Sally stepped aside to allow him to enter and let him upstairs to her room. The air was stale, and Sally opened a window. She wished she'd tidied. But there was no need to worry about tidy rooms, impressing Paul, or even whether to carry on with her research. She had an escape route and there was nothing to stop her from taking it.

"I'm going away," she said. "I've been thinking about it for a while. There are far more exciting places to be than here, and I'm going to make the most of them."

"Where?"

"Thailand probably, but then who knows."

Paul was quiet, not looking at her. Then he said, "is there any way I could persuade you to come back?"

"Yesterday there would have been."

"I'm so, so sorry I left, but now I'm ready to start again, talk about things, change them…" He reached out to take her hands and she let him.

"Why did you leave then?"

"Last night, that's not how I meant it to be. I felt so awful before, when we were students. You were so young, you deserved so much better than me taking advantage of you."

"You didn't take advantage of me, I was 21, not a child. And this time, yesterday, how was it meant to be? A peck on the cheek and a cold walk home?"

280

"No, I just didn't have the balls to tell you I loved you."

Involuntarily, Sally tightened her grip on his hands. "So leaving would make it better?"

"It wasn't to make things better, it was because I was finally able to do what I should have done a long time ago. I called Katie."

Recovering, Sally pulled away her hands. "You left and didn't even answer my calls so you could speak with your ex?"

"I called to tell her that I had met someone else, to make sure that if she still thought that one day we'd make a fresh start again, she now knew how fully it was over."

"What did she say?"

"That she knew when I left there was nothing she could do to change things. I guess she knew me better than I knew myself in that way. Anyway, she's back in the UK – I guess America didn't really work out for her in the end either."

"You could have let me know – at least a text. I thought you regretted what happened, that you'd never come back."

Smiling, Paul pointed to the constituent parts of Sally's phone, which were drying on the radiator. "I'd rather you deleted all my messages when they come through."

Sally scooped up the remains of her phone, embarrassed that he should know what had happened.

When she didn't speak, Paul continued. "Anyway, you left too, remember."

She couldn't pretend she had a monopoly on the moral high ground. "I always wondered what would have happened if I hadn't. I meant to leave a note, then I thought 'what's the point'. I guess I saved us from some awkward conversations in the morning."

Paul shook his head. "I could never explain to myself why I let it happen. I'm sorry."

"Even then, I didn't regret it."

"In some ways," Paul admitted, "nor did I."

He leaned forward and again they kissed.

Sally pulled back. "Look, let's get out of here. The sun's shining, let's go outside."

"I know a pub we can walk to, away from the city, away from everything. Then I can cook you supper again, if you'd like."

"That would be lovely."

"And, maybe, you'd consider bringing your toothbrush?"

Sally laughed and stood up. She reached out a hand to pull him up too. He put his arms around her, so her cheek was pressed against his shoulder.

She closed her eyes. "I didn't sleep much last night, you'll have to forgive me if I fall asleep before supper."

"I don't know that I slept at all." Paul squeezed her tighter. "I'm happy to scrap the pub and supper and go to bed now."

"Not so fast!"

"OK, we at least need a trip to the phone shop first."

Sally looked at the constituent parts of her phone. "I think this one may be beyond help."

Paul and Sally sat outside the pub, watching a child play ball with an over excited puppy. The wind was still cold, and Sally hid her hands in the sleeves of her jumper.

When they had drained the last of their drinks Paul asked. "What will you do? Will you still go to Thailand?" He didn't seem as concerned by the question as she had hoped he'd be.

"I've got myself through the last week by the idea of escaping to Thailand, so I want to go through with it. But not for long – I think we're going to try and rebuild the lab. If we've dedicated this much time to getting permission for GM field trials, we should actually plant them. I feel I'm in a strong bargaining position at work to get a long holiday first though."

"The joys of being needed."

"And you?"

"I have a house, a good job, a girlfriend maybe – what more could I want?"

Sally thought. "A cat?"

"Could do. How about Bernadette?"

"Why not!"

"Come on, let's go home."

Back at Paul's house, Sally helped him with the supper. Whenever there was a pause in the cooking they tentatively kissed, each time wondering whether to bother with the supper after all. While supper was in the oven, Paul went out 'to get a surprise for her', leaving Sally guarding the food. While he was gone, she sat on the sofa and imagined the house as theirs.

By the time Paul came home and placed Bernadette in her lap, Sally was fast asleep.

Chapter 26

Sally laid out her packing, while Mel looked on with a frown: insect repellent, suntan cream, torch, medical kit… Every conversation Sally had with Mel she was still distracted by the relief of regaining Mel's friendship, and the idea of a trip with no planning seemed less daunting with Mel looking on.

"You've oscillated wildly between going for 10 days or 10 months. Now you've booked your flights you must know?"

"Actually I've booked an open return, but if I get short of money you can sell my possessions to pay the rent."

"Huh, the proceeds of that won't get us very far."

Sally picked up the novels she'd added to her pile, testing their weight in her hands. "To be honest, I don't plan to stay too long. I think I will be ready to come back and see Paul."

"Sweet." Mel didn't sound entirely mocking when she said this. "And your job?"

"That I don't know. After all that's happened…" Sally wished she could tell her the whole truth, but their fragile friendship wasn't worth the risk. Guarding the secret was a price worth paying. "And with Vangelis gone I don't know that we can fix things."

"Before this all started, when good stuff was happening, what did you care more for, your results or Vangelis?" Mel came round the table so she blocked Sally's way, forcing her to concentrate only on their conversation.

"My results, but we couldn't get them without Vangelis."

"That's a way people keep power, making you believe you need them. From a purely practical point of view, can this project keep going?"

"Yes."

"Well do it then! You cared so much about the science and its potential. Christ, you even got me to quit my job in search of something I cared about. Where's that gone?"

"I still care, I just wonder whether it's already taken too much of me."

"Go to Thailand, come back refreshed." Mel let Sally pass and began to rearrange her packing for her. "Why don't you go and see Vangelis? It might be easier if you have his blessing."

"We've heard nothing from him."

"Then what do you have to lose?"

* * * * *

As Sally raised her hand to Vangelis's door knocker she remembered the first time she had stood outside Paul's front door, so scared she almost turned away. It was Vangelis's wife who answered, and she looked startled when she saw Sally.

"Hi," Sally said. "How are you?"

"We're fine," was Christiana's curt reply.

"Is Vangelis in?"

"No."

"When is he likely to be back, do you know?"

"I don't know."

Then it dawned on Sally: perhaps he wasn't coming back. Judith resigned; was it so she could be with him? Had it genuinely been love, not a careless affair? She looked down at the path where a trail of ants was moving nests, a stream of workers carrying ghostly-white grubs below their bellies. Sally moved her feet out of their way and was relieved when a child's head appeared round the door.

"Go back inside, Jonathan!"

"We made cakes." Jonathan smiled bashfully at Sally.

"Well done you, do they taste good?"

"They're for Daddy."

So maybe he was there, or perhaps this was a bribe to coax him back.

"Look." Sally returned her gaze to Christina. "If there's anything I can do, please let me know – babysitting, anything, my boyfriend's just done up his house, so he's useful…" She was speaking as if Vangelis was gone and needed to be replaced.

"That's very kind," Christina said more gently.

"Here, take my card, and if there's anything at all, just let me know." Sally fumbled in her handbag and handed over a tatty business card.

"So you're still working at the university?" Christiana asked.

Sally realised she had only given her work contact details.

"Here, let me write my mobile number on it."

Christina pulled back the card. "You will keep going, won't you? He thought the world of you, you know, and his research meant everything to him." Her intensity was such a contrast to her cold greeting that Sally took a moment to absorb what she was saying.

"I'm going away, to help decide, but I still care about it." Suddenly Sally realised that Christina had a stake in this too; she had given up her job so Vangelis could pursue his research. "I promise, whatever I decide, that it will be right. I know his research won't end here."

www.bramblebybooks.co.uk